*Praise f*

The
# GIFTED,
the
# TALENTED
and Me

'Probably the funniest and most authentic novel that I've
read about being an awkward, self-conscious teenage
boy since I WAS an awkward, self-conscious teenage boy!'
John Boyne, author of *The Boy in the Striped Pyjamas*

'Made me cry with laughter. A comic novel like this is
a gift to the nation'
Amanda Craig, journalist and author of *The Lie of the Land*

'So, so funny and recognisable – I immediately forced
it on my fourteen-year-old'
Jenny Colgan, *Sunday Times* bestselling author

'Sharp, witty and brilliantly observed … I haven't laughed out
loud like that for a long time'
Brian Conaghan, Costa Award-winning author

'Great characters, packed with wisdom and reminiscent of
Adrian Mole (and there's no higher praise, let's face it)'
Sathnam Sanghera, journalist and author of
*The Boy with the Topknot*

'It made me laugh out loud on the tube'
Patrice Lawrence, award-winning author of *Orangeboy*

'I blasted through this corker by William Sutcliffe … YA needs
more books like this'
Phil Earle, author of *Demolition Dad*

Yrs 11 – 13+

*Books by William Sutcliffe*

FOR ADULTS
New Boy
Are You Experienced?
The Love Hexagon
Whatever Makes You Happy

FOR ADULTS AND YOUNG ADULTS
Bad Influence
The Wall
Concentr8
We See Everything
The Gifted, the Talented and Me
The Summer We Turned Green

FOR YOUNGER READERS
Circus of Thieves and the Raffle of Doom
Circus of Thieves on the Rampage
Circus of Thieves and the Comeback Caper

# The
# SUMMER
## We Turned
# GREEN

# WILLIAM SUTCLIFFE

BLOOMSBURY
LONDON  OXFORD  NEW YORK  NEW DELHI  SYDNEY

BLOOMSBURY YA
Bloomsbury Publishing Plc
50 Bedford Square, London WC1B 3DP, UK
29 Earlsfort Terrace, Dublin 2, Ireland

BLOOMSBURY, BLOOMSBURY YA and the Diana logo are trademarks of
Bloomsbury Publishing Plc

First published in Great Britain in 2021 by Bloomsbury Publishing Plc

A catalogue record for this book is available from the British Library

ISBN: PB: 978-1-5266-3285-2; eBook: 978-1-5266-3284-5

2  4  6  8  10  9  7  5  3  1

Typeset by RefineCatch Limited, Bungay, Suffolk
Printed and bound in Great Britain by CPI Group (UK) Ltd, Croydon CR0 4YY

To find out more about our authors and books visit www.bloomsbury.com and
sign up for our newsletters

*For Saul, Iris and Juno*

*and for all the school climate strikers*

Summer 2019

# The sleeping bag

It starts with a knock at my bedroom door.

Without waiting for an answer, my sister walks in, closing the door behind her as if she doesn't want anyone to hear what she's doing.

Rose never comes into my bedroom. She barely even speaks to me, but I suppose this is normal, since she's four years older and thinks that compared to her seventeen-year-old friends I'm about as interesting as a dust particle, so I have no idea what to say when she appears, says hi, then just stands there smiling at me.

There's a weird silence, because she doesn't seem to know what to say, either.

'What's up?' I ask eventually.

'You all right?' she says.

'Yeah, fine.'

The room goes quiet again. Her eyes slowly pass over

3

my posters and shelves, and I get the feeling she's trying (and failing) to think of a topic of conversation. Then she says, 'You've got a sleeping bag, haven't you?'

'Yes.'

'Can I borrow it?'

'What for?'

'Sleeping in?' she replies, using the sarcastic statement-as-a-question intonation that drives our parents crazy.

'Are you going somewhere?'

'It's not important where I'm going, I'm just asking if you'll let me borrow it,' she says, with her eyes narrowing into a particular stare she has – the one that makes me wither and obey.

As always, it works, and next thing I know I'm rummaging under my bed, hauling out the sleeping bag and handing it over.

'Thanks, Luke. You're a star,' she says, already heading out of the room.

'When will I get it back?'

'When I've finished with it,' she replies, walking away without a backward glance, which feels much more like the sister I know than the strange, smiley person who walked in.

A few minutes later, I hear the front door open and close. There's no bell ring, just the sound of the clicking latch, followed by footsteps heading outside towards the

4

street, accompanied by the judder of small, hard wheels trundling over concrete.

I glance at my watch – it's nearly 9 p.m. – then jump up and look out of the window, just in time to see Rose cross the road and go into the house opposite, wheeling a small suitcase and carrying my badly-rolled-up sleeping bag under one arm.

I head downstairs. Dad is on the sofa in front of the TV, but he isn't really watching it because he's got an iPad on his lap, but he isn't really looking at that because he's got his phone in his hand, but he doesn't seem to be looking at that either, because his eyes are closed and his mouth is open and he doesn't notice me entering the room.

I head for the kitchen and Mum is in her usual spot at the table, gazing intently at her laptop, 'working' (browsing Facebook).

'Where's Rose gone?' I say.

'Nowhere,' says Mum, not looking up from her screen, which is showing a picture of a cousin she's always hated sitting beside a swimming pool holding a cocktail. Mum grimaces, mutters the words 'stupid cow', and 'likes' the picture.

'Are you sure?' I ask.

'How can she afford a holiday in Florida? She only just got divorced!'

'Er …'

5

'*That's* how she affords it. She just got divorced.'

'Mum …'

'Took him to the cleaners, and everyone knows she cheated on him first.'

'Do you know that Rose just left the house with a suitcase? I think she went over the road.'

This – finally – gets Mum's attention.

'What?'

'I saw it out the window.'

'When?'

'Just now.'

'Rose?'

'Yes.'

'Over the road?'

'Yes.'

'With a suitcase?'

'Yes.'

Mum springs from the table and charges up the stairs. I hear her open the door of Rose's room, close it again, then thunder back downstairs and charge into the sitting room.

I follow right behind her.

'I wasn't asleep!' says Dad, jolting upright as we walk in, sending his iPad and phone clattering on to the floor.

'Rose has gone,' says Mum.

'What?'

'Rose! She's gone!'

'Gone where?'

'I looked in her wardrobe and she's taken her clothes. We think she's gone over the road!' says Mum, with an air of tragic climax that Dad clearly can't make sense of.

'Er ...'

'With her stuff in a suitcase,' I say, translating Mum's panic into words Dad might actually understand.

'Oh!' says Dad. 'Right. So ... you're not saying she's popped out. You're saying she's ...'

'Gone!'

'Over the road?'

'She borrowed my sleeping bag,' I point out. Dad tends to need things explained to him very slowly, a bit like a small child but without the fun.

'SHE TOOK YOUR SLEEPING BAG!?' yells Mum, which is when I realise I should have kept this to myself.

I nod.

'WHY DIDN'T YOU TELL US!?'

'I'm telling you now.'

'After she's left! Why didn't you tell us when she took the sleeping bag?'

'Because she only took it two minutes before she went.'

'Why did you lend it to her?' says Dad.

'Because she asked for it.'

'That doesn't mean you just hand over a ... *sleeping bag* ... to a vulnerable teenager,' says Mum.

7

'What's vulnerable about her?'

'Everything!'

'She seems very confident to me,' I say.

'She's run away from home!' says Mum. 'You don't give a sleeping bag to a teenager who's on the brink of running away from home!'

'I didn't know she was going to run away.'

'What did you think the sleeping bag was for? A camping trip?'

'You always told me to be generous and share my things. Now I've done it and you're angry with me.'

'Not a *sleeping bag*!'

'That's not what you said. I don't remember you ever saying, "Be generous with your sister and share all your things except your sleeping bag."'

'We're getting off the point,' says Dad, turning back towards Mum. 'You're sure she's actually run away? You think she's not coming back?'

Mum sighs and for a moment her eyes glisten with tears. A heavy silence fills the room, and my parents stare at one another like two people who have just stepped out of a car crash and have no idea what to say or do next.

I should probably explain …

# The end of the world isn't our fault

Why the big drama about a seventeen-year-old girl crossing the road with a suitcase and a sleeping bag? Well, the boring street in the boring suburb where my boring home sits isn't as dull and safe as it used to be, because the house opposite, which used to be even more boring than ours, has become a magnet for every climate protester, anti-capitalist, extinction rebel, outcast and dropout in the country.

How?

Well, to explain this you have to go right back to when I was small. Nobody seems to know exactly when rumblings were first heard about a proposed new runway for the airport near my home. For as long as I can remember the project was on, then off, then on again, and there was always talk of a never-ending round of meetings and consultations that sometimes sent the whole street into a panic about threats of demolition, and at other times seemed like an endless drone of irrelevant background noise.

Then, roughly a year before the bizarre summer I'm going to tell you about, the project finally got a green light. On a morning that seemed like any other, the postman casually walked his usual route, unnoticed, delivering a small stack of dull-looking brown envelopes which would change the street forever. Twenty letters landed on twenty doormats that day, telling every family who got one that their home was going to be bought from them, whether they wanted to sell or not, then demolished. Ours was spared. All the houses opposite were condemned.

Local outrage ramped up as the row of buildings emptied out and got boarded up, and the story even got some news coverage. Then gradually the abandoned house opposite ours filled up again with squatters: anti-airport protesters, climate activists and, according to my parents, anyone else who thought it might be a laugh to hang out in a derelict house all day instead of going out and getting a job.

There's an old saying: *my enemy's enemy is my friend*. My street is a good test case for this idea, and, so far, it doesn't seem to be true. A more accurate version would appear to be: *my enemy's enemy is even worse than my enemy if he wears strange clothes and looks like he doesn't wash and makes noise late at night.*

10

Yes, since the protesters moved in over the road, all the nice, boring polite people on my side of the street simply don't know who to hate any more. They don't want their neighbours' houses demolished in order to build an access road to a new cargo terminal, but even more than that, they don't want weirdos waking them up at night with bongo drums, and they certainly don't want their daughters going to visit anti-capitalist communes and deciding they like it there.

That's why the loan of my sleeping bag (which, to be honest, I didn't really think through as I was doing it) was more than a little controversial, and why Mum ended up with tears in her eyes, staring at Dad in stunned silence, just because my sister had crossed the road pulling a suitcase.

'I'm going over there,' says Mum.

'What are you going to say?' asks Dad.

'What do you *think* I'm going to say? I'm going to tell her to come home.'

Dad pulls a sceptical face.

'Do you have a better idea?'

Dad shrugs.

'You're shrugging? How can you shrug at a time like this?'

'I just … I'm not sure telling her to come home is going to work.'

11

'Are you saying we should let her stay?'

'No,' says Dad, 'I just think telling her what she can and can't do doesn't seem to be very effective at the moment.'

'What's the alternative? Giving up and letting her do whatever she wants?'

'No … I … well, why don't you give it a try? We can see how it goes.'

'Thanks for the vote of confidence,' says Mum, striding to the front door and closing it behind her with a slam.

I head upstairs and pretend to go to bed after Mum leaves, but I'm listening out for the front door, and I hurry down to hear the news as soon as she returns, which is surprisingly soon.

'Well?' says Dad, who has jumped up from the sofa to greet Mum in the hallway.

Mum hangs her keys on the hook behind the door and slowly turns back towards us. Her face is pale, and the tip of her nose has gone white, which is what happens when she's trying to pretend she's not angry.

She looks at us as if we are far away and barely recognisable, takes a deep breath, then says, 'It didn't go well.'

'What happened?' says Dad.

'Well … she's in a very determined mood. I tried to take things gently, and I told her that I admire her open-mindedness, and I think it's good she's making friends with people from other walks of life, and that she can visit them as often as she likes, but for her own safety she has to spend her nights at home with us.'

'And … ?'

'She just asked what I meant by "other walks of life", and I tried to explain, but for some reason she didn't like what I said and I got a long lecture about why I'm a snob, and how ignorant and blind I am for having no clue about who the climate protesters are, and what they're trying to achieve, and how they're the only people facing up to the most serious crisis the human race has ever faced. I tried to tell her I wasn't talking about the end of the human race, I was talking about her coming home for bed, then she went off on one about how I wasn't listening to a word she was saying and how the whole conversation was a perfect illustration of why she has to move out. When I asked her what this meant, she just told me I'm impossible to talk to. Can you believe that? *I'm* the one who's impossible to talk to!'

'So what did you do?' asked Dad.

'I told her she was too young to be there, and it wasn't up to her, and she was coming home whether she liked it or not.'

'And … ?'

'Well, that's when things got a little heated. Honestly, where did she get that temper from?'

Dad and I avoid eye contact.

'So … what's the upshot?' says Dad, dodging Mum's self-answering question. 'That it *is* up to her?'

'No! But I can't physically drag her back! What am I supposed to do? I don't know what's happened to her. She's so *angry*.'

'About what?'

'Not sure. It's either global environmental meltdown or us telling her what to do. She talked a lot about both, but I think the main problem is us.'

'What have *we* done? The end of the world isn't our fault.'

'Well, Rose doesn't seem to think so.'

'How can it be *our* fault?'

'Well, not just us, but people like us.'

'People *like* us?'

'Our generation. We're complacent and selfish apparently, and we're destroying the planet.'

'That's ridiculous.'

'She does have a point,' I say. 'I mean, she's not wrong, is she?'

Mum and Dad glare at me.

'We're not complacent,' says Dad dismissively.

'Are you actually doing anything? To stop climate change?' I ask.

'We recycle,' says Dad.

I give him a slow round of applause.

'The end of the world isn't the point here,' says Mum. 'It's not our job to save the planet, but it *is* our job to save our daughter.'

'From what?' I ask. 'The people over the road?'

'Yes!'

'What is it you think they're going to do to her?'

'She's too young!' says Dad. 'You don't just move out of the family home on a whim one evening, aged seventeen, without even a goodbye.'

'Who says it was a whim?' I ask.

'We should have discussed it,' says Mum.

'You think you could have changed her mind?'

'I could have tried. Why didn't she talk to us about it?' says Mum, turning to Dad.

'Maybe she thought you wouldn't listen,' I say. 'Maybe she thought you'd forbid it. Anyway, how do you know she's moved out?'

'You told us yourself,' says Mum. 'She took a suitcase.'

'Haven't you noticed what day it is?'

Mum and Dad look at one another blankly.

'Last day of term,' I say. 'She waited till the end of the school year, didn't she? Then she made her move. And she clearly planned it. So maybe this is her version of a summer holiday.'

I watch this idea, which was obvious to me from the

15

moment I saw her trundle across the road, slowly percolate into my parents' slow-moving brains.

'A summer holiday?' says Mum. 'As in … a week or two?'

'Or longer. Who knows? She's been hanging out there a lot recently, so she must like it.'

'Has she? Since when? Why didn't you tell us?' says Mum.

'You didn't ask.'

'But she told you?'

'No, she never tells me anything. I just saw it. With my eyes.'

'When?'

'Often. Last few weeks mainly.'

'But … she can't move in there without even asking us. She's supposed to be looking after you. She promised. We're both working,' says Mum.

If Mum is thinking *this*, of all things, is going to keep Rose at home, she really does live in a dreamworld.

'I don't need looking after,' I say.

'We can't just leave you on your own.'

'Of course you can! I'm thirteen. And Rose is one minute away. I'll be fine.'

'What do you think?' says Mum, turning to Dad. 'Are we going to have to hire some childcare?'

He furrows his brow, pretending to be conflicted for a

16

few seconds, then says, 'Well, I suppose he should be OK on his own … if he promises to be responsible.'

'I'll be fine,' I say, trying to stop myself going saucer-eyed with glee at the idea of all the uninterrupted, unobserved, un-nagged hours of free time that are about to fall into my lap. 'As long as there's stuff to eat in the fridge, I can look after myself.'

'You're not to just gorge on snacks all day. You have to have proper meals,' says Mum, attempting to sound stern, though we both know her words are totally pointless.

'Of course,' I reply, attempting to sound sincere.

'Well – OK, then,' says Mum. 'Just for a while. Until we can talk sense into Rose and bring her home.'

'I'll go and have a word with her,' says Dad.

'What do you think that will achieve?' asks Mum.

'We have to try. Maybe there's a different approach.'

'Such as?'

'I don't know. How about we let her stay there tonight, and we leave her to do whatever she wants tomorrow, then after work I pay a visit and try again with something a bit less confrontational? It won't be long before she wants a hot shower and home comforts. She'll be back soon enough.'

'She can come here during the day and have a shower whenever she wants, then just go back,' I point out helpfully.

17

'It's late. You should go to bed,' says Dad.

'Or maybe I could stop her using the bathroom if you get me a Taser. But that might be a bit of a mixed message.'

'Bed!' says Dad.

I head upstairs, with a smile spreading across my face. Until now I've been strictly forbidden from crossing the road to see what the protesters are up to, but I can't exactly be prevented from going to visit my own sister, can I? Particularly with nobody watching over me every weekday. Besides, as of this evening, thanks to Rose, my parents' ability to stop me doing *anything* suddenly looks a lot shakier.

I've wondered for months about what it is that goes on in there, but up till now I haven't been able to satisfy my curiosity. All I know is that everyone on my side of the road seems to hate the protesters even more than they hate the airport expansion.

Helena, our next-door neighbour, is the one who seems most agitated about the whole thing. Every time I pass her on the street, I hear her complaining to someone about smells, behaviour or noises, and sometimes she goes suddenly quiet as I approach, as if the activities she's discussing are so twisted they can't be mentioned within earshot of a child.

All of which, of course, just makes me more curious.

What goes on in there that upsets Helena so much?

18

What can a group of seemingly peaceful hippies get up to that makes people like Mum and Dad so frightened of them? How did those people become the enemy?

Soon, I'll be able to find out. The question of why Rose has gone over there is less of a mystery. Obviously it's to annoy our parents.

And it's worked.

# The things they don't want you to hear

By the time I wake up, Mum and Dad are long gone. There's a note on my bedroom floor, which I can see from a distance is a numbered list of instructions in Mum's handwriting. I step past without picking it up, making a hazy mental note to myself that I should probably make an attempt to read it at some point before she returns.

I head down to the kitchen in my pants, gaze into the fridge, then eat a few fistfuls of Frosties straight out of the box. I slug some orange juice from the carton, dig out a packet of chocolate digestives that Mum has hidden not nearly well enough and wolf one down in a couple of bites, allowing the crumbs to land where they land, musing on the fact that already, just a few minutes into my new life of independence and self-reliance, I am in heaven.

Who would have thought that something so simple (being alone in the house) could be so amazingly and immediately enjoyable?

I stare out at the garden for a while, how long I have absolutely no idea because, after months of having my life parcelled up into a rigid hour-by-hour slog from lesson to lesson, time suddenly seems deliciously irrelevant, like a distant yapping dog, a dimly perceived irritation that is someone else's problem.

Gazing mindlessly at this view which is so familiar I barely even see it any more, I work my way slowly through the packet of biscuits, relishing the sensation of the summer holiday stretching ahead of me, as inviting as a perfectly soft, infinitely large mattress.

I check the fridge again, sample a few forkfuls of each of the various pots and tubs of leftovers, then head to the living room and power up my Xbox.

Gaming and snacking fill up the next few hours, until the point where my eyeballs begin to actually hurt, and I notice that a slice of crisp sunlight is leaking in through the crack down the middle of the living-room curtains. I decide to head outside with the carton of orange juice and get some sun while my eyes readjust to three dimensions, after which I figure I might be able to summon enough energy to put on some clothes and go to visit Rose.

I haven't been in the garden for long when Callum from

next door pops up at the fence and asks if I want to come over and hang out.

I've known Callum all my life, and everyone thinks of us as friends, mainly because if there's a kid next door who's roughly the same age as you it's almost impossible to avoid spending time with them, but the truth is that it's been years since I've actually enjoyed his company. He's the sporty, competitive type, and being with him usually involves playing whatever game is his latest fad while he gloats about how thoroughly he's beating me.

I shrug at him, making only the briefest eye contact, knowing he's not going to leave me in peace until I've caved in.

'Come on, I'm bored,' he says.

'I'm busy,' I say.

'You don't look busy,' he points out accurately.

'Dunno,' I say.

'Just for a bit,' he says.

I shrug again, but he nags and nags until eventually I agree to go over for a short while 'to see his new Swingball', because this is the only way to shut him up.

I reluctantly go back into my house, pull on a T-shirt and shorts and head next door. He thrashes me at Swingball with predictable ease, thumping every shot with the focus and force of a butcher wielding a cleaver, then digs out a rugby ball and says, 'Let's practise passing,' even though rugby is a sport I've never played. The ball flies at me like a torpedo, and each time I drop it (which is almost every time he throws it) he says, 'Don't flinch. You're dropping it because you're flinching.'

When I throw it back to him, he says, 'Throw it harder. As hard as you like. You have to spin it.'

This is Callum trying to be nice – he's not actively telling me I'm useless – but his conviction that I am a disappointingly feeble excuse for a male is somehow even more apparent in his attempts to coach me towards improvement than in his usual goads at my sporting failure.

I've always found it hard to walk away from Callum. There's something weirdly magnetic about his relentless determination to make me stay with him, while he simultaneously keeps up a running commentary on how substandard my company is. Again and again, over the years, I've found myself in his garden without wanting to be there, unable get away from him. But today feels different. While he rattles on about how he's going to be in the First Fifteen next year, my mind glazes over, and that vision of summer as an infinite mattress stretching to the horizon comes back to me. I'm not sure why, but it suddenly feels clear that a large empty vista of time without Callum in it is right there, in front of me, and all I have to do is walk into it. I can leave him behind.

I look down at the rugby ball in my hands, feeling its

rough, dimpled surface under my fingertips, and instead of throwing the ball back to him, I drop it at my feet.

His anecdote tails away. 'What are you doing?' he says.

'I'm off,' I say.

'Why? Where are you going?'

'Nowhere,' I say, walking away.

'But ... wait! We haven't finished!'

'I have.'

'What's wrong with you?' he snaps.

'Who knows?' I reply with a shrug, pausing at the patio doors to take one last look at his face, which is crumpled in bafflement and annoyance. This isn't how I'm supposed to behave. My role is to bend to his will, and it's obvious he can't understand what has just happened.

I go into their house, closing the doors on his droning, haranguing voice, walk through to the hall, and just as I'm about to leave, his cat, Blanche, appears at the bottom of the stairs. She looks up, greets me with a quizzical 'Brrrmow?' and yawns. Blanche is white, ridiculously fluffy, and isn't allowed outside because, according to Callum, she's 'too expensive'.

Every month or two there's a panic because she has escaped, and my family always gets roped into looking for her, even though we all secretly hope she's made a break for freedom.

Blanche figure-of-eights herself between my ankles,

24

rubbing the whole length of her flank and tail across my skin. I kneel down and stroke her, feeling her spine push up gratefully into my hand, then I bend right over her and whisper in her ear, 'Make a run for it.'

'Summer holidays, then!' comes a perky voice right behind me, making me jerk suddenly upright, sending the cat skittering away. It's Helena, Callum's mum, wearing her trademark outfit of fleece and ironed jeans. Her concession to the sweltering heat is that today her fleece is sleeveless. I didn't know sleeveless fleeces even existed until now, but you learn something new every day.

I nod and tell her I'm just leaving.

'Rose looking after you, is she?'

'Yeah, kind of,' I answer.

'Mmm,' says Helena sceptically. 'Do tell your mum I said hi.'

'OK,' I reply, letting myself out of the front door.

My step is light and my heart is full as I walk out into the street. I've spent so many long and unhappy hours in that house, for as long as I can remember, but now I'm struck by the realisation that if I don't want to, I never have to go there again.

I turn my head left and right, taking in the familiar but always strange sight of a row of semi-detached houses with neatly tended front gardens and family cars in the driveways, directly opposite a row of identical buildings,

25

all empty, abandoned and boarded up.

On the derelict side, only one house is different: the one everyone now refers to as the commune. Whether it really is a commune, or what that actually means, I don't know. As usual, the sound of enthusiastic but unskilled drumming is drifting from an upstairs window, or, rather, from where the window would be if there was one. A yellow and red sheet is draped across the space at night and for most of the morning, but the rest of the time there's just a cavity, through which I often catch glimpses of mysterious activity.

Just outside the front door, a girl with long, ragged hair is dangling by the backs of her bent knees from the lowest branch of a tree, upside down, staring at me. She's often there in that front garden, hanging around alone, reading, sketching in a little notebook she seems to carry around with her everywhere, or just looking bored.

I gaze back at her, wondering, for a moment, what she does all day. There's no sign of her ever going to school, even though she looks roughly the same age as me.

'Hi,' she says, with an upside-down wave.

At this moment, Mrs Deacon from a few doors down appears, pulling her ancient floral-patterned shopping bag on wheels.

'Awful, isn't it?' she says to me in a semi-whisper, which is an odd greeting, but more or less what you expect from Mrs Deacon.

'Isn't what?' I ask.

'Those people,' she mutters, wrinkling her nose and wafting a wrist in the direction of the commune. 'Such a shame.'

Then off she goes, inching away down the street at the speed of a dawdling earthworm.

'You've got a squeaky wheel,' I call after her. 'Would you like me to oil it for you?'

'Maybe another time,' she replies. 'I'm in a terrible hurry.'

I look across the street again and the girl is still there, still hanging from her tree, staring at me. I'd been about to visit Rose, but now I feel like I can't cross the road to the commune without this girl thinking I'm going to talk to her, and I can't think what I'd say, so I turn away and head back into my house.

Mum returns from work full of questions about my day alone in the house, and seems disappointed that I don't have anything to report beyond, 'It was fine.' If I tell her the truth, which is that apart from the interlude at Callum's the whole thing was total and utter bliss from start to finish, she might get suspicious, so I decide to say just enough for her not to worry that I'm unhappy, and no more.

I know I've pitched it right when she stops her litany of anxious questions and starts telling me to sweep up the Frosties from the kitchen floor.

Dad doesn't return from work at his usual time, so as Mum and I sit down for dinner she sends him a text asking him where he is, and reminding him about his plan to visit Rose. He replies straight away, saying he's already there.

'What's the news?' she texts back.

Her phone pings almost immediately. She stares at the screen for a few seconds, then reads aloud in a flat voice, 'All cool. I'll tell you later.'

'Your dinner's gone cold,' she writes.

'No probs. Eating here with the XR crew,' comes the reply.

Mum looks up from her phone and frowns. 'The XR crew? What's he talking about?'

'XR is Extinction Rebellion,' I explain.

'Is it? How do you know that?'

'How do you not know?'

'How does *he* know?'

'Everyone knows.'

'Do they?'

'Yes. Except you apparently.'

'Why's he having *dinner* with them?'

'Maybe that's just who lives there.'

'So is that what Rose is now? She's in the XR crew?'

'Mum, don't you know anything? XR means Extinction Rebellion – climate protesters. Crew is just a Dad word. That's him being clueless.'

'How do you know all this?'

'Because I don't live with my head in a bucket.'

'I … just … I'm very confused.'

'You don't say.'

When the doorbell goes, we both jump up, forgetting there's no reason why Dad would ring the doorbell of his own house. Turns out it's Helena from next door.

'Hi, Amanda,' says Helena. 'How are you?'

'I'm fine,' says Mum frostily. She doesn't like Helena.

'Just thought I'd pop over and check you're OK.'

'I'm fine,' she repeats, with an additional frosting of frost.

'I heard what happened to Rose,' says Helena, in a sing-song voice halfway between sympathy and gloating, reaching out a hand to squeeze Mum's forearm.

'Oh, really? What have you heard?' says Mum, taking a half-step backwards.

'That she's been … turned.'

'Turned?'

'By that lot over the road. They've got their claws into her somehow or other.'

'I don't think any claws were involved, Helena.'

'Is it true she's actually moved in there? That's what people are saying.'

'Which people?'

'Nobody in particular. Just …'

'You don't need to worry,' says Mum after a pointed silence. 'Everything's under control. But thanks for your concern.'

Mum begins to close the door, but Helena steps forward on to the doorstep.

'Do you think we should have a street meeting?' says Helena.

'About what?'

'Well … there are obviously safety issues. Regarding the other children on the street.'

'Rose isn't a child. She's seventeen.'

'Yes, but maybe this is just the thin end of the wedge. We can't all look the other way and pretend it hasn't happened.'

'What is it you're worried about?'

'Callum's fourteen. It's a very impressionable age.'

'I can't see him wandering across the road and joining a climate rebellion, somehow. Not unless they put together a rugby team, which I don't think is really how they operate.'

'Oh, it's not my family I'm concerned about! I just think that as residents, we should stand together. I'm thinking of starting a petition to the council demanding that they're evicted.'

'OK.'

'Your story is a powerful cautionary tale. It could form the heart of our case. Can I count on your signature?'

'Maybe. I'll have to talk to David about it.'

'Is he in?'

'No. He's actually at the commune.'

'He's there? Now?'

'Visiting Rose.'

'Oh! This whole thing must be awful for you! I'm so sorry.'

'Don't be. We're fine.'

'I admire your bravery. You're an example to us all.'

'I'm really not. But we've just sat down to dinner, so …'

'Yes, yes! Life must go on, mustn't it? In spite of everything.'

'I'll see you soon, Helena.'

'I hope so. Stay strong!'

'I'll try.'

An hour or two later Dad finally arrives home, walking in with the cheerful, relaxed air of a guy who's spent the evening in the pub with his mates.

'Well?' says Mum. 'How did it go?'

'I had a nice time, thanks.'

'I'm not asking if you had a *nice time*. I'm asking about the welfare of our daughter!'

'Oh, she seems fine.'

'Fine?'

'Yeah.'

31

Mum fixes him with a piercing stare. 'Are you drunk?' she says.

'No.'

'Are you sure?'

'Yes! I may have had a glass or two of mead.'

'Mead?'

'Yeah. It's not bad. Apparently it's one of the most ancient drinks there is. It's basically fermented honey mixed with—'

'How about we skip the novelty brewing lecture and you tell me about Rose?'

'Sorry.'

'Is she safe? Is she OK?'

'She's fine. Why don't we sit down? It's a long story.'

Mum follows Dad into the kitchen, turning back towards me to say, 'Go to bed,' which, obviously, I ignore.

'Well?' says Mum. 'What happened? Did you tell her to come home?'

'Er … I thought I'd try a different approach.'

'Such as what? Forgetting what you went for? Sitting around getting drunk with the hippies?'

'I'm not drunk.'

'You're suspiciously cheerful.'

'Since when is it bad to be cheerful? You're always telling me I'm grumpy, now I'm too cheerful! What am I supposed to do?'

32

'Your mood swings are not the point here.'

'Mood swings? What mood swings?' he says angrily.

'Rose – did you talk to her?'

'Of course I did.'

'And … ?'

'Well … she's clearly feeling very determined about the whole thing, so I think the best way forward, instead of trying to force her to do what we want, is just to spend some time over there, and show her that we're capable of listening, and that we respect her autonomy and the decision she's made. We can focus on keeping the lines of communication open, then if she gets in any trouble, or she begins to waver, we can help her out and try to bring her home.'

'What, so you've given up?'

'No. I just think we have to play the long game.'

'This is typical! It's just so lazy! She's our child!'

'I think we need to take some of the emotion out of this situation,' he says.

'*EMOTION!?*' Mum yells. 'Our daughter has run away from home and your suggestion is to feel no emotion! What's wrong with you?'

'I don't think this is very helpful.'

'Helpful!? She's moved in with a bunch of anarchists and dropouts! She told me that bourgeois values are murdering the planet and she hates everything we stand for.'

33

'That's normal at her age, isn't it?'

'No, it's not!'

'She's engaging with politics and the state of the world. It's not all bad.'

'How is it good?' asks Mum.

'I just think we have to work with this new passion of hers rather than against it. Maybe we can do some research into university courses which fit with these ideas that mean so much to her, show her what we find, and see if we can persuade her of the value of finishing her education.'

'Finishing her education? What are you talking about?'

'Did she not say that thing to you about finding her purpose in life?'

'What purpose? What life?'

'And how she's not sure she wants to go back to school next year.'

'WHAT!? But ... her A levels are next summer!'

'I know.'

'She can't not go back to school!'

'Well ... she *could*. We can't make her.'

'That's really what she said to you?'

'Yes.'

'Why did you not tell me this straight away?'

'I was building up to it.'

'This is a disaster! She's lost her mind!'

'Well, the more we act like it's a disaster, the more she's

34

going to carry on. That's how rebellion works. We're going to have to take it slow, stay calm and try to patiently win her back.'

'She can't leave school now! She can't just drop out! We can't do nothing and let her live in that dump with a mob of weirdos and freaks. We don't know who they are! It's not safe!'

'Well, I met most of them this evening, and they're not so bad. I thought they'd hate me and try to kick me out, but they were actually quite welcoming. They gave me a bowl of vegan chilli.'

'Vegan chilli?'

'It was pretty good. Have you ever thought maybe we shouldn't eat so much meat?'

Mum doesn't seem to hear him. All the blood appears to have drained from her face. Then she remembers I'm still sitting at the kitchen table with them, and tells me again to go to bed, this time as if she actually means it and will lose her rag if I ignore her again.

I stand, walk slowly to the door, then turn back and say, 'So that's it? She's gone?'

They both look at me, and neither of them speaks.

'Do you think she's going to be OK?' I ask.

There's a long pause, then Mum and Dad reply at the same instant: Mum saying, 'I hope so'; Dad saying, 'Of course she will.'

As I'm walking upstairs to bed, it occurs to me that even with just one person missing, the house feels eerily empty. I decide that tomorrow I'll head over the road and try to find out if what seems to be happening really is happening, or if Mum and Dad are just being hysterical. It sounds like a cool place. Maybe someone will offer me some mead.

# Who is this creature and when did it last wash?

The doorbell doesn't look promising. It's an old-fashioned brass one, heavily tarnished and is hanging by one wire from a hole in the wall. It looks more like a device designed to give you an electric shock than anything that might be used to announce the arrival of a visitor.

Someone has decorated the front door with an elaborate and beautiful swirling floral design. The stalks of the flowers are made of slogans written in bulgy green lettering. I tilt my head to read them: '*Leave your prejudices outside*' forms the stem of a dandelion; '*We tolerate everything except intolerance*' is what looks like a daisy; '*If you're not part of the solution, you're part of the problem*', complete with thorns, is supporting a multi-headed yellow rose.

The decoration must have taken days, but whoever did it clearly wasn't much interested in whether the door was capable of opening and closing, because it is hanging from only one hinge, at a skewed angle and wedged into the floorboards.

I step inside and, as my eyes adjust from the glaring sunlight, before I can see anything, I register the cool, dark air, heavy with a faintly fetid, sweetish smell.

'Hello?' I say, but there's no answer, and nobody appears. The only sign the house isn't abandoned is the sound of one lone voice, drifting down the staircase.

This is the biggest house on the street, and it feels like not so long ago that the Winters lived here. They were an old couple who barely spoke to anyone and were rarely seen, apart from occasional comings and goings in their silver Mercedes. I never went into their home, but it's a fair guess it didn't look like this. The hall floorboards are bare and ragged, roughly painted in blotchy streaks of lurid purple and green, and the once fancy wallpaper is only visible up near the ceiling, since all the walls are now covered in a mixture of murals, slogans and printouts of blogs, photos and news articles, all of which, at a glance, seem to be about the climate crisis. The only other remnant of the Winters I can see is the elaborate light fittings: big, old, swirly chandeliers now hanging incongruously above the stripped-out chaos.

I take a few tentative steps across the hallway, enough to see into the front room, which has the same painted floorboards and is furnished with a scattering of mismatched falling-apart chairs that look like they must have been salvaged from skips. Above the candle-filled fireplace is a wall painting of a globe inside an hourglass, dissolving like sand, crowned by an arc of white capital letters drawn to look as if they are melting, which say, 'HOW LONG HAVE WE GOT?' Underneath, forming a matching curve of writing, it says, 'THINK BIG. CHANGE EVERYTHING.'

Nobody seems to be around, and the house is strangely quiet. I can't even hear any drumming.

I walk on through the hallway, past the battered-looking staircase, following a tomatoey cooking smell to a room which looks out on to the junk-strewn, overgrown garden. A vast pot, big enough to bath a dog, is bubbling away on the stove, containing some kind of bean stew, and the sink is heaped with a teetering mound of dirty dishes. One more mug and the whole thing would collapse. An impressive amount of effort and skill has been applied to the task of a delaying this washing-up as long as possible.

Opposite the cooking area three pub-garden-style tables with built-in benches have been pushed together to form an eating area for twenty or so people. Behind the table is a large noticeboard thickly layered with colourful scraps of paper announcing craft workshops, jam sessions, discussion groups, meditation meetings, housework rotas, strategy forums, a bike-share scheme and more.

I gaze at the noticeboard, fascinated by this glimpse into

the world my sister has entered, filled with activities I've barely heard of, and certainly never participated in. I'm standing less than a minute away from my own home, but I seem to be in another dimension.

'Who are you?' A thin, high voice cuts suddenly though the air, making me jump and swivel towards the sound. In the doorway is the tree-hanging girl who greeted me yesterday. There's a streak of mud across one of her cheeks. I can see now that her hair reaches all the way down to her elbows and is filled with beads and tangled knots. A severe kitchen-scissors fringe just above her eyebrows is the only part of her hair that looks as if it's ever been cut.

Despite the heat, she is wearing a fluffy rainbow-striped jumper and a pair of loose cotton trousers with intricate embroidery at the ankles, just above bare feet which are whitish-grey on top, edging towards black at the toes and soles.

Seeing my face, she says, 'Oh, it's you.'

'I'm Luke,' I say. 'I live just over the road.'

'I know,' she says, after a long stare. 'How long have you lived there?'

This seems like a weird question, rather than, say, 'What are you doing in my kitchen?' but she doesn't look like the kind of person likely to ask what you expect, and, given the state of the front door, it's perfectly possible that random people could wander into this house every day.

'All my life,' I reply.

Her eyes seem to grow wider in their sockets. 'Wow!' she says.

After a long, uncomfortable silence, during which she stares at me as if I'm some sort of medical curiosity (which is kind of ironic, since the weird-looking person in the room certainly isn't me), she says, 'Your bedroom is the one upstairs at the front, isn't it? Over the front door. I've seen you.'

This girl is seriously strange. I decide to sidestep the stalking issue and get away as fast as possible. 'Listen – I'm here to visit my sister. She moved in a few days ago. Do you know where I'd find her?'

'I'm Sky,' she says, stepping towards me with an arm outstretched as if wanting to shake my hand.

'Great,' I say, tucking my hands into my pockets. 'Do you know where I'll find my sister? Seventeen. Longish hair dyed black. Black clothes. Always wears loads of eyeliner.'

'There's a house meeting upstairs,' says Sky. 'She'll be there.'

'Thanks,' I reply, edging out of the room.

As I turn to mount the staircase I glance back, and Sky is still in the same spot, with her neck twisted round towards me, following my every move with eerie, unblinking eyes.

From the upstairs landing I peer into the crowded room

where the meeting is taking place, examining the house's new inhabitants, who are perched on a jumble of rickety chairs and uncomfortable-looking stools or sprawled across the floor on cushions and rugs.

It takes me a while to spot my sister. She looks different, but it takes me a moment to realise how. Then I twig that it's her clothes, which, for the first time in ages, aren't black. But there's also something unfamiliar about her face. She hasn't been tattooed or pierced, yet she looks transformed. She looks happy. She's smiling, and not the weird, strained smile of the night she borrowed my sleeping bag, but a genuine one that actually fits with the rest of her face.

As soon as she spots me, this freakishly contented expression clouds over. She rearranges her features into a 'What the hell are you doing here?' look, and I respond with a shrug. She rolls her eyes, raises herself from the cushions she's curled up on and tiptoes through the tangle of sprawled limbs towards me.

'What do you want?' she says.

I probably should have thought of an answer to this question in advance. Bad planning on my part, there.

'Er … I came to see you.'

'Why?'

'Because you're my sister.'

'Why are you behaving like a moron?'

'I just wanted to say hi, and … Mum and Dad have gone totally off the deep end about you moving in here, so I thought I'd come and take a look. See what it's all about.'

'It's a climate protest. Why is that so hard to understand?'

'It's not.'

'I explained it to Mum, I explained it to Dad, now they've sent you. What's the problem?'

'They haven't sent me. I just came.'

'Why?'

'To see what you're doing.'

'I've told them what I'm doing. I'm taking a stand on the most important issue of our age.'

'OK. Right.'

'It's a global movement to face up to what's happening and actually change things, and I want to be part of it, instead of just ignoring the problem and distracting myself by buying more and more stuff while we all wait for the planet to die. I know Mum and Dad are freaking out and they think this is crazy, but what's crazy is *not* doing it. What's crazy is carrying on as if nothing's wrong.'

'You're right.'

'Well, if you think I'm right, why won't you leave me alone?'

'Who says I'm on Mum and Dad's side?' I say. 'I agree with you. I went on all the school strike marches.'

'Big wow.'

'I want to help.'

'Really?'

'Yes.'

'Why?'

'Because you're right. And because our street has split in two, and it's pretty obvious which side of the road is the boring one.'

She looks me up and down assessingly, then says, 'Well, the best contribution you can make is to keep Mum and Dad off my back. Tell them you visit me regularly, and I'm really happy, and everyone here is really nice and normal.'

'Are they?'

'Well, they're nice. And you don't have to *actually* visit me. That's just what you have to tell them.'

'Can I come sometimes?'

'If you have to. But I'm busy at the moment. This is a house meeting.'

'OK. Can I stay and listen for a bit?'

'I suppose. If you really want to.'

She gives me a quick half-smile and heads back to the cushions, returning to her spot next to a guy with a dense orange beard and a mop of ginger hair pinned up into a man bun, sitting as close to him as you can to another person without actually sitting on their lap.

I hover in the doorway for a while and take in the

intense discussion, which seems to be about refillable jars. Hoping that the debate will move on to a topic that explains a little more about how they are going to save the world, I look around at the commune members. Rose appears to be the youngest. There are lots of beards and dreadlocks, lots of tattoos, lots of shapeless garments in lurid colours, several adults in dungarees, and an extravagant peppering of piercings to ears, noses, lips and even the odd eyebrow. Most of them could pass for students, apart from one old guy with a long grey ponytail, wearing jeans, a lumberjack shirt and an ancient-looking leather waistcoat, and a pair of middle-aged women who both have long, curly hair and are sitting cross-legged on the floor.

Even though two shafts of sunlight are slicing in through the grimy windows, a nest of candles and tea lights is at the centre of the room, surrounding a smoking stick of vaguely armpity incense. Or maybe the room's odour is actual human armpits and the incense isn't cutting through. It's impossible to tell.

The topic of the meeting continues to be refillable jars for a very long time, way beyond my food container boredom threshold, and eventually I slink away, giving Rose a little wave as I leave, but she's too riveted by the discussion to notice.

In the front garden (or what was once the front garden

but is now the front junkyard) Sky is sitting on a chair made of builders' pallets. The instant I appear, she jumps up and walks towards me. Something about this strikes me as weird, so I keep walking and try to pretend she isn't there.

'Hi again!' she says, falling into step with me.

'Hi,' I say, stepping off the pavement and crossing the road towards home.

'Did you find your sister?' she asks.

'Yeah.'

'Was she in the meeting?'

'Yeah.'

'That's what I said, isn't it?'

'Yeah. Thanks.'

'She's nice, isn't she?'

'Sometimes.'

'She says everyone on your side of the street is terrified of the protesters.'

'She's exaggerating.'

'You're not frightened of us, then?'

'No.'

'So why are you running away?'

'I'm not,' I say, stopping and turning to face her. 'I'm just walking home.'

She smiles at me, and I look back at her, trying to form my features into an expression that says 'not frightened

46

but not particularly friendly either'. This is a tricky balancing act.

We're a similar height, probably roughly the same age, but she has the open and innocent face of someone much younger.

'Can I see inside your house?' she says. 'Since we're neighbours and everything.'

We're now only a couple of metres from my front door. The keys are already in my hand.

I don't really want this strange girl in my home, but I feel like she's cornered me, tricked me into a situation where her question feels like a test of whether or not I'm frightened of her.

For an instant, I wonder if maybe I am. Something about her makes me uneasy.

I take the last few steps to my door, open it and step inside. Sky remains where she is, staring at me in wide-eyed silence.

'Well?' I say eventually, which is quite a long way from 'Welcome, do come in and make yourself at home,' but this is how Sky seems to interpret it.

She walks in and gazes around, examining each of the walls and even the ceiling like a tourist awed by a cathedral, when in fact she's in a small suburban hallway. While Sky looks around, wonderstruck, my gaze falls afresh on this cluttered overfamiliar room, and it occurs to me that compared to the house I've just left this place has never looked more drab and dull.

After a while, Sky's eye falls on the hall mirror, which has old family photos and a jumble of postcards slipped in all the way around the frame. She examines every image one by one, in silence, with her mouth half open.

'Is that you?' she says, pointing to a faded photo I haven't really looked at for years, of Dad, me and Rose in a wooden rowing boat, on holiday in the Lake District. Rose and I are around ten and six, and we're pulling together on an oar, with Dad next to us operating the other oar, and all three of us are squinting into the sun. Rose and Dad are laughing at something, but I'm concentrating on the task of rowing, biting my bottom lip with a pair of chunky, oversized teeth.

'Yeah,' I reply, though it seems bizarre that this is true, and barely plausible that the cute child next to me in the boat is the same person as the scowling creature who has just run away from home to live with a gang of hippies.

Mum's voice, calling from the kitchen, breaks the momentary silence.

'Luke?' she says, 'Is that you?'

'I've brought someone round,' I say. 'From over the road.'

Mum appears and looks at Sky. She has her polite face on, but I can see what she's thinking: something along the lines of *Who is this creature and when did it last wash?*

48

# It can't be easy being her

Mum eventually stops staring and manages to say, 'And you are … ?'

'Sky.'

'What a lovely name,' she says, in a way that obviously (to me) means the opposite.

'Thanks,' says Sky.

'Well, Sky, *do* come in. It's lovely to meet you,' says Mum tensely.

'You have such a beautiful house,' says Sky, gazing around our messy IKEA kitchen.

Mum turns and glares for a moment, thinking this is sarcasm, but from the look of innocent admiration on Sky's face, it clearly isn't. Mum then glances at me, and I look back at her, and a silent *this-is-weird* flashes between us.

'Are you hungry?' asks Mum, switching her face back to Cheerful Hostess mode.

Sky nods, and Mum quickly assembles two sand-wiches, then sits at the table and watches us eat, gently probing Sky with questions about the mystery of what is really happening in the dilapidated house over the road.

Sky answers all her queries with a guileless simplicity that hides nothing but doesn't seem to reveal much, either. It turns out Sky is the only child there. Most of the protesters (though they prefer to be called climate rebels) are in their twenties and childless. The only exceptions are the three older people I spotted, who are veterans of other environmental campaigns. The place is supported in part by crowdfunding, and is striving to be a zero-carbon movement.

Sky, it turns out, has never lived in the same house for longer than a year, and is homeschooled by her mother.

'That must be fun,' says Mum, though I can see from her expression that just the thought of homeschooling makes her blood run cold.

'Not really,' says Sky, 'but most days it's pretty quick, so ...'

'And ... is she a good teacher?'

'It's not really like that,' says Sky cryptically.

'She doesn't teach you?'

'She does. Kind of. And other people, sometimes.'

'Who?'

'Just … whoever. I'd like to be at school, but Mum says …'

Sky tails away, looking as if this isn't a conversation she wants to be having. My mother isn't someone you can shake off quite so easily though.

'Your mum says what?'

'School isn't … suitable. For someone like me.'

'Like you in what sense?'

'Well … I'm different, and the way we live is different, and I need to value that instead of getting boxed in like other kids.'

'OK. I see.'

'She says schools are factories for conformism,' Sky adds, then looks up with those unnerving ice-blue eyes of hers, fixes her gaze on Mum, and says, 'Do you think that's true?'

Mum's cheeks flush. I can see that she knows she's been too nosy and has been caught out. She doesn't want to lie, but it's pretty clear she can't give an honest answer, either.

'I'm sure she knows best,' replies Mum unconvincingly, before swerving as quickly as she can to a new topic. 'And … er … you must have got to know my daughter, Rose. She's just moved into the commune.'

'A bit.'

'How's she getting on?'

'OK.'

'And do you have a sense of … well, of … what it is she does all day?'

'Just … normal stuff.'

'Such as … ?'

'Don't know. Chatting.'

'Anything else?'

'Just normal things. Like everyone else. Drinking tea. Having meetings. Do you have a bath?'

'Pardon?'

'Do you have a bath?'

'Of course.'

'Can I have one?'

'Now?'

'Is it OK to ask, or is that rude?'

'No, it's … it's fine. I'll show you the way and find you a towel.'

Mum and Sky head upstairs, and through the ceiling I hear the sound of water pounding into the bathtub.

After a while, Mum reappears carrying Sky's clothes at arm's length, pinched between finger and thumb. She puts them in the washing machine and slams it shut.

'I've given her some of your cast-offs,' she says.

'OK.'

Mum washes her hands, then sits next to me and whispers, 'Why did you bring her here?'

'I didn't. I went to see Rose and she just followed me home.'

'How is Rose?'

'Fine.'

'Fine? Is that all?'

'We didn't talk much.'

'Why not?'

'She was busy.'

'Doing what?'

'Having a house meeting.'

'About what?'

'Jars.'

'Jars?'

'Yes. They were talking about jars.'

'What is there to say about jars?'

'A lot apparently, but don't ask me to tell you what it was. Anyway, Rose seems fine – happier than when she was living here, anyway.'

'Thanks,' says Mum. 'Very sensitive.'

'You asked me how she was! You want me to lie and say she's miserable?'

'No, I just … never mind.'

Mum gets up from the table, fishes some ingredients out of the fridge, then passes me a pile of potatoes to peel.

I've just finished when Sky walks back into the kitchen with wet (but still straggly and tangled) hair, wearing one of my favourite hoodies and a pair of grey tracksuit trousers that only reach three-quarters of the way down her shins.

'Thank you,' she says to Mum. 'That was lovely.'

'No problem.'

'You're very kind.'

'It's nothing.'

Sky smiles at her, looking as if something is on the tip of her tongue which she can't quite get out, then she takes a couple of steps forward and says, 'Carrots.'

Mum looks up from the carrots she's chopping. 'Yes. Would you like one?'

'Thanks. I like carrots.'

Mum passes her a carrot and tosses another one to me.

After a couple of noisy bites, Sky says, 'Can I watch TV now? I've seen it through the window. You've got a huge TV, haven't you?'

'Not huge. Just normal size,' says Mum.

'Can I watch it?'

'Er … OK. Luke will put it on for you.'

I lead her into the living room and show her our old, average-sized TV.

'Wow! It's massive!' she marvels.

'What do you want to watch?'

'Something good.'

I open up Netflix and put on *Brooklyn Nine-Nine*. She stares at it, transfixed, standing in the middle of the room.

54

'You can sit down if you want,' I say.

She reverses on to the sofa and sits without taking her eyes from the screen. After a while, I go next door to talk to Mum.

'You gave her my best hoodie!' I hiss.

'It's worn out. There are holes in the elbows.'

'It's my favourite.'

'Sorry. You've got lots of others. Without holes.'

'Not like that one. And why did you tell her she could watch TV? Next thing she'll be staying for dinner, then she's going to think I'm her friend and I'm never going to be able to shake her off.'

'She asked! I couldn't just say no.'

'Why? She's not my friend!'

'You don't like her?'

'She's a freak!'

'Well, I think we should make an effort to be nice to her. It can't be easy being her. She said she's the only child living there.'

'That's her problem. I'm not going to be her social worker.'

'Nobody's asking you to be her social worker. But you can at least be kind.'

'Why?'

'Because it's the right thing to do.'

'I thought you hated those people. Now you're saying I have to be nice to them.'

55

'I never said I hate them. I just don't want Rose to live with them.'

'Because you don't want her to become like them, because you hate them.'

'Keep your voice down. And has it occurred to you that having someone from across the road visit us occasionally might be our best chance of finding out what's going on over there? Rose isn't going to tell us anything, is she?'

'Are you saying you're going to invite her *again*?'

'I'm just saying she's our neighbour. She's been living right over the road from us for weeks, and she's obviously lonely, so we can at least be pleasant to her.'

'Out of charity, or so we can use her as a spy?'

'It doesn't cost anything to be nice.'

'She gives me the creeps.'

'You just need to get used to her.'

'I don't want to get used to her.'

In the end, Sky did stay for dinner, and she stayed while we did the clearing-up, and she stayed while we all stood there in the empty kitchen waiting for her to leave. Eventually Mum said, 'I think it's time for you to go.'

Only then did she get the hint (if you can call that a hint) and go home.

## ✳ Things just happen to you, then that becomes your life

Though it just felt weird at the time, when we tell Dad about Sky's visit later that evening, the whole thing suddenly seems funny. Mum and I have trouble explaining it in a way Dad can follow, because we both keep cracking up. I do an impression of Sky's awestruck face as she sees the TV that almost makes Mum fall off her chair, and when I mime Mum carrying Sky's clothes at arm's length with her head turned away, they both lose it.

This garbled story must have stuck in Dad's mind though, because it's the first thing he asks me about as we drive to visit Grandpa on Saturday, which we do every other weekend. I'm not really sure how I got into this routine – Rose hardly ever goes, and Dad doesn't seem to mind when I skip it – but I've always felt close to Grandpa, and I quite like the trip. The drives to and from the care home are the only time I have Dad's undivided, undistracted attention, with him actually listening to what I say and asking follow-up questions.

We have a game we play in the car where he plays me the terrible music he used to like when he was young, alternating with me playing him the stuff he ought to like but doesn't because he's too old and stuck in the past and obsessed with outdated things like guitars and melody.

Near the care home there's a kebab place that Dad loves, so we always stop there after seeing Grandpa and pick up a takeaway to eat in the car. Part of the ritual is that every time Dad takes his first bite he says, 'Still the best!' and I roll my eyes at him. I'm not sure why, but we do this every single time.

All in all, the visit to Grandpa is a pretty good option for a Saturday morning.

'So that kid from over the road,' Dad says, barely a minute after we set off. 'What was she like?'

'Weird.'

'In what way?'

'Every way. Even how she looks at you is weird. She just stares all the time.'

'Who invited her in?'

'She invited herself. Couldn't keep her out.'

'Must be a strange life for her in that place. She's always hanging around, looking bored, isn't she? The amount of time she spends in that front garden, just drawing or doing nothing ...'

'What goes on in there?' I ask. 'What do those people actually *do*?'

'Hard to say. It's a bit of a mystery.'

'Why do you think Rose has gone?'

'Well ... teenagers like to rebel. It's just what happens.'

'This is kind of extreme though, isn't it?'

'I suppose.'

'It might make sense if she hated life at home, but she doesn't, does she?' I ask, turning towards Dad.

'I don't think so. Which is good. It means she hasn't really run away from us – she's run towards them.' Dad glances away from the road to meet my eye, and gives a tentative smile.

'Why though? I can see it might be fun to visit, but to *live* there! The place is a dump.'

Dad goes quiet for a few seconds, then says, 'Well ... I can kind of understand it.'

'Really?'

'I can see that being there is more interesting than being at home with me and you and Mum. It's different.'

'Don't you think they're all weirdos though?'

Dad brakes for a traffic light and turns to look at me. 'Is that your word for anyone who's different from you?'

'No!'

'I did a lot of travelling when I was younger, backpacking around.'

'Yeah, I've heard the stories.'

'Well, it was years and years ago, but I ended up spending time with a few people like that, and they're OK. Part of me admires them.'

'Admires them?'

Dad turns back to face the windscreen as we accelerate away from the lights. 'They've got the guts to be different and make their own rules, when everyone else just becomes a slave to work and money without even thinking about it.'

'Last I heard, you and Mum were going crazy about Rose living there, now you're saying you like them.'

'I never said I *like* them, but they're making a stand for something they believe in, and I respect that.'

'So you don't mind Rose living there?'

'She should come home. But that doesn't mean I think the people in the commune are evil.'

'Does Mum?'

'No! But she is a bit more upset than I am.'

'Why?'

'She and Rose just have a more … intense relationship. She feels kind of wounded by Rose leaving like that, without even talking to us about it. And she's worried.'

'She cares more,' I say, half a question, half a statement.

Dad doesn't respond to that, but he appears to be mulling it over as we drive the rest of the way in a silence that only breaks as he reverses us into a parking space and mutters, 'I sometimes wish I'd done things differently.'

'Different to what?'

He switches off the engine and yanks up the handbrake, but makes no move to get out of the car.

'Don't know,' he says, looking straight ahead at the dirt-splattered van parked in front of us. 'You only get so many choices in life, and the really big decisions don't even feel like you're consciously making them. Things just happen to you, then that becomes your life.'

'Like what?'

'Work mainly. I don't remember ever actually wanting a job in insurance, but here I am … twenty years doing the same thing. On and on.'

'Wow, you're a barrel of laughs today.'

'Sorry. Am I moaning?'

'I guess it's my job to cheer up Grandpa, then?'

'OK, let's go,' says Dad, pushing open his car door. 'You do the cheering-up, I'll do the moaning.'

'Same as always, then?'

'Very funny,' he says, as we step together on to the path to the care home.

'Also true.'

'Now it's not funny.'

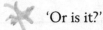'Or is it?'

'I have no idea what we're even talking about now,' says Dad, pressing the security buzzer with a jab of his thumb, but I can see that he's smiling.

Grandpa has been living in an old people's home for over a year now. He coped for a while on his own after Grandma died, and never complained, but when it became clear he was losing weight and not looking after himself properly, he reluctantly agreed to move somewhere where he'd get more help.

His body is much healthier now, but his mind isn't what it was. He almost seems to be trapped inside himself these days. When we visit, I can sense him struggling to peer out at the world and make sense of what he sees. Glimmers of the old Grandpa still shine through, but you never know when that's going to happen.

We head for Grandpa's stuffy little room, through corridors which smell of bleach mingled with whatever vegetables they're boiling that day. I don't know what it is they cook, but any time of day you go there, that's the smell: boiled vegetables and bleach. Even now, with the sun beating down outside, all the radiators seem to be churning out heat.

Grandpa is the only other person in the family who likes games, so I always take a pack of cards with me, and his lined, sagging face brightens a little whenever I sit down next to him and deal. Whist and crazy eights are his favourites, and the only time I ever hear him laugh these days is when he beats me. I love hearing the raspy, wheezing sound of his old man's cackle, so sometimes, if a game is close, I let him win, just like he used to do for me when I was small.

Chess was our game back then. He'd sit with me for hours, teaching me moves and strategies, chatting contentedly in the lilting, throaty East European accent he's never lost, every game ending with him saying, 'Ach, you beat me again!' in mock annoyance, which delighted me every time.

I have a feeling he'd be upset if he knew how the tables have turned, but I'm always subtle about it and he never guesses.

After a few hands of cards, I retreat to the window seat to play games on my phone, and Dad takes over the chair next to the bed for their fortnightly chat. I don't usually listen to what they're saying, but when Dad starts trying to explain about Rose's move into the commune, I find myself tuning in. He doesn't appear to notice I'm listening, because the story he tells Grandpa about his visit doesn't match the version he gave Mum and me. It's clear that he likes the place much more than he admitted to us.

After a relatively short and unconvincing account of

Rose's rebellion, and the possible reasons for it, he starts talking about the other people who live there, in particular a guy called Clyde, who sounds like some kind of guiding light for the commune, a veteran of 'the struggle' (whatever that is). Dad goes on to explain that he and Clyde have figured out that they would have been at university at exactly the same time, and even visited India in the same year, but their lives took opposite paths, with Clyde having travelled all over the world, living hand to mouth from a string of temporary jobs, keeping himself going where necessary by busking.

'He's just done whatever he wants, for his whole life,' says Dad, with something that sounds a little like awe. 'Whenever he's begun to feel bored or restless, he's just picked up and gone somewhere new.'

At this point, Grandpa, who has been silent ever since Dad took over the chair next to him, pipes up. 'Moron!' he barks.

'Who, me?' says Dad, with an embarrassed glance in my direction, as if he's only just remembered I'm in the room.

'No – this idiot friend of yours. What a waste of a life!'

'Well, maybe I've explained it badly,' says Dad. 'He's a nice guy.'

'It's no use being nice if you're lazy,' says Grandpa. 'I can't stand people who are lazy.'

'I know, Dad, I know,' replies my father wearily.

I often feel, watching these two talk, that their conversations inevitably end up falling into a groove that bores them both, as if they've already had all the conversations they're ever going to have, and the only question is which one it will be this time.

'Biscuit?' says Dad, raising a plate of chocolate digestives towards Grandpa in an obvious bid to change the subject.

I jump up and take three.

On the way home, we stop for our usual takeaway in the car. Dad's staring out of the windscreen, lost in thought as he unwraps the food and takes a mouthful, and still has the same dreamy expression on his face when he leans forward and silently takes a second bite.

'Still the best?' I say.

'Yeah,' he mumbles. 'Still the best.'

# Space

My first full week with the whole house to myself turns out to be less exciting than I'd hoped. The thrill of unsupervised solitude wears off surprisingly fast, and my enjoyment of uninterrupted days of nag-free gaming soon fades.

Seeing people would help, but everyone in my group of close friends has gone away on holiday, and it would feel weird to contact anyone else. I know I could always go next door and have balls thrown at me by Callum, but that never feels tempting.

The days soon begin to seem long, empty and slightly lonely. By the middle of the week, I realise that I'm starting to look forward to Mum getting home from work.

On Wednesday morning, Mrs Gupta, our other next-door neighbour, wakes me up with a ring on the doorbell at the highly antisocial hour of ten o'clock, but I manage to forgive her because it turns out she's delivering a homemade cake, along with the message, 'This is for your mother. Tell her I'm thinking of her.'

What kind of a mad person delivers a cake to a teenage boy who hasn't even eaten breakfast, in an empty house, and tells him the cake is for his mother? Does she know nothing? What planet does she live on? How I'm going to find the restraint to reach the end of the day with anything more to hand over than an empty tin with a few crumbs in it I have no idea.

'And do ask her if there's anything I can do to help,' she adds.

'More cakes,' is the obvious answer, but I manage to hold this in and just nod politely, until it occurs to me to say, 'Help with what?'

'Something has to be done. Everyone's been saying it for ages, but now … well … this was bound to happen sooner or later. I'm just so sorry it happened to Rose. She was such a lovely girl. I remember when she used to babysit for the boys …'

'She's not dead. She's just crossed the road.'

'Your family is being so brave. I admire that, I really do. It's terribly sad, what's happened to this street. Those people coming here, turning a lovely house into a filthy hovel.'

'It was empty.'

67

'Yes, and now look at it! God knows what goes on in there! Such a shame.'

Mrs Gupta turns and walks away. I stand in the doorway, holding the cake tin, watching her go, and just as she's getting to the pavement, I say, 'Why does everyone hate them so much? What have they actually done?'

She stops, turns, looks at me, thinks for a few seconds, then says, 'Well – they're dropouts. Anarchists.'

'What's an anarchist?'

'Someone who doesn't believe in anything.'

'If they don't believe in anything, what are they protesting about?'

'This is a conversation you need to have with your own parents. It's not my place. Just … be careful. You don't want to go the way of your sister. And don't eat all the cake!'

'Of course I won't,' I say, closing the door with one hand and opening the cake tin with the other.

That afternoon, feeling directionless and bored, I cross the road to visit Rose again. As I enter the commune, I hear the sound of guitar music wafting into the hallway – the kind of sleepy/bluesy thing I always make Dad switch off in the car, but it's obvious this isn't a recording coming out of a speaker. This is someone in a nearby room plucking an actual instrument with amazing skill and delicacy. The sound of it makes me freeze and listen, momentarily floating me away to a faraway place – somewhere empty, hot and dry.

I follow the drifting shimmer of notes and find myself in the kitchen, along with a dreadlocked couple sitting at the table, staring at their mobile phones in silence, and a bearded man swathed in layers of sack cloth and leather who is stirring a vat of something that smells like curry. He looks like he might be in fancy dress as an innkeeper in a children's fairytale. On a stool by the window is the grey ponytail guy, plucking an ancient-looking acoustic guitar with a dark patch in the wood under the strings from years of strumming. Everyone ignores me as I stand there staring at the guitarist, watching the spidery dance of his fingers on the fretboard.

Only when I step closer and stand a couple of metres in front of him does he acknowledge my presence with a brief nod, before returning his full attention to the guitar.

This guy is obviously Clyde. He looks like the kind of man people would talk about when he's not there and listen to when he speaks. There's something about him that looks simultaneously old and young, wizened and carefree. His hands are huge, hairy and rough-looking, but they move with fluid precision on his guitar strings, every motion smooth and perfectly coordinated, each finger sliding from note to note without the slightest flicker of hesitation or unnecessary movement. The expression on his face is one of serene, blissed-out concentration. I don't normally like sad music, but watching him produce these sounds in front of my eyes is mesmerising, and I lose all track of time as I watch him play.

Eventually, allowing his strings to reverberate on a long chord that sounds like both a whoop of delight and a howl of despair, he stops playing and looks at me. We listen together as the sound fades away. 'You like blues?' he says, after a while.

I shrug, since I never liked it before now. 'Are you Clyde?' I say.

He nods, seemingly unsurprised that I know his name without any introduction, then looks me up and down. 'So you are … ?' he says, in the gravelly voice of a lifetime smoker.

'Luke,' I say. 'From over the road. I'm Rose's sister. I mean she's my sister. I'm her brother. You know Rose? She's moved in here. For a while. Or maybe for good, I don't know.' Something about this man's level, unblinking stare is making me gabble like an idiot.

'I know Rose,' he says. 'She's a good kid. Lots of ideas.'

'And I think you know my dad.'

'Yeah, he visited.'

'He's told me about you,' I say.

Anyone else would ask what had been said, but not Clyde. He just nods and smiles, with a distant look in his eyes, as if he's not so much smiling at me as through me.

'Hi!' says a voice from the doorway.

I turn, and my heart sinks at the sight of Sky, still wearing my favourite hoodie and the too-short tracksuit trousers, giving me a geeky wave.

'Hi,' I say reluctantly.

'So you two are friends?' says Clyde, giving me a pointed stare, as if the question is some kind of test.

'Yes!' says Sky, but Clyde keeps his eyes fixed on me, with one eyebrow fractionally raised.

'I suppose,' I say, after a while. 'We only just met.'

Clyde gives a tiny nod of approval. 'Was it you that gave her the clothes?'

'It was my mum.'

'That was kind,' he says, less as a compliment than a judgement, then he casts his eyes down and begins to pluck a quiet tune.

'Do you know where I'd find my sister?' I ask.

Without taking his hands off the guitar strings or saying a word, he briefly flicks his chin upwards, a gesture that seems to mean *upstairs somewhere – not my problem*.

I don't want Sky to follow me, so without looking at her, I head out of the room and up the mud-streaked staircase.

I eventually find Rose sharing a hammock in a tiny bedroom at the back of the house. When she sees me, she scowls, hastily extinguishes a roll-up cigarette, and tumbles out of the hammock with all the elegance and grace of a cowpat exiting a cow.

At first I can see only the feet of her hammock companion, and a dangling tress of red hair. It's immediately obvious from the atmosphere in the room that I'm interrupting something.

'What are you doing here?' says Rose, straightening her clothes.

'Just came to say hi,' I reply.

'Again?' she says, as two hairy legs emerge from the folds of the hammock, followed by a long, skinny body. Sure enough, it's Ginger Man-Bun Boyfriend Suspect from the house meeting. He's wearing nothing more than a pair of cut-off jeans and a Celtic arm tattoo.

'Yo, blud,' he says.

I try to smile at him, but I don't really manage it because I'm too busy trying to calculate how crazy my parents would go if they knew Rose had a boyfriend in the commune, let alone the owner of a tattoo and a man bun.

'So you're the famous brother,' he says.

'Famous?'

'I was being ironic.'

I have no idea what this means and look towards my sister for some kind of explanation, but she's still just staring at me with *go away* eyes.

'Space,' says the boyfriend, extending a hand.

'What?'

'*Space!*' snaps Rose. 'That's his name.'

'Space?' I say.

'Yeah,' he replies.

'This is Luke,' says Rose.

'Space as in ... outer space ... or just space? Like a parking space,' I ask.

'Who can say?' replies Space, with a knowing smirk.

'Is that a nickname?'

'Used to be,' he replies. 'Shall I leave you two to catch up?'

'No,' says Rose hurriedly. 'Luke isn't staying.'

'Aren't I?'

'Did Mum and Dad send you here to spy on me?'

'No.'

'What do they want?'

'I don't know. I haven't asked them. I just came to see you.'

'Why?'

'Why do you keep asking why I'm visiting you?'

'Why do you keep visiting?'

'Because you're my sister. Mum and Dad don't even know I've come.'

'Dad keeps on hovering round here too.'

'Does he? I thought he only came once.'

'No – he keeps turning up.'

'When?'

73

'All the time! Why can't you just leave me alone!'

'That's not very friendly.'

'It's spying that's not friendly.'

'I'm not spying. I …'

'Can I say something?' interrupts Space, stepping forward and taking Rose by the hand, then, bizarrely, taking my hand too.

'The nuclear family unit is nothing more than a social convention, but brotherhood and sisterhood are part of our human geology,' he says. Then he puts my hand into Rose's and steps back.

I cannot remember the last time I held her hand – it's probably around a decade ago – and for some reason this feels like one of the most embarrassing moments of my life.

We can't look at each other, and can't instantly recoil from one another's touch, but neither of us can think of anything to say, either, so for a while we just stand there, hand in hand, staring at the floor.

'I should get home,' I say, mainly because this seems like the least weird way to let go of her and step away. 'Is there anything you want?' I add. 'From over the road, I mean. Or any message you want me to pass on?'

'Just … tell them not to worry. And to leave me alone. I'm fine.'

'OK.'

'And don't say anything about Space.'

'Don't say that he exists, or don't say he's your boyfriend, or don't describe him?'

'Just say nothing.'

'All right. My lips are sealed.'

As I'm walking out of the room, having pretty much given up on ever getting a friendly reception from Rose in her new home, she says, 'What about you? Are you OK?'

I turn back and see an expression on her face that now seems free of hostility, possibly even almost apologetic.

'I'm all right,' I say, with an attempt at a smile. 'Mum and Dad are a bit out of their tree, but that's no big deal. Got the house to myself all day, which is nice.'

'Yeah – Mum's been hassling me about not babysitting you, but you don't need that, do you?'

'No – course not.'

'Cool. Well, if you want to pop over again, text me first, and maybe we can hang out.'

'All right.'

'It's good here,' she says. 'We're doing something important.'

I nod.

'There are other ways to live,' she adds. 'Different to Mum and Dad. And that's OK.'

'I know. It's Mum and Dad that don't get it.'

'They will eventually,' she says.

'So you're going to be here for a while?'

'Probably. Can't think why I'd leave.'

Whether this is something Mum and Dad have already figured out, or is news that would break their hearts, I have no idea. Either way, it doesn't feel like information I'm in any hurry to pass on.

'You understand why I'm here, don't you?' says Rose.

'I think so.'

'Even if we don't stop the airport expansion happening, it's important to stand up for what you believe in, isn't it?'

'Totally.'

'We're planning things. Protests. Stuff is going to happen.'

'Well, if I can help …'

'Maybe you can. When it's time, I'll tell you.'

'OK.'

'Good. See you soon, yeah?' she says.

I smile and set off home, feeling surprisingly good about the way the visit panned out, until I step outside, and there's Sky. Waiting for me. Not even doing anything else while she waits, but just standing there, looking at the front door like a dog outside a supermarket.

'Hi!' she says, as if we're old friends and it's an extraordinary coincidence we've bumped into each other.

'Hi,' I mumble, heading home without breaking stride.

Inevitably, she follows me.

Callum is in front of his house, chucking a tennis ball

against his garage then catching it on the rebound, and I know immediately what will happen next.

Sure enough, as soon as he's made the next catch, he turns and positions himself to block the way to my front door.

'Who's this?' he says.

'I'm Sky,' says Sky, with clueless friendliness.

Callum smirks. 'What kind of a name is that? Are you called after the TV channel?'

'No, I'm called after the sky. Up there,' she says, pointing upwards. 'What's your name?'

'Callum.'

'You live next door to Luke?'

'Yeah.'

'Nice house.'

'It's OK.'

'It's big.'

'Not as big as yours. But then mine isn't filled with homeless people, is it?'

Sky's face freezes as she begins to sense the hostility in the air. Her eyes flick anxiously towards me for a moment, looking for clues as to what is going on, but I can't think of a way to explain it.

'Let's go,' I say, but before Sky moves, Callum takes a step towards her, sniffs the air, and says, 'What's that smell?'

Sky stares at Callum with a look of bewilderment.

'I can't smell anything,' I say.

'Must be both of you, then,' says Callum, turning back to me. 'Are you going to move into the freak house with your sister?'

'They're not freaks, they're climate protesters,' I say, stepping around him and heading for my door, but before Sky can follow, Callum says 'Catch!' and chucks his tennis ball straight up into the air.

Sky stands under the rising then falling ball with her hands cupped together, but I can tell by her awkward stance and worried expression that it is going to bounce free of her grasp, which is exactly what happens.

Sky hurries after the ball as it skitters away into the gutter, goes on her hands and knees to fish it out from under a car, then scampers back and hands it to Callum, who tosses it from hand to hand without breaking eye contact.

'Butterfingers,' says Callum.

Sky squeezes past him and follows me to my door.

As I unlock it, Sky says into my ear, 'Mum says I have to get my clothes back. The ones your mother took.'

'I'll get them for you,' I say.

I'm about to ask her to wait on the doorstep, but Callum is still right there, staring at us, bouncing his ball against the pavement with a sinister look in his eye. I have no desire to invite Sky into my house, but I sense that I can't leave her out there at Callum's mercy, so I usher her in with a wave of my arm and close the door behind us.

By the time I've found the clothes, which are in a neatly folded pile on top of the washing machine, she's sat herself down on the sofa and put on the TV. She has the same rapt expression on her face as last time, except that now she's watching one of those mind-numbingly boring programmes about doing up houses.

I hand Sky the clothes, but her eyes don't budge from the screen.

I stare at her for a while, feeling as if I ought to say something about Callum, sensing that I owe her an explanation of what just happened outside my house. I want Sky to understand that Callum is someone who zeroes in on other people's weaknesses, and that Sky, of all people, should give him a wide berth, but I don't want her to think I'm her ally or protector. I don't want her to mistake me for a friend.

I can't think of any way to put this into words, so instead I sit with her for a few minutes in front of the boring show as a gesture of low-grade companionship, then slip upstairs, leaving her in front of the TV. Mum can get rid of her when she gets home from work.

# The wrong chair

I'm not sure how much time has elapsed when I hear Mum calling me down for dinner. My room can be something of a black hole when it comes to the passage of time. Once I'm behind that door, hours can disappear without me having any idea what I've even been doing.

When I come down, after being called a couple more times, I've almost forgotten that I left Sky in the living room, and I'm certainly not expecting to find her chatting over dinner with Mum and Dad as if they are old friends. It's true that I didn't exactly hurry downstairs, but the sight of the three of them eating happily together, with Sky sitting in my seat, immediately makes me bristle.

'This is very cosy,' I say, pulling out the chair Rose usually sits on.

'You have to try this food,' says Sky. 'It's incredible.'

'Should I? I was planning to just sit here and watch.'

Sky stares at me blankly, as if I'm talking in a foreign language. Why did I invite her in? What was I thinking?

'Sky's been telling us all about the commune,' says Mum. 'Apparently there are rotas for everything, and everyone has to do their share of cooking, washing-up, cleaning and other household chores.'

'Cleaning? I don't think that's on the rota,' I say.

'It is,' says Sky.

'There's also a skill-share pool,' says Dad, 'where everyone in the commune contributes their time to teach a skill to other people in the house. There's yoga, music, carpentry, cooking ... lots of things.'

'What's Rose teaching?' I ask. 'Whining?'

'She's been helping me with my schoolwork,' says Sky. 'She's really nice.'

'Never helped me with *my* schoolwork,' I say. 'But I'm only her brother, so ...'

'And ... what's her boyfriend like?' asks Mum, in an unconvincingly offhand manner. I haven't told her anything about Space, but news of his existence must have filtered through, either from Rose herself or from something Dad has spotted on one of his snooping trips. Or maybe she's just fishing – acting like she already knows there's a boyfriend as a way of tricking Sky into revealing whether or not there is one.

'He's OK,' says Sky, cutting herself a large mouthful.

Mum gives a small nod, glances at Dad, then says, 'What do you mean "OK"? Is that OK as in not nice?'

Sky shrugs.

'How old is he?'

Sky shrugs.

'Is he … are you saying you don't like him?'

'He's OK. He does a lot of drumming.'

After that Mum and Dad grill Sky for the entire duration of the meal about who lives in the commune, whether they have jobs, what they used to do before they moved in, and various other coded questions to try and figure out if they have criminal tendencies or dangerous habits. Sky somehow manages to answer all my parents' questions without giving anything interesting away, but I get the feeling this isn't because she's concealing something, it's because she genuinely doesn't know anything about anything. If the commune is a hotbed of drug abuse and subversive behaviour, Sky is clearly oblivious to it all. In her world everyone is either 'nice', 'OK' or (for a couple of people who are obviously beyond the pale of awfulness) 'not very nice'.

Reading between the lines of Sky's vague comprehension of what people other than her do all day, none of the residents of the commune have actual jobs, but thanks to crowdfunding and other mysterious sources of money, there's always food on the table (eaten communally and cooked according to a rota), though some of it is 'free-cycled' from past-sell-by-date supermarket stock. A few things have been planted in the garden, some by Sky herself, but nothing has been successfully harvested yet, apart from some cress that she grew on a piece of kitchen towel on a window sill.

Mum seems to have learned her lesson about the difficulty of getting rid of her, and at the end of the meal, with Dad still quizzing Sky on every detail of life in the commune, Mum stands up and says, 'It was nice to see you, Sky, but now it's time for you to go home.'

This, it turns out, is just about direct enough for Sky to get the message. She thanks Mum, lifts her plate, licks off the last dregs of food, then leaves.

'Poor kid,' says Mum as the front door closes.

'She's so weird. I wish you'd stop inviting her,' I say.

'I didn't invite her. She was here when I got home.'

'You didn't have to give her dinner though.'

'It's amazing how they're just over the road, but it's like they're in another world,' says Dad dreamily, more to himself than to us. 'All the things we do without even thinking about it, just blindly going along with what everyone else does, and they ... don't.'

'Parenting, for example,' says Mum.

Dad looks at her for a moment, then turns his head and gazes pensively into space, his eyes clouded over with some distant private thought. The warm orange light of a summer evening is slanting into the room, casting a skewed shadow of my father across our plates and glasses, and for an instant the room seems paused, like a photograph. I have a strange sense of this insignificant moment dropping itself into my memory and taking root, and as this happens, I'm struck by a feeling that everything is about to change.

Mum breaks the spell with a weary sigh, saying, 'I don't think anyone's looking after that child.'

'That doesn't make it your job,' I say.

Sky getting mocked by Callum may have stirred my sympathies, but the sight of her being mothered by my mum has had the opposite effect. The fact that Mum let her sit in my chair feels ominous and unsettling.

'That's heartless,' snaps Mum, fixing me with a cold stare. 'You don't know how lucky you are.'

I look back at her and, for the first time ever, this tedious parental mantra doesn't just bounce off me. In a flash, as a sudden revelation, I see that my boring, predictable house and family are, in fact, a blessing which has been bestowed on me, and not on kids like Sky. If it had never been given to me, I'd be someone else entirely.

An instant after this idea hits me, it seems to merge with a returning sensation of vague anxiety. I'm not sure exactly what it is that has happened, or what might be coming next, but I feel tugged in the pit of my stomach by a feeling that the straightforward family I belonged to until the moment I lent Rose my sleeping bag has begun to dissolve.

I cannot, of course, say any of this, so I roll my eyes at Mum and head upstairs.

# The wigwam controversy

A couple of days later, towards the end of another listless afternoon, I hear the sound of drumming pulsing out of the commune. This, in itself, is nothing unusual, but the sheer volume sounds different, as if not just a couple of people but everyone who lives there is playing the drums at once.

I head over the road to see what's going on, and when I place my hand on the rickety front door, I can feel the sound reverberating through the wood. In the hallway, the floorboards under my feet also seem to be trembling in time with the ear-splitting racket emerging from the kitchen.

I go in, and even though, until this moment, I had no idea what a drumming workshop was, it's clear that I'm looking at one now. Space is standing in the middle of the room with an African drum in front of him, held in place by a loop of purple and yellow rope which is slung over one shoulder. Scattered around him are ten or so people, squatting on the floor or perched on stools, each playing drums of different shapes, sizes and musical styles. But that's not the weird thing. There's something else, a sight that at first I can barely believe or comprehend.

My dad, playing the bongos.

He's red-faced, drumming furiously, and seems to have worked up a sweat which has led him to strip off his shirt.

This is among the most alarming things I have ever seen. It's like a crack has opened up in the surface of the Earth and swallowed up my home. It's like gravity has decided to operate sideways instead of downwards. It's my dad, in a vest, playing the bongo drums in a room full of hippies and, apparently, enjoying it.

I'm not sure how much of the sheer horror I'm feeling is visible on my face, but when Dad sees me, he smiles, waves and beckons me over. His whole body is rocking to and fro with his drumming. Even Grandpa, who has been certified mentally infirm by doctors, has never looked as mad as this.

I tiptoe through the aural carnage of slaps, booms and thwacks towards the grinning, sweat-soaked freak who used to be my father.

'WANT A GO?' he yells, barely audibly, into my ear.

I pull a *what-is-going-on-here-and-who-the-hell-are-you?* face at him, but he doesn't seem to understand.

'IT'S FUN!' he shouts, beating out a failed attempt at a jazzy rhythm. His palms, I notice, are the colour of beetroot.

'What are you doing?' I say.

'WHAT?'

'WHAT ARE YOU DOING?'

'DRUMMING!'

'I can see that, but …'

'Can't hear you,' says Dad, biting his bottom lip and twitching his neck in time to the beat (except not in time).

'WHY AREN'T YOU AT WORK?' I ask.

He grins at me, executes a little bongo flurry and says, 'TOOK THE DAY OFF!'

'WHAT … FOR *THIS*?'

'PARTLY. AND I SAID I'D HELP CLYDE PUT UP A WIGWAM IN THE GARDEN. DO YOU WANT TO SEE IT?'

Yes, I really did just hear my dad ask me if I want to see his wigwam. The man who fathered me truly spoke those words.

'IT'S ALMOST FINISHED!' he yells proudly.

I stare at him, slack-jawed, and it dawns on me that the weirdest thing of all is how content and carefree he looks. I don't think I've ever seen him this happy.

'DOES MUM KNOW YOU'RE HERE?' I ask, attempting to burst his balloon of insanity by reminding him that he's an adult, with a family.

'I'LL TELL HER LATER. OOH, LOOK! THERE'S SOME MARACAS. DO YOU WANT THEM?'

The maraca request is too much. I take a final look around the room to see if Rose is there – she isn't, unsurprisingly, since if she saw what our father was doing she'd probably go into an embarrassment-induced coma – then make a hasty exit. I take a quick tour of the house, and though I do find Clyde (who is either asleep sitting up or meditating, I can't tell), and a roomful of women who seem to be reading poetry to one another, there's no sign of my sister.

Stepping out of the commune into the bliss of drum-free open air, I feel momentarily as if I have just walked away from being beaten up.

Mum's car is now back in the driveway.

Should I try and explain to her what I've just seen? Would that even be possible? Are there words to describe the horror? Or, given that Dad is clearly having some kind of crack-up, should I just stay out of the way and leave her to make sense of it? Dealing with this situation, whatever it is, really shouldn't be my job.

I head home, and I'm still wondering whether to tell Mum about Dad's personality crisis when I walk into the kitchen and find her standing at the counter chopping a tomato, doing spelling drills with Sky, who is at the table in front of an exercise book, gripping a pencil and writing something down with such intense concentration that she doesn't notice me entering the room.

'B – E – L – E – I –,' she says.

'No,' replies Mum, not even looking up or greeting me. '"I" before "E" except …'

'After "C"! So it's B – E – L – I – E – V – E?'

'That's it! Spot on!'

'What are you doing?' I say.

'Oh, hi, love,' says Mum. 'I'm giving Sky some help with spelling.'

'Why?'

'Because she asked me to.'

'So you're her teacher now?' I say.

'Oh, Luke! Stop being so sulky! You're acting like you're jealous, or something.'

'Of *her*!?'

'Maybe you're just hungry.'

'Your mum's an incredible cook,' says Sky.

'Oh, really?' I reply, with enough sarcasm to wilt a plant. 'Is there anything else you'd like to tell me about my own mother that I might not be aware of? Since you're such great pals.'

'Luke!' snaps Mum. 'Come with me! Now!'

She slams down her knife, grabs me by the arm and marches me into the living room.

'You have to stop this! It's beneath you!' she says, in an angry whisper.

'What's beneath me?'

'The way you're behaving to Sky. Can you not see what she's been through?'

'No, I can't.'

Mum lowers her voice another notch. 'Nobody's ever looked after her! Nobody's given her any proper schooling or decent clothes or even a haircut, and I'm sure she'll move on soon enough, but for the moment, she's our neighbour, and our house has become some kind of sanctuary from whatever madness it is she has to live with. And that leaves us with a choice. We can either be selfish and cold and ignore her and throw her out, or we can share a little bit of our good fortune and be pleasant to her and, maybe, in some tiny way, help her.'

'How do you know nobody looks after her?' I say.

'It's obvious!'

'You just assume that everything those people do is terrible, but you don't know. You won't even go there.'

'We're not talking about them. We're talking about us,' she says. 'We're talking about you. What kind of a person do you want to be?'

I shrug.

'How do you think you'd want to be treated if you were her?'

I force myself to meet her gaze and rearrange my scowl

into a reluctant half-smile. 'I'd probably want loads of spelling tests,' I say.

Mum lets out a chuckle and gives me as much of a hug as I'll let her. 'How about you play a game with her? Give her some attention?'

'A game?'

'Monopoly or something.'

'*Monopoly!?*'

'Or something else.'

'I suppose I could teach her to play *Fortnite*. But only if it doesn't count as part of my screen time. Because it's not for me.'

'You are such a lawyer.'

'It's only fair!'

'OK. If that's what it takes.'

I cannot tell you how grateful Sky is to be taught how to play a video game, or how eyeball-shatteringly useless she is at it, but it's touching to see how much she enjoys playing, even when this involves getting slaughtered every few minutes.

At first it seems pointless playing with someone so useless, but there's something infectious about her unguarded enthusiasm, and after all the hours I've spent gaming on my own since school broke up, I have to admit it is more fun to be playing alongside someone else, with an actual human being, not just a voice in a headset.

The strangest thing of all is that her habit of making over-intense eye contact, and the way she constantly issues a stream of bizarre questions, slowly begin to seem endearing rather than annoying. I'm not saying I start to *like* her, but I do find myself understanding in a new way the hissed pep talk Mum gave me in the living room a short while earlier.

I've never before met anyone so open – so nakedly and unashamedly innocent – and once I notice this, being mean or unfriendly to her somehow seems as cruel and unthinkable as kicking a puppy.

Sky ends up joining us for dinner again, of course, but that doesn't mean there isn't a surprise guest, because Dad walks in (still sweaty, but fully dressed again, thankfully) accompanied by Rose, who makes it immediately clear she's 'just visiting'.

'Rose!' says Mum, in response to the unexpected sight of my sister turning up in her own kitchen. 'How lovely to see you!'

'Dad persuaded me to come round for dinner. Like, a social call.'

'Wonderful! You're welcome *any* time,' says Mum.

'Obviously,' replies Rose. 'Did Dad tell you he bunked off work today to put up a wigwam?'

'What did you say?' asks Mum, seemingly unable to comprehend the words that have come out of Rose's mouth.

93

'Yeah, he's stalking me. Can you tell him to stop?'

'I'm not stalking you,' says Dad.

'So what *are* you doing?'

'Just … visiting.'

'Oh, and me being there is a coincidence?'

'I hardly saw you all day.'

'Yeah – because I was hiding from you.'

'You were there all day?' says Mum.

'Yes,' says Dad sheepishly. 'I was going to tell you, but Rose beat me to it.'

'You weren't at work?'

'I told you, he was putting up a wigwam all day with Clyde,' says Rose.

'Who's Clyde?'

'Dad's new boyfriend. They're having a massive bromance, which is literally the most embarrassing thing in the world. If you saw the way Dad looks at him, you'd puke. Literally puke.'

'Rose, don't be ridiculous,' says Dad.

'I'm ridiculous!? You're the one who just spent an hour playing bongo drums!'

'An hour playing the bongo drums?' says Mum.

Dad's face flushes from the neck upwards. 'I …'

'At least an hour. Maybe two,' says Rose.

'On a work day?' asks Mum. 'Why?'

'Yeah,' says Rose. 'Good question. Why, Dad?'

Dad takes a deep breath and has a long think. Sky stares at us all with a face even more bemused than her usual permanently bemused one. 'I … visited the commune … to see where you'd gone, and check that you're safe, and find out what you're up to, and … I didn't know what I'd find, and … to my surprise … the people there are … I mean, even though I'm a middle-aged man in a suit, they seem willing to not make any assumptions about me and … well, they're just friendly. I like them. Not all of them, but it's like a breath of fresh air. Everyone I've met, for years, they're all kind of basically the same. But those people aren't. It's interesting.'

'So you took a sickie to spend the day putting up a wigwam and playing the bongos?' says Mum. 'That genuinely happened?'

'It sounds weird if you put it like that,' says Dad.

'How can I put that so it wouldn't sound weird? What other way is there to say it?' says Mum.

'I was just helping a friend.'

'So this Clyde person is your friend now?'

'HE'S NOT YOUR FRIEND!' spits Rose. 'Nobody there is your friend. They all feel sorry for you and they're just too nice to say it to your face. Clyde's nice to everyone – that's his thing – he loves everybody and everybody loves him, and you thinking you're now his special buddy is just totally tragic and you DON'T BELONG OVER THERE!

IT'S MY PLACE AND THAT'S WHERE I LIVE NOW AND YOU GOING OVER THERE ALL THE TIME IS JUST TOTALLY PSYCHO! WHY CAN'T YOU LEAVE ME ALONE!? IT'S MY LIFE AND IT'S UP TO ME WHAT I DO!'

With that, and without having eaten a single mouthful, Rose stands and marches out of the house, slamming the door behind her.

'So,' says Mum eventually. 'That conciliatory approach of yours – how's it working out for you?'

# The double-down

Saturday morning. Mum, Dad and I are eating breakfast together, and without Rose it's weirdly quiet. You can hear our spoons against the cereal bowls. When Dad spreads his toast, the sound of his scraping knife fills the room.

Mum's sitting in front of a half-eaten portion of muesli, staring out at the cloudless blue sky, but from the expression on her face you'd think she was gazing at November drizzle. The grass in our garden is losing its colour, slowly turning khaki and becoming spiky underfoot. Through the open window, I can hear the steady thump, thump, thump of Callum playing Swingball on his own, battering his tethered tennis ball round and round in circles with brutal determination.

Dad crunches his toast and looks at Mum, as if he's trying (and failing) to figure out what she's thinking. There's a strange, tense atmosphere. I have a feeling Dad spent the night in the spare room.

After a while, he pushes his chair back from the table and announces, 'I've got a plan!'

Mum turns towards him, but slowly, already doubtful. 'What?'

'We double down!' he says proudly.

'What does that even mean?' she asks.

'It's when you double your stake on a bet to try and recover your losses.'

'I know what the phrase means,' she says. 'I just don't know what *you* mean.'

'I'm talking about Rose. She clearly doesn't like me being at the commune. It annoys her.'

'Just a bit,' says Mum.

'And we want her to come back here, don't we?'

'Yes …'

'So how about instead of doing what she asks and leaving her alone, I do the opposite. I've got a week's annual leave from the office that I haven't used yet, and there's a room at the top of the commune nobody's using. I could go over there and move in for a few days.'

'What? Why?'

'Flush her out.'

'Flush her out?'

'Yeah. If she hates me being there as much as she says she does, and I move in, what's the logical next step? She'll come back here.'

'You think?'

'It's worth a try.'

'Is it?'

'We have to do *something*.'

'Even if it's futile and pointless?'

'It might not be. You never know.'

'I don't understand why you'd want to do this. Is there something you're not telling me?'

'No,' says Dad.

They stare at one another for a while, Dad stretching his mouth into a nervous smile, Mum looking like she's chewing something too unpleasant to swallow.

'So,' says Dad, turning towards me. 'This room I'm thinking of is currently filled with junk. Will you help me clear it out?'

I look back at him, feeling a jolt of mingled dread and excitement at the sight of my dad losing his marbles. He's never before been someone likely to do anything unexpected, and I have no idea whether this transformation is a calamity or a joke. If nothing else, at least this version of him is more interesting than the old, predictable, sane one.

'OK,' I say, less out of any real desire to help him than because I want to find out what on earth he's up to.

Dad hurries upstairs, and comes back down wearing an old T-shirt, hiking boots and a pair of faded, bizarrely misshapen jeans which are tight in all the places they should be baggy and baggy in all the places they should be tight.

'Feeling strong?' he says, clapping his hands together, seemingly unaware that he is wearing trousers which are so bad they should probably be illegal.

'Ish,' I say, momentarily catching Mum's eye. She gives me a little nod, which seems to mean, '*Go with him and keep an eye on him,*' so I stand up and head to the commune with Dad.

We go into the kitchen first, where Clyde is eating breakfast with a small group of bearded/dreadlocked/tattooed people. Dad greets everyone by name, and they all respond as if they're both pleased and unsurprised to see him. One of them even gives him a fist bump.

Clyde tells us to help ourselves from the vat of lumpy porridge on the stove and, even though it looks about as appetising as bin juice, Dad scoops himself out a portion and sits at the table with his new friends (who look exactly like the kind of people he'd usually cross the street to avoid).

He introduces me to everyone, announces that we're going to clear out the junk room at the top of the house, and asks if it's OK for him to stay there for a few days. Unlike Mum, the commune members seem quietly welcoming towards Dad's suggestion. I'm not sure what it is you'd have to do to make these people believe you're behaving strangely, but apparently this isn't even close.

The conversation turns inevitably to recycling, and what should be done with the abandoned and broken furniture that's currently filling the room. Dad's suggestion is to put it in his car and take it to the dump, but after a while Clyde speaks up and says he has a better idea. 'How about we upcycle and make something out of it?'

'Like what?' says Dad.

'Brilliant!' says one of the previously silent porridge-eaters around the table – a woman with so many nose rings that she tinkles like a wind chime when she moves her head. 'A sculpture! A monument to waste!'

'How about we go for verticality?' says Clyde. 'Make a kind of totem pole. To go next to the wigwam.'

This idea is so enthusiastically embraced that we soon have a team of eight people emptying out Dad's new bedroom and carrying the contents to the commune's back garden. When everything is out there in a big heap on the dry and faded unmown grass, Dad heads home for his toolkit and all the nails and screws he can find.

Within a couple of hours, the garden is dominated by a huge structure, which is christened *The Waste Totem*. It consists of an ancient wardrobe underneath a tower made from the nailed-together remnants of a broken bed, an upside-down office chair and a child's desk, topped with a hat stand and a standard lamp. It's tethered down with a few guy ropes attached to nearby shrubs and trees, and when I look up at the finished sculpture, it strikes me that it is both brilliant and possibly lethal. When the wind gets up, anything could happen.

Every member of the commune now seems to be out in the garden, cheering on the people who are up ladders adding finishing touches to the top. Someone appears with tins of green and yellow paint, and I join in with the group who now take over the project.

I don't notice that Dad has slipped away until he suddenly reappears, poking his head out of a top window, shouting, 'It's beautiful!'

Someone calls back asking if he needs any help with his room, and he says he's almost done, so I head up to check out his progress. I'm intercepted halfway up the stairs by Rose, who grabs my T-shirt and pulls me into a bedroom.

'What's going on?' she snaps. Her eyes have narrowed to snake-like slits.

'We're making a totem pole.'

'Don't piss me around, Luke. What's he up to?'

'Dad, you mean?'

'Obviously!'

'Er … he's clearing out a room.'

'And?' she says, her nostrils flaring with barely contained rage.

'I think … have you spoken to him?'

'Of course I have! He says he's moving in! MOVING IN! HERE!'

'Why are you asking me what's going on if you already know?'

'Not what's going on as in what is he physically doing, but what's going on as in WHAT THE HELL IS GOING ON!? WHAT'S HE PLAYING AT?'

'Did you ask him that?'

'Of course I did!'

'And?'

'He said I'd inspired him.'

For some reason, this makes me laugh. It's probably just the tension, but Rose is not impressed.

'Funny, is it?'

'No,' I say, struggling to wipe the smile from my face.

'This is insane! This is so twisted! You have to stop him!'

'Me? How?'

'I don't know. You and Mum have to get him out of here. He's gone totally rogue and there is just no way he can do this! It's not OK! Can you imagine what this is like for me?'

'Not really.'

'Well, try.'

'Is it that bad? He seems … happy.'

'THAT'S NOT *HAPPY*!' yells Rose. 'THAT'S PSYCHOTIC! THAT'S A MAN WHO NEEDS TO BE

CARTED AWAY AND LOCKED UP! HE CAN'T DO THIS!'

'How am I supposed to stop him?'

'Everybody here thinks he's nice!' she spits. 'None of them can see what's going on. He's pulling the wool over all their eyes and nobody gets it. Even Space! Even my boyfriend! "Hey, yeah, don't stress, he's a decent guy." *It makes me want to throttle him!*'

'Who, Space or Dad?'

'Both of them! If he moves in up there, I ... I ... I'm going to go crazy.'

'I thought you said he was the one going crazy.'

'I'm going to go crazier. Just watch me.'

With that, she turns and stamps out.

We used to be such a normal, happy family. Now, suddenly, we seem to be competing to outdo each other for insanity.

I carry on up the stairs and find Dad on his knees, next to a bucket of grey water, scrubbing the floor with a wooden brush.

'What do you think?' he says.

'Nice room,' I say. 'Apart from ... you know ... being totally empty.'

'Let's go and get a mattress,' he says.

'From where?'

'The spare room at home. Can't be bothered with the

bed, but at my age you do need a proper mattress.'

Without waiting for my answer, Dad clatters down the stairs in his big, geeky shoes, clearly in no doubt that I'll follow. As we cross the road, I notice that even the way he moves now is different: it's faster, bouncier, more alive than the heavy-seeming, slow-moving father I used to have.

Dad slips his key slowly into the lock of our front door, gestures with a finger to his lips, and we step into the house as quietly as we can.

It turns out that carrying a mattress down a twisting staircase in silence is almost impossible, particularly when you knock two pictures off the wall and topple a lamp.

Mum's in the front hall, standing by the door with her arms crossed, when we get back downstairs.

'Hi,' says Dad, doing a very unconvincing job of looking pleased to see her.

'How are you getting on?' says Mum icily.

'Fine,' he replies.

'We made a totem pole,' I say, because I find it very hard not to stir, even when I know I should keep my mouth shut.

'Lovely,' says Mum, in the tone of voice you'd use to congratulate a toddler for successfully filling a nappy.

'See you later,' says Dad, opening the front door and beginning to haul the mattress outside.

'Is that later as in later today?' says Mum. 'Or later this week? Or just some non-specified time in the future when you get the urge to pop into your own home?'

'Soon,' says Dad. 'Don't worry. Everything's fine.'

'Half the family has now moved out, and you're telling me everything's fine?'

'I haven't *moved out*. It's just a temporary adjustment to the sleeping arrangements. For the sake of our daughter.'

'That's who you're doing this for?'

'Of course! Who else would it be for?'

'It's just very out of character. All this. I can't really tell what you're up to.'

'I'm not up to anything!' says Dad, with a nervous laugh.

'Apart from spending the day making totem poles with your hippie friends. That's totally normal behaviour, is it?'

'Oh, normal, normal, normal,' says Dad. 'What's so great about being normal?'

'Mmm,' says Mum. 'That, right there, is what I'm worried about. Is this a midlife crisis?'

'No!' says Dad. 'Don't be ridiculous.'

'*I'm* being ridiculous? That's what's happening here?'

'I don't have time for this. Come on, Luke, let's get going.'

Mum shakes her head and walks away, slamming the kitchen door behind her.

'Don't worry,' says Dad, under his breath. 'I'll smooth things over later.'

'How?' I say.

'That's between me and your mother.'

We lift the mattress and begin our clumsy hobble over the road, but halfway across we're intercepted by Helena, who, as is her habit, seems to appear from nowhere exactly when you least want to talk to her.

'Hello, David!' she says cheerfully.

'Hi, Helena,' he replies, without much enthusiasm.

'Is that a mattress?' she asks, looking at the mattress.

'Hard to say,' says Dad.

'Is it for Rose? Very generous of you to help her get so comfortable over there.' It's pretty obvious she's using the word 'generous' to mean 'stupid'.

'It's not,' says Dad.

'Oh,' she says, her brow furrowing in puzzlement. 'Who's it for, then?'

'Me. I'm sleeping with the enemy. Very hush-hush. Don't tell a soul.'

'I … you … what?' says Helena. She clearly has no idea if he's telling the truth or winding her up.

'Anyway – must dash,' says Dad.

'Wait,' she says. 'I just wanted to say, have you heard the news about the demolition crews?'

'Just a few rumours.'

'Less than a month, they're saying. I think we should have a street meeting. We need a strategy. That lot over there, are they planning to … resist?'

'That's why they're here.'

'Well,' says Helena, 'I think maybe the two sides of the street should find a way to communicate, don't you?'

'It's not hard. You just go over there and talk to them,' says Dad.

'I'm not sure that's where my talents lie,' says Helena.

'So have a meeting at your place, then,' says Dad. 'If the bulldozers are coming, you're right. We all need to work together.'

'Absolutely,' says Helena.

'Let me know when it's happening, and I'll see who I can bring along,' says Dad, lifting his end of the mattress and beginning to walk away.

'Watch out for bedbugs,' Helena calls after us. 'I'd burn that rather than taking it back into your house, if I were you.'

Dad and I carry on up to his bedroom, returning home briefly for a duvet and pillow and a dust-covered guitar I've never seen before, which he retrieves from on top of a wardrobe. When we've finished, Dad looks around at his cell-like new residence with the kind of self-satisfied smile you'd expect to see on someone's face after checking into a five-star penthouse suite.

'How long do you think you're going to stay here?' I ask.

'Oh, not long.'

'And you're doing this to push Rose back home?'

'Yes.'

'Do you really think that's going to work?'

'It's worth a try.'

'So you definitely haven't come here for the same reason as Rose?'

'What do you mean?'

'I can't really see the difference between what she's doing and what you're doing. It's only me and Mum left at home now. Isn't that kind of weird?'

'Is weird always a bad thing?'

'I just feel like Mum doesn't believe that you're here for the reason you're saying you're here.'

'What *other* reason could there be?'

'Maybe you like it here.'

Dad fixes me with an intense stare, and I can see him trying to figure out whether to be impressed or annoyed by my suggestion. I get the feeling he's mainly annoyed. Life must be far simpler when you can lie to your children without them realising.

'I'm not going to pretend I hate it,' he concedes. 'I mean, I thought I would, but … when you've been doing the same job for years and years, and it's not necessarily a job you even liked that much in the first place … well, you get bored. And if something turns up that's different from the daily grind, it kind of … wakes you up. Maybe everyone here is a bit nuts, but … it's fun. I don't know when I last had any fun.'

'So you admit it?'

'Admit what?'

'You coming here is basically a holiday.'

'No!'

'You're saying it's for Rose but it's really for you.'

'No! And you mustn't say that to Mum. What I told you just now is private – father-and-son talk, man to man – just between me and you.'

'Mum knows anyway.'

'Does she?'

'Yeah, it's obvious.'

'Is it?'

'Totally.'

'Well … it's just a week. Can't do any lasting harm. Maybe I'll change Rose's mind about things and she'll go home, and I'll follow her, and thanks to me we'll all be back to normal before we know it.'

'Or maybe the opposite will happen.'

'That being … ?'

'Who knows?'

At this moment one of the two middle-aged women in the commune appears at the top of the stairs. She's wearing an orange and gold jumper that has clearly been hand-knitted by someone who doesn't know how to knit.

'Just thought I'd say hi,' she says to Dad. 'I heard you're moving in. I'm Martha.'

'Hi,' says Dad, reaching out to shake her hand, then changing the gesture into a wave when he realises a hand-shake is too uncool. 'I'm David. Or Dave. Most people call me Dave.'

'Nice to meet you, David or Dave,' she says, with a knowing smile.

'And I'm not so much moving in as just … you know … visiting for a while.'

'We're all only visitors wherever we are, I always say,' says Martha, in her throaty, honey-smooth voice.

'Very true,' replies Dad, though I can tell that he has no idea what she's on about, and also that me being there, watching him introduce himself to Martha, makes him uneasy. It's hard to tell with people who are the same age as your parents, but I get the feeling that long, long ago, Martha would once have been quite attractive.

'And this is my son, Luke,' he adds. 'He's helping me get set up.'

'Hi, Luke,' says Martha, beaming her large green eyes at me. 'You're Sky's new friend, aren't you?'

'Well … kind of.'

'I've heard all about you.'

'Have you? There's not much to say, is there?'

'You should never put yourself down, Luke. Never,' she

says in a low and serious voice, bangles and bracelets clanking together as she sweeps a tress of curly hair over one shoulder. This is when I notice that she gives off the sweet and delicious scent of freshly sawn wood.

'Anyway, there's soup in the kitchen if you want it,' she adds, flashing a smile at Dad and heading back downstairs.

'I'm starving,' I say.

'What?' replies Dad, staring at Martha's retreating form, lost in a deaf dream.

'I'm hungry,' I repeat.

This time he hears me, and his eyes snap back into focus. 'Me too,' he says. 'Let's eat.'

We head down and are immediately given steaming bowls of pus-coloured lentil soup and bread rolls which are as heavy as a handful of mud. Outside, a totem pole inauguration celebration is in progress, which seems to involve fire, dancing and greased torsos.

This doesn't really feel like my scene, so after I've finished my soup and found a hiding place for my cannon-ball of a bread roll, I say goodbye to Dad (who is now regaling Martha with his favourite well-worn backpacking anecdote, about meeting a holy man in a Himalayan cave who would say a prayer for you in return for a Coke), and head home in search of a second dinner.

'Perfect timing!' says Mum as I walk in the front door. 'Sky and me have made roast chicken.'

# Barrel Woman

We've just sat down to eat when an angry banging at the front door interrupts us. There's a perfectly workable doorbell, with a cheerful two-note chime, but that's apparently not the greeting this visitor wants to give.

Mum throws me a puzzled glance, and I shrug back at her. The doorbell now sounds five times in a row, transforming the happy 'ding-dong' into something crazed and aggressive, then the banging resumes. Frowning, Mum gets up from the table and heads to the hall.

As soon as the door opens, I hear a voice snarl, 'Is this where she is, then?'

Sky's face immediately falls.

I follow Mum into the hallway, and am greeted by the sight of a muscular, barrel-shaped bulldog of a woman, dressed in tight ripped jeans and a garish tie-dyed T-shirt, with one side of her head shaved to reveal a spiderweb tattoo on the scalp, while the other side sports shoulder-length clumps of red, blue and black hair. She's standing on the front step looking as if she is about to throw a punch at my mother.

'Where who is?' says Mum, in a reedy, high-pitched voice I've never heard before.

'Don't piss me about,' says Barrel Woman. 'You know exactly who.'

'Sky?'

'SKY! COME OUT HERE!' she yells.

Sky appears behind me, clutching a chicken drumstick.

'So it is you,' says Barrel Woman, staring at Mum. 'Sneaking her off! Stealing her clothes! Trying to take over her homeschooling!'

'Take over?' says Mum. 'And I didn't steal any clothes. I just gave them a wash.'

'Oh, so we're not clean enough for you now, are we?'

'I ...'

'Think you're better than us, do you?'

'No, I ...'

'Think I don't know how to educate my own child?'

'I just gave her a bit of help with her spelling.'

'I don't need your help. I can teach her to spell just fine.'

'So why's my spelling so useless?' says Sky, stepping out from behind me and eyeballing her mother.

'No, it isn't. It's very good,' insists her mum.

'It's embarrassing. I want to go to school,' announces Sky.

Barrel Woman stares at her, blinking in disbelief. This is clearly not where she was expecting the conversation to go. Only a couple of seconds earlier she was happily monstering my mum, now she's confronted by her daughter demanding a major life change.

'What did you say?' she asks, even though it's obvious that she heard.

'I said I want to start school. I want to learn what other people learn.'

'Is this *her* doing? What's she been teaching you?'

'Lots of things,' says Sky defiantly. 'Maths, for starters.'

'I teach you maths!'

'About once a month. And it's got nothing to do with her. It's what *I* want.'

'Since when?'

'Since now! You always said that school is bad because I need to learn to think for myself. Well, I've been thinking for myself, and what I think is that I want to go to school.'

'Well ... er ... that's a big decision, but ... if that's how you feel, it's certainly something we can talk about.'

'There's nothing else to say. I've decided.'

'Why don't you just come home with me and we can talk about this in private.'

'No.'

'What?'

'I said no. I'm staying here.'

Sky then turns and walks up the stairs.

Mum and Barrel Woman stare at one another for a while, and it's not immediately clear who is unhappier with this outcome.

'I could have you up for kidnap,' says Barrel Woman, wagging a finger in Mum's face.

'It's not really kidnap, is it? I haven't even invited her. If you can get her out, be my guest.'

'You think you're so clever.'

'Not really. I genuinely want you to get your child out of my house. She's not my responsibility.'

'This isn't over!'

'Of course it isn't over. *Your* child is in *my* house! What am I supposed to do if she won't leave?'

'Oh, so you're the victim here, are you?' says Barrel Woman accusingly.

'No – Sky is the victim. She needs an education! And a parent who actually looks after her!'

'And you'd know, would you? If you're such a great mother, how come *your* daughter's run away to live in *my* house?'

'It's not your house. It's a squat.'

'It's the same thing and you know it.'

'It's completely different! Now if you'll excuse us, we're trying to eat dinner.'

'For your information, Sky's a vegan.'

'Not any more she isn't,' says Mum, closing the door.

We return to the dining table and our now cold chicken. Sky doesn't reappear.

It's unlike her to skip a meal, so after a while Mum and I go upstairs to look for her. We find her in Rose's bed, asleep, like Goldilocks, though in this case it's Brownshapelesstangledlocks.

Mum gently takes off Sky's shoes, tucks a duvet around her and draws the curtains. As we're leaving the room, she whispers, 'It looks like we've got ourselves a squatter.'

# Shorter!

The next morning, at breakfast, Mum tells Sky that we can't be her family, and she can't move in with us, but that she's always welcome, and she can spend the night in our home whenever she wants.

Sky's eyes widen with amazement when Mum says this, and she nods vigorously, but doesn't speak.

'Any time,' says Mum, adding, 'Isn't that right?' with a pointed look in my direction.

'If we're in,' I say reluctantly. 'And not busy.'

'Rose isn't using her bedroom at the moment. That can be a little refuge for you. Whenever you need it. Would you like that?'

'A room? For me?'

'Just until Rose wants it back.'

Sky's face breaks into a huge grin. She launches herself at Mum and wraps her in a bearhug that almost topples

118

them both off their feet. Mum holds her for a few seconds, then steps free, announces that the Xbox is going to stay off this morning and asks Sky if she knows any board games. I may have entered a new, liberated world of gaming freedom, but Sundays, unfortunately, are still ruled over by the outdated, repressive laws of the old regime, and Mum, I can tell, has suspicions about how I've been spending my weekdays.

Sky shrugs at the board game question. Mum puts a firm hand on my shoulder and says that I will teach her.

'Mum!' I say. 'I haven't played board games for years!'

'Well, now's your chance.'

'No way!'

'Just till lunchtime, then you can do whatever you want.'

'No.'

'In that case, the Xbox is staying off all day.'

'WHY!?'

'Because that's what's happening.'

'THAT'S NOT AN ANSWER!'

'It's the answer you're getting.'

'*BOARD GAMES!?*'

'Yes. You and Sky.'

'Why?'

'Or cards. You could play cards.'

'*Cards!?*'

119

'You play cards with Grandpa.'

'That's different! He's old!'

Mum opens the games cupboard, rifles through the heap of dusty boxes and brings over Monopoly, Cluedo, chess and Risk.

'You ever played any of those?' Mum asks Sky.

'My mum had a boyfriend who taught me chess once.'

'Perfect,' says Mum, walking out of the room before I can make an objection.

I stare at the pile of games, then at Sky. She looks back at me apologetically.

'You don't want to,' she says.

I shrug.

'Sorry,' says Sky.

With a sigh, I brush a stripe of dust off the top of the Monopoly.

'Do you hate me?' she asks.

'What kind of a question is that?'

'You think I'm weird.'

'You are weird, but I don't hate you,' I say.

She thinks for a while, staring at me with her huge blue eyes, and says, 'Thank you for telling the truth. I know I'm weird. Will you teach me not to be?'

'How?'

'I don't know, but I want to learn, so it's easier to make friends.'

While I'm trying to think how on earth to respond to this, she adds, 'I've never spent much time with people my own age, so I know I get things wrong.'

It's awkward that she's just thanked me for telling the truth, because I can't think of an honest reply to her request that is remotely tactful or helpful, but she just sits there, waiting for me to speak, so eventually I have to say something.

'Well,' I begin, '… er … I suppose the main thing is just to not try too hard.'

'Not try too hard?'

'If you seem desperate, or follow people around and don't leave them alone, you put them off. If you want people to like you, you have to play it cool.'

'Play it cool?'

'Yeah. Just … let people come to you instead of you chasing after them.'

'Was what I did with you chasing? Is that how you knew I was weird?'

'Kind of. And the way you look at people – you can be a bit starey. Try not to be so starey.'

'Oh. OK. Is there anything else?'

'Maybe … a haircut? Just cut out the knots and lumpy bits. If you want to look a bit more normal.'

'OK. A haircut. Is that it?'

'That's probably enough to start with.'

'Shall we play chess, then?'

'I suppose.'

'Thank you,' she says, with a smile spreading across her face. 'It's kind of you to help me.'

I unfold the board, open the box of pieces and smile back, not because I'm happy, but because somehow it's impossible not to.

'Do you think I'm funny?' Sky asks as we lay out our ranks of chessmen, sounding more curious than offended.

'No. You're just ... different.'

'Is that good or bad?'

'Don't know.'

'My mum always says that's the best thing you can be. She says most people live like robots, and that consumerism eats your soul.'

'She might be right.'

'She might be wrong,' says Sky, fixing me again with that intense stare.

I move my queen's pawn forward two squares. 'Let's play,' I say.

When Mum reappears in the kitchen an hour or so later (by which time I have managed to lose three games in a row), Sky immediately says, 'Can I have a haircut?'

'Well ... I can try to make you an appointment,' says Mum.

'Aren't hairdressers expensive?' asks Sky.

'It depends where you go.'

'Could you do it?'

A chain reaction of surprise, weariness and amusement flashes across Mum's face.

'Me?'

'That would be brilliant! Can you do it now?'

'Now?' she says.

'Nothing fancy,' says Sky casually. 'Just a chop. Tidy it up a bit.'

Mum stares at her, scrutinising the tangles and knots that crown her head, and I can sense her fingers itching to grab a pair of scissors and get started.

'I'm not really … I mean, I did do Rose and Luke when they were small, but I haven't cut anyone's hair for years.'

'Brilliant! Oh, thank you so much!' says Sky, lifting her chair and placing it in the middle of the room, popping back to take one of my knights, then saying, 'I'll sit here, shall I?'

For someone so seemingly guileless and innocent, Sky is amazingly adept at getting people to do what she wants.

Mum gives me a *how-did-this-happen?* glance, sighs and, with a mixture of reluctance and eagerness, pulls the kitchen scissors and a tea towel out of a drawer.

She starts by cutting out the worst of the matted clumps, some of which fall with a clatter to the kitchen floor.

'Do you want to keep those beads?' Mum asks.

123

'No,' replies Sky.

Within a few minutes, she looks like a different person. An outer layer of the strangeness that hovers around her seems to fall away and land at her feet.

Mum slowly brings Sky's hair to a vaguely horizontal line at her shoulders. Sky examines herself with a hand mirror and smiles. She suddenly looks older, as if she's flipped, in front of our eyes, from childhood to the very edge of becoming a teenager.

She lowers the mirror. 'Can I have it shorter?'

Mum takes the hair up to her neck.

Sky looks again, trying out different facial expressions and angles, alternately pouting, frowning and smiling regally at herself. I'd be embarrassed for anyone to see me looking at myself in the mirror like this, but embarrassment doesn't appear to be a concept Sky understands.

'Shorter,' she says.

This happens twice more, until Mum says, 'If I take any more off, people might think you're a boy.'

'I don't care,' says Sky. 'I think it looks nice.'

'It does. So how short do you want it?' asks Mum.

'Like his,' says Sky, pointing at me.

'Er … well, it might look a bit odd if you two are walking around with exactly the same haircut, so how about we aim for something a bit … softer. I could try to give you a pixie cut, if you like.'

'I don't want to look like a pixie.'

'That's not what it is. It's just a style that's short but still kind of feminine.'

'That sounds nice. Can I have that?'

Mum snips away for a while longer. When she's finished Sky looks almost unrecognisable, and actually pretty cool. She examines herself in the mirror for ages, sucking her cheeks in to study her newly prominent jaw and cheekbones, then gives Mum an intense hug and tells her she loves her.

Mum doesn't seem to know how to react to this, and says, 'I'm very pleased you like it,' patting Sky gently on the back.

# The house of cards

My family never adopted Sky, but for a while it seems like she has adopted us, whether we like it or not. Without actively choosing the role, both Mum and I somehow end up being recruited for the job of teaching Sky how to behave in the real world.

Some days I resent this, other days I find it surprisingly fascinating. Sky may sometimes be maddening but she's never boring, and with her now more or less living in Rose's bedroom, the two of them having effectively swapped places, if I think about the change in terms of friendliness and entertainment value, this exchange is definitely an upgrade. Also, me being pleasant to Sky becomes the key to Mum turning a blind eye to my weekday shattering of all screen-time rules. Neither of us acknowledges what is happening, but the arrangement holds itself precariously in place without anything needing to be said.

With a few friends now back from holiday, I have other places to go, and a group of us sometimes meets up in the park or at each other's houses, but I never bring anyone home. The whole situation, with Rose running away and my dad going rogue and a weird girl always hanging around the house, is something I don't want to have to explain. It seems easier to make sure my friends never know, simpler to keep all the strangeness quiet until some kind of normality returns.

My friends have never seemed particularly conformist in the past, but, knowing Sky, and having learned a little of how the world looks through her eyes, this familiar group of boys now feels different. I notice, for the first time, the mockery that bubbles up when anyone slips up or steps out of line – just stupid jokes, but with a force that pulls everyone back to some invisible centre. And the fact of me beginning to notice this makes me wonder if that centre is no longer quite where I belong.

I can picture exactly how they'd react to Sky, and it's ugly.

It's not like anyone asks, so if I keep them all away from my house, nobody need ever find out that my family has temporarily (I hope) imploded. Given half the chance, Callum would spread an exaggerated version of the story to anyone who'd listen, but he goes to a different school and doesn't know any of my friends, so for the time being, as long as I keep my home and school worlds apart, that problem is contained.

As for Dad's only partially explained week off work, this remains a mystery. He doesn't come home once, and Mum doesn't go to visit him. It's hard to be sure, but it seems like they're not talking to each other.

I visit the commune most days that week, and usually find Dad hanging out with Clyde in the garden, sitting in mouldy deck chairs and talking about music, films, books, places they've been and Funny Things That Once Happened To Them or having conversations about the evils of capitalism.

Dad always seemed quite keen on the evils of capitalism in the past, but I don't bring this up. When Dad's talking to Clyde, there's no way in. You can either sit there and listen, or you can walk away. For obvious reasons, I always opt for the latter.

On one occasion, there's not a single person anywhere in the commune, and for a moment I wonder if the whole place has been abandoned, but a text from Dad explains that they've all gone on a march somewhere.

Another time, I find him being taught how to knit by the curly-haired woman who introduced herself to us on the day Dad moved into the commune. He looks slightly guilty when I find him in her room, but attempts to cover this with a very long speech about how knitting is 'actually quite relaxing' and is 'proven to lower your blood pressure almost as much as having a dog'. She and Dad then go off into a long discussion about dogs, during which he conspicuously fails to mention that he hates them, so I wander away in search of Rose. As usual, I find her 'in a meeting' (i.e. lolling around on cushions, chatting) and therefore 'too busy' to talk to me.

Though there's plenty of evidence that Dad's cracking up, the only ongoing visible symptom is that he looks alarmingly – no, freakishly – happy. I've never seen him like this. Not just happy, but also relaxed. Hanging out, chatting: I had no idea he even knew how to do those things.

There's something unsettling about Dad being this content. You can't help wondering where it will lead. In the long run, it surely can't be a good thing.

Sky rarely comes with me on my visits to the commune. She prefers to stay in my sitting room watching TV, staring at it with the rigid attentiveness of a nerdy pupil in a favourite lesson. She doesn't so much watch TV as actually study it, like she's revising for an exam on How People Behave.

My family does everything it can to keep up a nobody-mention-that-everyone-has-fallen-out act, so the only open confrontation during this strangely tense week happens when Mum, Sky and I are halfway through a

peaceful dinner and a familiar banging at the door interrupts us. From the speed and volume of the thumps, we all
instantly know it's Barrel Woman, and that she's even
angrier than last time.

Mum rises reluctantly from her seat, dabs her mouth
with a napkin and heads for the door. I follow a short
distance behind.

'WHAT DID YOU DO TO HER HAIR!' yells Barrel
Woman, by way of a hello.

'Cut it,' says Mum, who is not easily intimidated. In
fact, she's rarely calmer than when someone is trying (and
failing) to boss her around.

'HOW DARE YOU! YOU DON'T HAVE THE RIGHT!'

'She asked me to,' says Mum.

'I asked her to,' echoes Sky, positioning herself next to
Mum.

'You made her look like a little Tory!'

'It's what she asked for.'

'I like it,' says Sky.

'You can't just go around cutting people's hair without
permission. Who do you think you are? The Queen?'

'I don't think that's something the Queen does, is it?'

'That's not what I said!'

'And I did have permission,' says Mum.

'Not from me! Her hair was beautiful. We've been
growing it for years!'

'*We?*' says Sky. 'It's my hair!'

'Not any more it isn't. It's in the bin now, thanks to her.'

'It's longer than yours,' says Sky. 'Half your head is shaved.'

'Yes, but the other half is long.'

'That whole bit is bald! I can see the skin.'

'This side goes down to my shoulders. I don't look like Little Lord Fauntleroy.'

'Who's Little Lord Fauntleroy?' asks Sky.

'He's ... I don't know ... someone posh who thinks he's better than everyone else.'

'So it's posh to not want an itchy bird's nest on your head that people stare at?'

'If you wanted a trim, all you had to do was ask me.'

'Did you choose *your* haircut,' says Sky, 'or did you ask your mum's permission before you got it?'

'That's different! I'm not eleven!' snaps Barrel Woman.

'Neither am I. I'm twelve.'

'That's what I meant.'

'And so what if you don't like it. You always told me I shouldn't worry what other people think.'

'I was talking about *other* people. Not me. I'm your mother.'

'Is it because you think I look like a boy? Are you trying to police my gender?'

'No! Of course not! You're completely twisting my words!'

131

'Well, you're telling me what I can and can't do with my own body!'

'OK. Sorry. That isn't what I meant. It's not you I'm angry with. I love your hair. It's her that's out of line – Miss Fancy Pants Corporate Trouser Suit Bossy Boots muscling in and tidying you up so you don't spoil the view in her perfect living room.'

'Is that me you're referring to?' says Mum. 'Miss Fancy Pants Corporate Trouser Suit Bossy Boots is me, is it?'

'I asked her to do it!' insists Sky. 'It was my idea! So leave her alone! And leave me alone!'

'She is not your mother and this is not your house. This whole thing has gone too far. You need to come home now. It's dinner time.'

'I'm already eating dinner here, and it's spaghetti bolognaise, and it's literally the nicest thing I've ever had.'

'You can't just …'

'And there's an empty bedroom here for me, with a comfy bed and clean sheets and a duvet and everything.'

'You've got a bedroom?'

'It was his sister's,' says Sky, pointing at me, 'but she's over the road now so they said I could use it.'

'What's your game?' says Barrel Woman, squinting at Mum. 'Do you often go around trying to nick other people's kids?'

'No. And to be strictly accurate, she started using the

bedroom without even asking me. All I've done is allowed her to carry on.'

'Whatever it is you're playing at, it's not normal.'

'Oh, and that is?' says Mum, pointing across the road towards the commune.

'There's a difference between alternative and just *weird*,' says Barrel Woman.

'Which one are you? I'm confused,' says Mum.

'You *are* confused. Going round thinking you're superior to everyone who doesn't have a fancy car and a big house, when in fact it's selfish people like you who are destroying the planet.'

'Selfish? I'm giving time and attention and food and a bed to your lonely and unhappy daughter and you're calling *me* selfish?'

'We're not like you, and we don't want to be. She doesn't belong here. And she's not unhappy. Sky – it's time for you to come home.'

'No,' says Sky, crossing her arms over her chest.

'Now!'

'No.'

For a few seconds nobody moves or speaks, then Barrel Woman turns to Mum. 'See what you've done!' she snaps.

'What *I've* done?' replies Mum.

Barrel Woman ignores this and turns her attention back to Sky. 'All right, you can have dinner here, and I suppose

133

it's OK to stay for a few sleepovers, if that's what you really want, but you have to come and visit tomorrow. This isn't your home.'

'So where is my home? Have I even got one?' says Sky.

Another tense silence falls, mother and daughter staring at one another across the threshold. For a while the air seems to thicken.

'Come over tomorrow, and we can talk about this in private. Please. If you won't talk to me, how can I sort this out? I hate it when we argue.'

Sky looks down at her feet and stays silent.

'I haven't seen your sketchbook for ages. I'd love to see what you've been up to. We could go for a walk somewhere and do some sketching.'

There's still no response from Sky, so her mother presses on, tilting her head to try and make eye contact. 'We've always talked, Sky. Whatever it is you want to change or be, that's OK, but I can only help you if I know what you're thinking. You have to talk to me.'

Sky finally lifts her gaze from her feet to look at her mother, but still doesn't speak.

'Please.'

'OK,' says Sky, in a voice so quiet it's barely audible.

'Good,' says Barrel Woman, forcing the corners of her mouth upwards into an attempt at a smile.

'Right,' says Mum. 'I'll make sure Sky heads your way tomorrow morning. Shall we say seven a.m.? Eight?'

'Mid-morning might be better.'

'Fine. I'll do that.'

Barrel Woman scowls at her, then blows a kiss to Sky, whispers, 'Night night,' and walks away.

# Whoever I am when I come out the other side

The following morning, which is a Saturday, Sky and I cross the road together, her to see her scary mother, me to visit my crazy dad. I'm under instructions from Mum to find out 'how far gone he is', and when he's coming home. As I'm heading out of the door, Mum tells me to remind Dad that it's only two weeks till Spain and that he has to do the check-in and print the boarding passes.

When I arrive in the commune, Dad is at the stove, stirring an enormous vat of grey sludge. He's wearing his shouldn't-be-legal jeans, leather sandals and a too-short black T-shirt emblazoned with the inexplicable words 'Guns N' Roses'. I'm going to skate over the embarrassing subject of what is visible between the too-short T-shirt and the too-low jeans. Just imagine hairy dough and you're most of the way there.

This look clearly means something, but I have no idea what, other than that my dad is a man in crisis. Have those jeans been lying at the back of a wardrobe, hidden away for decades, waiting for this moment to come? And where did the rest of the outfit come from? Did he sneak back into the house during the week and dig it out from a secret '90s fashion drawer? Borrow it from someone in the commune? Buy it online? Did he *go clothes shopping*? None of those things seems plausible.

When I remind Dad that it's our day to visit Grandpa, he looks at me with a dismayed expression, a spoonful of 'porridge' paused halfway to his mouth. 'Is it Saturday?' he says mournfully, as if this is unexpected and terrible news. 'Already?'

If my task is to find out how sane he is, the fact that he has no idea it's the weekend seems like a symptom I should remember and report. As I'm thinking this, it strikes me as strange that after all my denials to Rose that I've been sent by our parents to spy on her, I now appear to be spying on Dad to gather information for Mum.

The discovery that it's Saturday causes Dad's mood to plummet. His flow of chat stalls, and he quietly finishes his breakfast, then reluctantly agrees that we should head for the care home.

After walking out of the commune, at the edge of the pavement he hesitates, as if it takes an effort of will to cross the road back to our house. In our front drive, he pats his pockets, thinks for a few seconds, then suggests that 'things might be quicker' if it's me who goes into the house to fetch the car keys.

'I'll wait out here,' he says, taking a few steps back and positioning himself behind a lamp post. If he ever had the physique of a man who could hide behind a lamp post, that was a long time ago. Perhaps way back when he bought that Guns N' Roses T-shirt.

Mum either doesn't hear the door, or chooses to ignore me, because I manage to get in and out of the house without incident.

I try to start the car journey with some of our usual chat, so it doesn't sound too obvious that I'm on a covert mission to assess the progress of his mental collapse, but I can't think of anything normal to talk about. There is no normal any more.

Having failed to think of a roundabout way to broach the subject, after a few minutes of silence I abandon any attempt at subtlety and dive in with, 'You're going back to work again next week, then?'

Though I can tell by Dad's face that he hears me, he doesn't reply.

'You said you were using up your week's holiday. That was a week ago,' I say.

'Mmm. A week can go so fast, can't it?' he replies.

'You're coming home again, right?'

'It's a very fluid situation.'

'What does *that* mean?'

'I've been doing a lot of thinking lately, and I've decided the best thing is if we all just take this one day at a time.'

'Take *what* one day at a time?'

'I've spent too much of my life afraid of the future. And you know what? It never comes. By the time the future arrives, it's the present.'

'Mum's concerned about you. She thinks you're losing the plot.'

'You mustn't worry. Everything's going to be fine. In fact, it's going to be better than before.'

'I never said I'm worried. I said she's worried.'

'Well, are you? Worried?'

'Should I be? You are behaving kind of weird.'

'I'm happy! How can that be bad?'

I shrug, because although I can't think of an explanation, I know for sure that it certainly isn't good.

'So are you coming back home on Monday, then?'

There's a long silence.

'Not Monday, no. I haven't … there's still … as I said, one day at a time,' says Dad, reaching out and flicking through a series of radio stations in search of music, eventually stopping on a twangy song which is so dire that after a few seconds I lean forward and switch it off.

139

I have no idea what Dad is talking about. All I know is he's hiding something.

'So when are you coming home?' I ask.

'Soon,' he says. 'You mustn't worry.'

'Mum told me to remind you that it's two weeks till Spain and you have to do the boarding passes,' I say, my mind suddenly jumping ahead to the resort where we go every year, imagining us all on the beach together, a normal family again. 'Maybe going away will sort things out,' I add.

'I'm sure it'll help,' says Dad, pulling into the care home car park. 'But ... you know Rose is refusing to go?'

'Where?'

'To Spain.'

'No. Nobody told me that.'

'She says you can't live in an anti-airport climate change protest camp, then jump on a plane for a week's holiday to the Med. We've tried to talk to her about it, but she's adamant that she's not a hypocrite and she won't go.'

'So we're going without her? You're not cancelling, are you?'

'No, no. It's much too late to cancel. The whole thing's paid for. But ... anyway, I'm going to be popping in this evening to finalise plans with Mum.'

'What is there to finalise?'

'Oh, nothing major. You don't need to ... it just ... might

140

be best if you give us half an hour or so to chat in private. You know – boring grown-up stuff.'

'OK,' I say, though I have never been more certain that everything is very much not OK.

In Grandpa's stuffy little room, I deal out the cards for a hand of rummy, but he seems distracted, and asks me twice about school, forgetting almost immediately that I've told him it's the school holidays.

After a couple of games, I retreat to the window nook with my phone and pull up my photos from last year's summer holiday: a selfie of all of us on the beach, giving sunburned grins; one of me and Dad carrying plates heaped with multiple desserts from the buffet; another one of Mum and Rose falling off a two-person paddleboard. I scroll from picture to picture, thinking how long ago this seems, and how different the trip will be this year, partly because Rose won't be there, and partly because the atmosphere in the whole family feels spiky and off-kilter.

At the same time, Dad goes through the questions he always asks Grandpa about his health and what he's been up to, and Grandpa gives his usual downbeat replies.

Dad usually then gives a quick rundown of what has happened to the family in the two weeks gone by, before opening a newspaper or magazine and reading aloud some things he thinks might catch Grandpa's interest, but today their conversation takes a different course. From the sound of Dad's voice, I can immediately tell he's not just skipping through the usual superficial summary of his fortnight but is saying something he actually means in a slow, reflective tone I don't think I've heard him use before.

I keep my head turned aside and tilted down towards the screen of my phone, so he can't see I'm listening, but I tune into every word, searching for clues to explain what he's really up to and when he might be returning to normal.

Dad starts by reminding Grandpa about Rose moving into a protest camp, then goes on to explain how he's followed her there to try and 'edge her out'.

'But,' he continues, 'things haven't quite panned out that way. All that's happened is I've taken a week off work, and during that time we've both been in the commune, and now she won't speak to me. So it wasn't really very productive. But ... I suppose ... I knew that's what would happen. Anyway, it was worth a try. Maybe I had other reasons for going.'

There's a long silence at this point. I glance in his direction and see that he's lost in thought.

'Maybe, if I'm honest, I actually wanted to be there,' he adds. 'I mean, I know I'm supposed to be disapproving and angry about Rose dropping out and spending her time with hippies, but part of me admires her for it. When have

I ever made a personal sacrifice and stood up for something? What have I really done with my life? How did I end up as a suburban dad, trudging out to the same old boring job year after year? How did that happen? I don't remember ever choosing this, but life just kind of boxes you in without you even noticing it's happening.'

Dad's gazing dreamily into the middle distance as he talks, but I notice that Grandpa is staring at him with a pinched look clenching together his wrinkled features. I can tell that he's shaping up to make one of his rare pronouncements. He takes a few short, fast breaths in preparation, then says, 'You don't know how lucky you are!'

'Lucky? Me?' says Dad, with a sarcastic laugh. 'If you knew how bored I am!'

'Bored?' spits Grandpa, as if the word burns his tongue.

'And I'm supposed to go back to work again on Monday. Back to the same old desk and the same old tasks and the same old people, on and on forever. Honestly, I just can't do it.'

'Can't do it?' says Grandpa, sitting upright in his chair now, looking agitated. A curl of white foam has formed in the corner of his mouth.

'I'm thinking of staying longer,' Dad says. 'I've run out of holiday leave, so my boss won't like it, but I think I'm beyond caring. What's the worst they can do?'

'Sack you.'

'Maybe that would be a good thing. Give me a chance to think about what I really want from life.'

'What you *want from life*?' says Grandpa, his voice clearer and louder than I've heard for years, ringing with contempt.

'Yeah.'

'What on earth is wrong with you?'

'I'm bored is what's wrong with me.'

'Boredom is a luxury! I came here with nothing – fleeing for my life from the most horrific war the world has ever seen, escaping by the skin of my teeth …'

'Yeah, I know all this, Dad.'

'And you talk to me about how awful it is to be *bored*?'

'Everything's different now. You can't compare …'

'My whole life I worked and worked and worked, without question, to give you and your brother a safe home, a secure home, a chance to make something of yourselves, and I considered myself the luckiest man in the world to be able to do that – because that's what a man does. He provides for his wife and children. That's what a man *is*. Now you're telling me you're *bored* and you want to get the sack!'

'That's not what I said.'

'I'm not so old and stupid that I didn't hear what you said.'

At this moment Dad looks up and catches my eye. His

144

face seems to flinch with embarrassment at me having heard him talking (and being talked to) like this. A spark of shock also passes between us at the vehemence of Grandpa's response. It's months since I've seen him so animated, and this ought to be a cause for celebration, but the fact that he's only perked up to attack Dad somehow takes the joy out of it.

'I didn't raise you to pull this kind of idiotic stunt,' says Grandpa.

'You didn't raise me at all,' replies Dad. 'You were always at work.'

'Oh, very clever, smart guy. Very clever. I'd like to see what would have happened to you if I hadn't always been at work. If I'd been too busy drifting around worrying about my *feelings*.'

Dad stands, pushing back his chair so roughly that it topples with a thump on to the hard carpet. 'Well, it's good to see you so perky, Dad,' he says. 'I'll come again soon.'

'Leaving already?'

'I have to go.'

'Don't like someone talking sense to you, do you? Never did.'

'Come on, Luke.'

Dad walks out. I follow him, pausing first to pick up the fallen chair. In the doorway I turn back to Grandpa and say goodbye with a tentative smile. He responds with a wink, and an expression that could be a scowl or could be a smirk. I've never seen him wink before. It's hard to know what this gesture means, but my best guess is that he's trying to communicate something along the lines of, 'Don't worry – everything's going to be OK.' Or maybe it's, 'Did you see? I won the argument!'

There's always something a little edgy between Grandpa and Dad. In the days when Grandpa used to visit our home and play board games with me, I once overheard Dad say to him, as a joke that was also clearly not a joke, 'You never let *me* beat you at chess.'

I still remember Grandpa's response, which was to laugh at him with a scornful, open-throated cackle that made Dad turn on his heel and leave the room.

It's hard to put my finger on it, or remember specific examples, but I often feel that Dad resents Grandpa for something, and that him being kinder and more attentive as a grandfather than he ever was as a father is Grandpa's attempt to make amends. Even when they're trying to be nice to each other there's a crackle in the air, a static electricity of unfinished arguments and unspoken criticisms.

As I follow Dad back to the car I still can't figure out if Grandpa was genuinely angry or was just enjoying an opportunity to put Dad in his place. Part of me even wonders if Dad's strange behaviour at the moment has something to do with Grandpa, and is in some way part of this lifelong argument they're always having about what it means to be a man. Could it be that Dad is copying Rose in more ways than one – that even at his age, he's *still* rebelling against his parents?

Maybe Dad told Grandpa about what he's doing because provoking that reaction is one of the reasons he's doing it. Maybe Grandpa snapped out of his oblivion because he saw Dad's change of priorities as a new manoeuvre in their endless battle, which necessitated a counter-attack. Maybe this is their only way of showing their love for each other: by fighting.

When I get in the passenger seat, Dad is sitting behind the wheel, staring dead ahead, his face expressionless and rigid. I sit there for a few seconds and he doesn't speak or move.

'Shall we go?' I say.

He starts the engine.

We don't talk until I notice that he's driven past the kebab place, which he's never done before, and I point out that he's missed it.

He mutters something inaudible, does an angry U-turn which causes a van driver to hoot and swear at him, and we head back.


'Is there a reason why you and Grandpa don't get on?' I ask, as we're finishing off our meal.

Dad gives a dry bark of laughter. 'There's more than one.'

He doesn't elaborate, but I keep looking at him, waiting for him to say more.

'It's ancient history,' he says eventually. 'I just don't want to make the mistakes he made.'

'He didn't go and live in a commune, then?'

'No, he did not. Can you imagine? And I'm not living there. I'm just visiting.'

I chew through the last few bites of my kebab, then, without looking at him, I say, 'Why are you doing this?'

'It just feels like something I have to do,' he replies.

I look up and he's staring at me and also somehow through me, as if he's either willing me to understand him or is indifferent to what I think. I can't tell which. 'What's happening with your job?' I say. 'Is Grandpa right that they could sack you?'

He leans back in his chair and sighs, as if bored and disappointed by my response. 'It'll be fine. They'll under-stand,' he says with a casual swat of his hand.

'Really?'

'It's very hard to fire people these days. You don't need to worry.'

'What does Mum think about all this?' I ask.

'Well, we haven't been … things are a bit … we're

going to talk everything through this evening. Clear the air.'

Dad takes a sip of his drink, and seems to have trouble swallowing it. 'The best thing is always to be honest,' he adds eventually, in a slightly strangled voice.

# If you put it like that, I suppose you can come in

It's clear that Dad's meeting with Mum has the potential for a volcanic outcome, so, for the first time in years (or possibly ever) I put myself to bed early. Darkness gradually falls as I lie there with a book in front of me, not reading, just listening for the sound of the front door.

Eventually I hear a key slide into the lock, and a quiet rumble of voices begins to come up through the floorboards, but the pitch of the voices soon rises, until first Mum, then both of them are shouting. Dad's plan to stay longer in the commune has gone down exactly as badly as I was expecting.

After a while, there's an ominous crash, which sounds like a plate smashing.

My door creaks open and Sky appears, silhouetted against the landing light. She stands there in silence for a while, then says, 'I can't sleep.'

'Me neither.'

'What are they arguing about?'

'I don't know, do I?' I reply sharply.

'Is it … ?'

'Just go back to bed! Go!'

I turn to the wall, and after a while I hear her walk away.

Time seems to stretch while I listen to the pitch of the argument rise and fall, so I have no idea how long has passed when I finally hear the front door open, then click shut.

I jump out of bed and slip myself behind the closed curtains so I can look down on the street.

Dad crosses the tarmac, then stops and stands there, still, turned back towards our house with his face cast into long shadows by the street light above his head. He looks small and far away.

After a while, he tilts his head and looks up at me, but the light is off in my room and I'm not sure if I'm visible, because he doesn't wave or smile or give any indication that he's seen me.

We stare at one another through the closed window and the hot summer darkness, neither one of us giving any sign that we can see the other. A flash of jittering shadow that may or may not be a bat flits between us, then vanishes.

Dad lowers his face, turns away and walks to the commune.

\* \* \*

The next morning I wake early, and instead of lying there trying to get back to sleep as I would on a normal day, I head downstairs to assess the fallout.

Mum is quiet and, unusually for her, still. She sits for a long time at the breakfast table, lost in thought, sipping at a mug of tea cradled in both hands. The skin under her eyes is shiny and slightly grey. She says nothing about Dad's visit, except to ask me if I'm aware that he's decided to stay longer in the commune.

I'm not sure if I'm supposed to know this or not, and I have a moment of panic, but Mum lets me off the hook by adding, 'And he says he's coming back soon, but he won't say what "soon" means.'

'What do you think it means?' I ask.

She thinks for a long while, so long that it begins to seem she might have forgotten the question, then eventually says, 'I don't know. I just don't know.'

She stands up, kisses me on the forehead and busies herself for the rest of the day with chores: vacuuming the whole house, going to the supermarket, even mowing the lawn. She doesn't sit down once.

By the time I wake up on Monday Mum has already left for work. In fact, by the time I get out of bed, she's probably on her lunch break.

For the next few days she continues to seem incapable

of sitting still, and carries around with her a buzzing cloud of brittle energy. Then, on Wednesday evening, I'm watching TV with Sky when Mum comes in and tells us she's going next door for a street meeting.

'At Helena's?' I ask, muting the telly.

'Yes.'

'I thought you hate Helena.'

'I don't hate anyone.'

I raise an eyebrow at her.

'OK, I'm not a fan of Helena,' she says, 'but it isn't a social call. Apparently the demolition team is assembled and they're moving in any day now. There's a meeting to decide what we're going to do.'

'What *are* you going to do?'

'I don't know. Watch?'

'You're not going to fight it?' says Sky.

Mum looks at her, puzzled. 'How?'

'There's a million ways,' says Sky. 'Chaining yourself to bulldozers, gluing yourself to buildings, throwing things, climbing trees and refusing to come down, hunger strike, human chain, lying in the road till you get arrested … loads of stuff. That's just the basics.'

'Is this what was on your homeschooling curriculum, then?'

'Kind of.'

'Are the commune people invited to the meeting?' I ask.

'Invited by Helena? I doubt that.'

'Well, they should be,' I say.

'This is what they do,' adds Sky. 'I mean, I'm sure they already have a plan, but they should coordinate with your side of the road. That's obvious, isn't it?'

'I'm not sure how feasible that is.'

'What, crossing the road to have a conversation?'

'Relations are a little strained,' says Mum.

'OK,' I say. 'You go to the meeting, I'll go and fetch Dad and Rose and Clyde and Barrel Woman and the others.'

'Who's Barrel Woman?' says Sky.

'Oh, er … just … whoever made your garden furniture. Out of barrels.'

'They aren't barrels. They're pallets.'

'Really?'

'They don't look anything like barrels.'

'No. I … er …'

'I'm not sure fetching the people from the commune is a good idea,' says Mum.

'Of course it is. Come on, Sky,' I say, heading out of the room and across the road before Mum can stop us.


Dad and Clyde are in the garden, as usual, but for once they're not sitting around on deck chairs, regaling one another with traveller's tales. They're on their feet, standing in a group with five or six others, staring intently at a twisted knot of mangled railings and scrap metal. Clyde is holding a large grey mask in one hand and something that looks like a huge dentist's drill in the other.

Nobody notices us arriving, even when we join the circle of metal-starers.

'What are you doing?' I ask Dad, pulling at an arm to get his attention.

'Welding,' he replies.

At this moment, Clyde steps forward, kneels, lifts the mask over his face and touches his dentist's-drill-type contraption to the whatever-it-is lying on the ground in front of him. A high-pitched crackle fills the air, white flame shoots out, sparks fly.

'Welding what?' I ask, when Clyde pauses to examine his handiwork.

'Barricades,' says Dad.

'Cool,' says Sky, clearly understanding what's going on before I do, which is the first time this has ever happened.

'What are barricades?' I whisper in her ear.

'Things you use to block roads,' she replies, with a hint of surprise in her voice, as if she can't quite believe I don't know how to construct a roadblock.

I pull Dad's arm again, since he seems to have already forgotten I'm there, and say, 'I came to tell you something.'

'What?' he replies absent-mindedly, light from the

welding torch flashing against his face as another series of buzzes and crackles rises up.

'There's a meeting,' I say, 'at Helena's house. Now.'

'OK,' he says, obviously not listening. It's hard to compete with the shooting flame and sparks.

'It's a street meeting. Everyone is gathering to decide what to do about the demolition. Which is any day now, isn't it?'

'That's what they're saying.'

'So maybe you should go.'

Clyde, who up until this moment has given every impression of being totally absorbed in his metal-melting activities, turns to me, lowers his welding mask, stares for a few seconds, then looks across at Dad.

'He's right,' says Clyde.

'About what?' asks Dad.

'The meeting. You should go. We should all go. The whole street should act together. This side and that side. If we're separate, they look like Nimbys, we look like extremists, and it's easy to dismiss us both for different reasons. If we stand together, we're much stronger.'

Dad doesn't have much chance to respond to this, because the whole welding crew immediately starts noisily and vociferously agreeing with Clyde, some of them already dispersing through the house to gather people for the meeting.

This isn't the response I'd anticipated, and it certainly

156

isn't what Helena would have been expecting when she put out her invitation, but within minutes I find myself crossing the road at the head of a gang of crazily dressed and weirdly excited hippies, showing them the way to the front room of my most uptight and neurotic neighbour.

As I ring the doorbell, Sky wriggles between the people surrounding me and appears by my side with a mischievous smile on her face.

'This is going to be fun!' she says.

Callum answers the door. He looks at the crowd standing on his doorstep, then at me, and says, 'What do you want?'

'We're here for the meeting,' I reply.

He doesn't move. His jaw muscle twitches a couple of times, then, without taking his eyes off me, he shouts, 'MUM!'

'What is it?' calls an irritated voice from the living room.

'Come here! You've got … visitors,' he replies, with about as much enthusiasm as someone saying, 'You've got fleas.'

Helena comes to the door with a *welcome-to-my-home* smile, which freezes in horror when she sees who is there.

'Can I help you?' she says, through gritted teeth, with one hand placed firmly on the door frame and the other holding tight to the latch, as if to stop us barging in.

'It's me,' says Dad, stepping out from the crowd. Helena stares at him blankly, so he adds, 'David, from next door.'

'I know exactly who you are,' says Helena, in a tone of voice that makes it clear this isn't a compliment. 'And you don't need to tell me where you live. Or maybe you do. I hear you've moved elsewhere.'

'I'm just trying to … er … coordinate efforts on the street.'

'What efforts?' asks Helena.

'Exactly,' says Dad. 'Not enough is being done. We've got the residents on one side who have been living with this threat for a long time, and this team of seasoned protesters on the other, and with the demolition crew right on our doorstep we need to start working together.'

'Working? I wasn't aware that was a word these people understand.'

'With all due respect,' says Clyde, appearing alongside Dad, 'I've been working for various environmental causes all my life, right back to the Twyford Down and M11 protests in the 1990s, and I've acquired some useful experience along the way. I'd very much like to share that knowledge with everyone living here in the shadow of the building work that could commence any day now, and I'd also like to hear your stories. We have a common goal, and we're far stronger if we stand together. Collaboration between residents and environmentalists is what this whole movement is built on. The protests of the '90s changed government policy on road-building. Air travel has to be the next target if we want to save the planet from irreversible climate breakdown. This, right here, is one very small battle in a conflict that is going to define the future for humanity. There's nothing that can't be changed if enough people stand up and fight for it. My name's Clyde, by the way. It's a pleasure to meet you, and to have a chance to contribute something to your campaign to protect this street.'

Clyde extends his arm for a handshake and gives off a thousand-watt smile. Helena looks down at Clyde's hand for several long seconds, then her eyes drift up for a moment towards his shoulder muscles, which are bulging from his vest top and are much more pronounced than you'd expect on a man his age.

Clyde's charisma does to people what heat does to butter. With a sigh, Helena shakes his hand and says, 'Well, if you put it like that ... and if you promise that none of you will sit on my soft furnishings ... I suppose you can come in.'

'That's much appreciated,' replies Clyde, giving a full display of his surprisingly perfect teeth.

Helena lets go of the door and steps back, a confused expression furrowing her brow, as if she already can't quite remember what she has agreed to or why.

The noisy (and frankly also slightly smelly) crowd pours into her house. As I pass Callum, who has positioned himself at the foot of the stairs, he hisses, 'Your dad's lost it.'

'No, he hasn't,' I say.

'Is it true he's moved in with the nutjobs?'

'No. He's just helping out Rose.'

'Yeah, right.'

'It's true.'

'Who are these weirdos? What do they want?'

'Did you not understand what Clyde said?'

'Course I did.'

'Then you don't need me to explain it, do you?' I say, following the others into the living room.

Bowls of crisps, nuts, biscuits, olives and sausage rolls have been laid out neatly on various coffee tables and sideboards. These are picked clean within seconds.

Mum stares at me with a *what-have-you-done?* look on her face.

I smile back at her.

# Diplomat!?

'Thank you for inviting us into your beautiful home,' Clyde says to Helena, picking a Pringle crumb from his chest hair and popping it into his mouth.

She doesn't reply, but her pursed lips seem to say, 'I didn't invite you into my home.'

'We understand,' continues Clyde, 'that you've been living with the threat of this airport expansion for a long time, and we know this place is very precious to you. It's where you've raised your families, and tended your gardens, and invested your hearts. I can feel how special this street is to you, and I realise we must look like interlopers – jumping on your cause for reasons that may seem incomprehensible or even misguided. It's completely understandable that you think we don't belong here, and we appreciate that our lifestyle may not be to your taste. This is your community, not ours. But as the threat of

161

demolition approaches, we'd like to offer our skills and experience as protectors of the environment to your cause. We'd like to work together with you to stop the construction work which, if we do nothing, could start in a matter of days. It's clear there's a culture gap we'll have to bridge, but I'd like to put forward David, here, as somebody who I believe can do that.'

Clyde stretches out an arm and puts it around my dad, which is probably the first time I've ever seen him being hugged by another man. Weirdly Dad doesn't seem to mind. This looks like further evidence that he's had his brain reprogrammed. The factory settings version of my dad would be more likely to hug an electric fence than a man in a vest top.

'David is, as you all know, a long-time resident of this street,' Clyde goes on, 'but he's become a valued and trusted member of our community too. I think he'll be an excellent go-between – a sort of diplomat and interpreter in the struggle that lies ahead.'

'*Diplomat!?*' says Mum.

When everyone turns to look at her, an expression of surprise and alarm flashes across her face, as if she only intended to think this and didn't mean the word to actually come out of her mouth, especially not at that volume.

Clyde ignores her outburst and carries on. 'But first,' he says, 'we'd like to hear your plans. This is your street. We're just guests here. The best thing we can do is simply enhance the work you're already doing.'

Clyde then sits cross-legged on the floor and looks up at Helena, across whose cheeks a hot-looking blush slowly spreads.

'Well … thank you … for that,' she says. 'And … I suppose … thank you also for coming to support our cause.'

In response to this, Barrel Woman lets out a whoop, and a wave of applause accompanied by a chorus of whistles spreads through the commune-dwellers, who are all now either sitting on the floor or perched on the backs and arms of Helena's chairs (yes, including the soft furnishings).

This turns Helena's cheeks even redder and, though I can see she's trying not to smile, she can't quite help herself. I get the feeling it's a long time since she last got a round of applause.

'And as to our plan,' she continues, 'well, my husband, over there …' (Laurence, dressed in his usual off-work uniform of beige chinos, brogues and collared T-shirt, gives a little wave from the armchair where he is seated at an awkward angle, leaning away from the purple-legging-clad buttocks of Barrel Woman) '… is a long-standing member of the local Conservative Party, and has extensive business experience in dealing with the law and various regulatory matters, and he is in the process of writing a very stiffly worded letter to our MP.'

If she's hoping for another round of applause, it doesn't come. After an uncomfortable silence, with everyone still staring at Helena while she looks around the room, waiting for someone else to say something, she speaks again. 'And … er … well, this is why we've called the meeting. To gather together as local residents and think about what else we can do to stop or delay the demolition. Anyone? Any thoughts?'

'Do you think maybe we should write to the council?' says the man from number five, who washes his car with a massive yellow sponge at least once a fortnight and pretends he's out every Halloween.

'Did that already,' says Laurence.

Another silence descends.

'Maybe we could put together a Facebook group,' says Mrs Gupta.

'I started one months ago,' snaps Helena.

'How many people have joined?' asks Mrs Gupta.

'Seven. But maybe now's the time to ramp things up.'

'What about the local press?' says Mr Deacon, from number fourteen. 'Should we get them involved?'

'The local newspaper went bust years ago,' says Helena.

'Did it?' says Laurence.

'Yes! Didn't you notice?'

'No. Passed me by.'

'Anyone for a top-up of tea?' says Helena. 'Callum – could you pop to the kitchen and replenish the nibbles. I seem to have underestimated demand.'

Callum, who has been leaning against the door frame, watching the meeting with a sceptical scowl, sighs and shuffles away towards the kitchen. On the back of his hoodie is the name of his fancy school and the cryptic marking 'U16 1st XV'.

After another awkward silence, Clyde says, 'So what we have is a stiff letter to your MP and waiting for a response from the council to a request they've so far ignored?'

'It's just a start ...' says Helena. She doesn't mention that her letter to the council was in fact a petition to get the inhabitants of the commune evicted.

'The thing is,' replies Clyde, 'the bulldozers are on your doorstep. Our planning group has been talking about a few direct actions that we think are appropriate as our resistance enters a proactive final phase. Would you like to hear what we have in mind? And if any of you want to participate or contribute, that would be great.'

'OK. Go on,' says Helena.

'Well,' says Clyde, 'we're a free-standing single-issue collective that has formed for this specific protest, but we all have different backgrounds and alliances, so between us we're already plugged into all the obvious networks for

Extinction Rebellion, Reclaim the Streets, Earth First, Plane Stupid, Plane Mad, Flying Matters, Climate Rush, Camp for Climate Action and Airport Watch. Many of us are frequent contributors to their blogs, newsletters and social media feeds. Add those groups together and there are hundreds of thousands of activists to tap into. We think it's time to put out the call for a street occupation. If we get significant numbers, it'll attract national media, and we can reach out to them via various press contacts to increase exposure when we expect clashes to take place, since unfortunately that's the only way to initially generate interest. No spectacle no news story is the way it usually goes. Modern protesters have to think like film directors. It's a visual culture, and the only way to get ideas across these days is by translating them into something that tickles the eyeballs of people with short attention spans. As for the actual occupation, we're thinking some basic barricades would be a good start.'

'Barricades! Ha!' barks Laurence, as if he thinks this is a wonderful joke. Everyone ignores him, especially his wife.

'Their practical use is limited,' continues Clyde, 'but physical barriers make for a potent photogenic representation of resistance to state violence which plays well on social and traditional media. The first phase would be the old stalwarts of chaining ourselves to things, gluing ourselves to sites slated for demolition, or even to the ground in the path of bulldozers and police cars. For anyone unwilling to go that far, mass lie-ins are effective, though we always advise not to actively resist arrest but simply to go limp, which makes a human body surprisingly hard to lift and carry away. This creates maximum inconvenience for the police, and annoys them, and also plays well in front of the cameras.'

'And it's a good laugh,' adds Sky's mum. 'If you go like jelly it can take six of them to lift you. It's hilarious.'

'Drumming's useful too,' says Space.

'I'm getting to that,' says Clyde. 'We want a clear confrontation, but of a non-violent kind that keeps us on the moral high ground. All the organisations we're allied to are committed to policies of strict non-violence, and it's imperative we adhere to that. Music and dancing are also cool, for obvious reasons.'

'Specially drumming,' mumbles Space.

Clyde nods patiently and carries on. 'Depending on how things develop, we'll be looking for volunteers to attach themselves to the bulldozers – a bike D-lock round the neck works well and is very tricky for the police to remove – but that can put you in line for a criminal damage charge, so it's best to keep that in reserve for the next escalation, when the time comes. We should probably hold off on the gluing and chaining until we have a bigger media presence and the demolition is looking imminent. The more of us who participate in that the better.'

Clyde looks around the room, and everyone who has been listening to him intently suddenly looks down. Nobody wants to be the first to respond.

'Excuse me,' says Mum, just at the point where the lack of any reply to Clyde's long speech is hitting peak awkwardness. 'Can I ask a question?'

'Sure,' says Clyde.

'Is the idea of gluing and chaining yourself to things that it stops the demolition work, or just that it makes a spectacle and gets on the news?'

'Both,' says Clyde.

'It might delay things for a while, but surely that won't stop anything,' continues Mum. 'If you want to actually stop it, you have to have a media campaign that gets enough attention to build support outside the bubble of people who usually care about this kind of thing. Only then will politicians and decision makers even begin to consider changing course.'

'Exactly,' says Clyde, nodding enthusiastically and looking at her as if he's seeing her for the first time. This is when I remember that Mum works in marketing. What she does all day, and what marketing even really is, I have no idea, but I think this has something to do with why she's speaking up now.

'Well,' says Mum, in the purposeful tone I recognise as her taking-a-work-call-on-her-mobile voice, 'effective public messaging is my area, and if you want this protest to be noticed, what you're going to need is something people haven't seen before.'

'Such as?'

'If people like you do that stuff, nobody is going to be very surprised, are they? But if the person glued to the ground in front of a bulldozer was someone like … I don't know … Laurence, for example – pillar of the local Tory Party and all – that would get much more attention.'

'Me?' says Laurence. 'Glued to the road?'

'For example,' says Mum.

'Or a building,' adds Clyde.

'What an extraordinary idea!' says Laurence. 'To stop the bulldozers?'

'And generate a media response,' says Clyde.

'Gosh,' says Laurence.

'Ridiculous!' says Helena.

'House prices on this street are going to take a huge hit when the building work starts,' says Mum.

'I know, but—'

'Are you honestly suggesting …' interrupts Helena.

'The thing is …' continues Laurence, '… it might be rather fun.'

'What did you say?' barks Helena, staring aghast at her husband.

'I think whatshername's right,' says Laurence, wafting

a hand towards Mum, who has been his next-door neighbour for more than a decade but whose name has evidently never sunk in. 'If a bunch of hippies do that kind of thing, nobody's going to give it a second glance, are they? We've seen all that before. If I do it, people might actually notice. These days, news is all about those funny little whatnots that get shared around, isn't it? That's the only way to get people to pay attention. It's moronic, obviously, but if I become one of those, it might be helpful.'

'It certainly would,' says Clyde, with a grin spreading across his face.

'I might become a ... what's it called? A memmy?' says Laurence.

'Do you mean a meme?' asks Rose.

'That's the one!'

'But ... you ... he's talking about *gluing yourself to the road*!' says Helena, an octave or so higher than her usual speaking voice.

'Yes, I heard him, darling.'

'You can't do that!'

'Why not?'

'What will people say?'

'I think they'll be impressed,' says Dad.

'Oh, and you'd know, would you?' snaps Helena.

'I'll be chaining myself to the tree in front of the

170

commune,' says Dad. 'The more residents that take part in the direct action the better.'

'Laurence, have you gone stark raving bonkers?' says Helena.

'I don't think so, darling.'

'How will you eat?'

'Soup,' says Clyde.

'If you think I'm feeding you soup while you're glued to the road in front of our house, you've got another thing coming.'

'We'll feed you,' says Rose gleefully. Ever since the time her pay was docked for breaking a glass while babysitting, Rose has disliked Helena even more than Mum does.

'One question,' says Laurence. 'How would I ... relieve myself?'

'You have to be in loose-fitting clothes you can slip out of when you need to go for a wazz, and you have to time it for when nobody's there trying to arrest you,' says Sky's mum. 'Then you come back, slip into the clothes, and you're glued down again. That's how they normally get you in the end, to be honest.'

'How bizarre. Well, I'll give it a try,' says Laurence.

Another round of whooping and cheering thunders through the room. Sky's mum tries to fist-bump Laurence, but he clearly has no idea what this means or how to do it, and they settle on an awkward cross between a high five and a vertical handshake. Laurence's decision to join the direct action transforms the atmosphere of the meeting. Soon the whole place is buzzing with ideas, suggestions and offers of help.

Following on from Mum's point about the importance of local residents spearheading the media campaign, Clyde ends up proposing Dad not just as cross-street liaison guy but as public spokesman for the whole operation – someone with a foot in both camps, who will be harder for the media to dismiss as a crazy hippie than the other residents of the commune.

Dad seems surprised to be pushed forward in this way, but everyone in the room (except for Mum) gets behind the idea, and he ends up accepting the role.

It takes me a while to screw up the courage to speak, but eventually, as the meeting is quietening down and moving to a close, I pitch in with my own idea. 'A lot of this stuff has to happen at the last minute, doesn't it?' I say. 'As the bulldozers are preparing to roll in. I mean, you don't want to chain yourself to stuff until you really have to, do you? So what you're going to need is a lookout.'

Everyone stares at me, suddenly quiet, clearly surprised that a kid has spoken up. I swallow hard and make myself carry on. 'So how about we build a treehouse at the top of the big oak in front of the commune? Me and Sky will man it, and we can message everyone if we see movement from the bulldozers. Or the police.'

For a moment I think everyone's going to laugh at me, or that one of my parents is going to tell me to stop embarrassing them, but the idea is immediately embraced, and a team of carpenters is put together with the car-washing Halloween-hiding man, who works in construction and says he can get hold of a supply of timber.

The funny thing is, I always wanted a treehouse, until a couple of years ago when I grew out of the idea, but now that one might actually be built specifically for me and Sky, I realise I've never stopped wanting it after all, especially one that's high, dangerous and built not for playing in but as a strategic outpost in an eco-war. I mean, who wouldn't want one of those?

By the end of the evening there's a buzz of excitement in the air that feels almost like a party, as if the threat of demolition is somehow a cause for celebration rather than regret.

As I'm leaving, passing by Callum, who has returned to his vantage point at the bottom of the stairs, I lean towards him and whisper, 'Your dad's lost it.'

# I didn't know that was even possible

The next day, Mum's out at work and Dad is doing whatever it is he does to pass the time in the commune, so after a late breakfast and a couple of slightly aimless hours in the park with some school friends, I settle in with Sky for a marathon gaming, TV and snacks session. We also fit in a game of chess, because I've been looking up tactics online and am determined to beat her – but, yet again, I don't manage it.

Even more annoying than losing to her at chess is the fact that while she's deciding on her moves I stare at the board, plotting and scheming, but while I'm thinking about mine, she turns her attention to the sketch pad she always carries around with her and scratches away at drawings of birds and dragons that usually end up as good as any illustration you'd find in a book. Maddeningly she often looks as if she's thinking harder about the drawings than the chess.

It's late afternoon before we eventually step outside into the dazzling sunlight and discover that work has already begun on the treehouse. A heap of timber has been dumped at the foot of the huge oak in the front garden of the commune, with a pulley rigged up on a loop over the top branches.

At the bottom, the pulley is being operated by Rose and Space, who we find tying a stack of planks to a rope. Rose's T-shirt is dark with sweat, and Space is wearing only sandals and a pair of shorts whose camouflage pattern is almost entirely camouflaged by blotches of dirt. The only thing Space ever seems to wear on his top half is his drum.

When she sees me, Rose smiles, wipes a forearm across her brow and says, 'Hi – how are you doing?'

I can't remember the last time she greeted me with anything that isn't a version of 'What do you want?', so for a moment I'm thrown by her unexpected friendliness.

The first reply that occurs to me is, 'Why are you being nice to me?' but instead I settle for a simple, 'Good.'

'The treehouse is taking shape already,' she replies, pointing upwards.

It's hard to see through the foliage, but a couple of people seem to be high up in the tree, tied on with harnesses and ropes. A web of joists has been nailed into place and a platform is beginning to be laid on to them.

'That's high!' says Sky, squinting up into the sun.

'Your mum's at work with a team in the garden making a rope ladder,' replies Rose. 'You can go and see, if you want, or you can give us a hand here.'

Sky heads round to the back of the house to see her mum (or maybe just to see the rope ladder), but I stay put to help Rose with the pulley.

'Who's up there?' I ask, as we set to work securing the next plank.

'Clyde and Martha.'

'Martha?'

'You know – the one that fancies Dad.'

'Someone fancies Dad? *Who?*'

'Old. Long curly hair. Terrible jumpers.'

'Her? She fancies Dad?'

'She hasn't *said* anything, but it's pretty obvious. She's always hanging around him.'

'But … why?' I say.

'No idea.'

'I didn't know that was even possible.'

'People are weird.'

'Dad's always with Clyde. It must be Clyde she fancies.'

'You'd think. But I can sense a vibe.' She turns to Space and adds, 'I'm right, aren't I?'

'I have a … theory,' says Space very slowly, 'that … actually … in some way … everyone fancies everyone. It's the human condition.'

'Do you fancy everyone?' says Rose, with an edge to her voice.

'No, of course not!' says Space rapidly. 'OK, it's not a very good theory.'

Space puts his head down and goes back to tying planks together.

'And that's Martha up there now, building the tree-house?' I ask.

'Yeah. Apparently she was an academic, then she retrained as a psychotherapist, then as a carpenter now she lives here. She's the one who pointed out the totem pole was going to kill somebody and fixed it.'

'And you really think she fancies Dad?'

'Can we please stop talking about this?' she says. 'It's gross!'

'I don't think he and Mum are talking. They had a huge row a few days ago.'

'Really?'

'You didn't know?'

'No.'

'Well, maybe you should talk to her,' I say.

'I am talking to her.'

'You can't be. If you were talking to her, you would have

177

talked to her about how she isn't talking to Dad. The argument was on Saturday.'

'It's been a few days. I'll give her a call.'

'Just go and see her!'

'It's easier on the phone,' says Rose. 'And I'm not not talking to her. It's Dad I'm not talking to.'

'Do you think it would be better for the whole family if we could all … just … ?'

'No. Take this rope. Hold tight.'

I squeeze the rough, twisted surface of the rope. Rose and Space grab it behind me and the three of us haul together, yanking a bundle of planks jerkily up the tree.

I'm still working at the pulley, and have built up a sweat myself, when Mum gets back from work and reverses into the driveway. She steps out of the car, watches from our front garden for a while, then crosses the road and joins us at the foot of the oak.

'Treehouse is looking good,' she says, peering up into the foliage. 'You're fast workers.'

'No time to waste,' says Rose.

'Well … it's impressive,' replies Mum, smiling at Rose.

'Not just a bunch of useless slackers, then?' she replies.

'I never said you were.'

'You thought it though.'

'You don't know what I think, Rose.'

'Yes, I do.'

178

'Maybe I'm capable of changing my mind.'

'Are you?'

'Yes,' says Mum.

The two of them share a moment of intense eye contact, then, suddenly, as if things weren't awkward enough already, Dad's there, still wearing his illegal jeans.

Mum looks at him, expressionless, not speaking, probably wondering, among other things, where he got his trousers.

'It's taking shape, don't you think?' says Dad. 'The treehouse.'

Mum nods.

'Great idea of Luke's, wasn't it?'

This time Mum doesn't even nod. She just looks at him and frowns.

'There's going to be a barrier at the edge. We'll make sure it's safe.'

'You'd better,' says Mum, with all the warmth and tenderness of a polar blizzard.

Knowing he's beaten, Dad turns to me and says, 'You looking forward to going up?'

I'm desperate to say something that might dispel the tense atmosphere, but a brain freeze gets the better of me, and all I manage to come out with is, 'Yeah. It looks good.'

'I'm heading home to make dinner. Want to join us?' says Mum, angling her body so it's clear her invitation is to

Rose and not Dad. 'Both of you,' she adds, gesturing towards Space. 'You look like you could do with a break.'

'No, thanks,' replies Rose. 'We're on the rota tonight for washing-up, so …'

'Maybe tomorrow,' says Mum.

'Maybe.'

'I'll make something veggie.'

'We're vegan.'

'That's what I meant. OK. Bye, then. See you tomorrow, maybe.'

'Bye.'

Mum walks home, and almost immediately Dad heads off in the opposite direction, back into the commune.

Rose and I look at one another.

'That was weird,' I say.

Rose shrugs. 'It's not *my* fault,' she says.

I hadn't said (or thought) that it was, but now she's jumped so rapidly to deny it, I can't help feeling that maybe the whole thing *is* her fault. If she hadn't come into my room that night, borrowed a sleeping bag and moved out, everything would be different. At the very least, we'd all be living in the same house.

There's no point in saying anything though. Who is to blame for the ongoing family hostilities is irrelevant now, and there doesn't seem to be much to gain by confronting or accusing Rose, especially with her beginning to show

180

signs of recognising that I am an actual human being – a sibling, even.

A voice calls down from above requesting more planks, and the three of us get back to work.

'Family, eh?' says Space, after a while. 'Can't live with 'em, can't live without 'em.'

I have no idea what he means, and no desire to ask.

'You live without yours,' says Rose.

'Yeah, well, I'm lucky,' he replies.

# The nest

Within a couple of days the treehouse is finished, complete with built-in seating, a roofed area for shade and rain shelter, a safety rail to stop us falling out, a basket that can be lowered to the ground for sending up supplies, and access by a long snaking rope ladder which can be raised to keep out intruders.

As I climb up there for the first time, my heart races with a mixture of fear and excitement, which, by the time I'm halfway up, turns into just plain fear. The higher I go up the swaying rope ladder the more convinced I become that, instead of getting closer, the treehouse is retreating skywards with every step I take, but if I pause to catch my breath, the slippery treads under my feet lurch forward, leaving me hanging at a painful and frightening angle. Higher and higher I go, wondering what I've got myself into, cursing myself for coming up with the idea, because, having thought of it, there's no way I can bail out now. However terrified I am and however much I hate it, there's no option except to press on to the top.

The transition from the rope ladder to the platform is the most sickening part of all, with my hands struggling to find a good grip while my legs sway and judder on the top few rungs. I somehow manage to clamber on, and immediately lie flat on my stomach to recover something resembling a normal heart rate.

When I finally build up the confidence to look down, I'm convinced that I am now twice as high as I thought I'd be when I was looking up from below. My eyeline is level with the rooftops. If I fell out, I'd die.

'How is it?' Dad yells up from the foot of the tree.

It's a while before I can summon enough breath to answer. I don't want to say anything negative, but I'm reluctant to lie, so I just say, 'High!'

'Does it feel safe?' shouts Martha.

'Er … it feels solid. I need to get used to it.'

'You will!' says Clyde. 'Are you ready for Sky?'

'OK.'

She starts her climb confidently, but I'm relieved to see that she appears to hesitate in the same way when she hits the midpoint. Her face is pale and bloodless when she appears at the top of the ladder. I grab her upper arms and help her with the final scramble on to the platform.

A chorus of whoops and cheers rises up from below.

'You OK!?' yells Rose, cupping her hand beside her mouth.

'Fine!' I lie, peeping over the edge and waving back. The people at the bottom look alarmingly small, and I'm still wondering if this whole treehouse plan was a good idea.

'Well done, Sky,' shouts her mum. 'You did great!'

I'm sitting up now, but Sky is lying flat, hugging the boards underneath her. She doesn't look like she can speak.

'Tell them I'm fine, but I'm catching my breath,' she mutters hoarsely.

I pass on the message.

'Take your time!' calls Clyde. 'There's no hurry!'

'This is really high,' says Sky quietly.

'It is, isn't it.'

'Do you think we'll get used to it?'

'I hope so. I feel about as relaxed as you look.'

'How do I look?'

'Terrified.'

'Are you all right?' calls Dad. 'Do you want me to come up?'

'No! We're fine!' I call back. The idea of another body up here on the cramped area of flooring, particularly a large and clumsy one, feels petrifying. As things stand, there's space for Sky and me to spread out while we get used to the dizzying height.

184

After a few minutes Sky sits upright, and not long after that she inches herself to the built-in bench, crawling on all fours, then slowly pulling herself up.

'Look at this view!' she says, staring out through the crown of the tree at the roofscape spread out around us.

Now that Sky has made it to the bench, I decide that I ought to try and summon the courage to stand up. I grip the safety rail and slowly pull myself on to my feet, straightening my legs in tiny increments, then uncurling my spine and finally lifting my neck. As I stand there, holding the wooden rail with both hands, my knees feel strangely loose and unreliable, barely strong enough to support my weight, so I shuffle towards Sky, sliding rather than lifting my feet, and sit next to her.

A churn of anxiety is still squelching in my stomach, but now, looking down on the world, I begin to sense for the first time that the fear and discomfort might all be worth it. To be this far above my everyday life, my house and family, the streets I walk every day, feels like being lifted out of myself, almost reborn.

Looking out over my city, an ocean of roofs that stretches as far as I can see, all those thousands of people scurrying around on the ground seem small and slightly ridiculous as they rush from task to task like overgrown insects, with no idea how tiny they really are.

I soak up the view, sensing the tension leave my body

and float away on the breeze rustling through the branches around us. I look across at Sky, and neither of us needs to say anything. We just smile at each other.

And as I sit there, in this elevated, secret place, it occurs to me that I know I will never bring my school friends here. Though I haven't known Sky for long, I'm in no doubt that she'll stay calm up here and not take any risks or attempt any stupid, dangerous pranks. I don't think I could trust my friends in the same way. They'd either be overconfident or, if they became frightened, they'd get competitive with anyone who was less frightened, then anything could happen. Also, there's something about Dad and Rose moving into the commune, and the impossible-to-explain place that Sky now seems to have in my life, that feels private.

On my street and in my house nothing is what it was, and I sense that nothing is going to stay how it is now, either. I don't want anyone to see the soap-bubble fragility of my new life, and I'm not sure why but I have a sense that maybe, if nobody sees it, the bubble won't burst.

The next day starts with a short house meeting where a messaging system is put in place to coordinate what we should do if we see any suspicious activity in the building site at the end of the street. It's expected that a demolition team will move in fast, with no prior warning.

A string of numbers is programmed into my phone, while the curious culinary pairing of my dad and Sky's mum serve up a stack of pancakes, which are brown for some reason but taste OK if you cover them in enough sugar. The sugar is also brown, by the way. Unless I say otherwise, just assume that all food in the commune is brown.

When we've eaten our fill, Sky and I head up to the treehouse to begin our first day as lookouts. At first there's the same jolt of fear verging on panic, but this time it settles down faster into the state of hushed other-worldly peace that our treetop hideaway seems to generate.

We spend the day going up and down the rope ladder, hauling cushions, blankets, food and books up there to transform the platform into what feels like a homely den. For someone who lives in a hovel, Sky has a surprising flair for interior decoration. I don't know how she does it, but the cramped space, despite now being filled with stuff, ends up feeling bigger than it did before. She creates defined areas: a lookout corner; a relaxation nest lined with the sleeping bag I reclaim from Rose; a dining area with a low table (a snack-filled cool box covered in a blanket); and we even add a hanging bucket in case of emergency calls of nature during a ladder-up situation.

Hours pass in a flash as we refine and perfect our new temporary home, the thought of lunch not even occurring to us. Then suddenly Mum is standing at the bottom of the tree calling us down for dinner.

She watches anxiously as we descend, and gives us both a relieved hug when we return to ground level.

Over the meal she quizzes us on the safety of the tree-house, asking how much time we're intending to spend up there, and not very subtly trying to persuade us to do something else.

She says that when it was discussed in the meeting, she had no idea how high it would be, and she seems annoyed that something so dangerous was built without her permission.

I point out that she visited during the construction work, when maybe it could have been altered, but she swats away my comment with a wave of her hand, saying, 'Nobody would have listened to me.'

When I confess that I've relocated most of the family supply of snacks to the top of the tree, bracing myself for a telling-off, she just gives a resigned shrug, as if she thinks the whole project is mad, but is somehow not her problem. This seems to be the position she's reached on everything to do with the commune, including Dad.

'Just be careful up there,' she says.

'We will,' I assure her, but I can sense that she doesn't believe me. Even so, she doesn't argue back or try to forbid us from going back up there, which seems uncharacteristically easy-going and passive.

Now I look at her – at the pallor of her skin and the bags under her eyes – and realise that I've never seen her look so tired. My mother, who has always been a source of boundless energy, looks, for the first time ever, like someone who can't be bothered to fight her corner.

'We'll be careful. I promise,' I say.

She smiles at me, but it isn't really a smile.

Later that evening, as I'm putting myself to bed, Mum comes into my room and hands me a dark brown leather case the size of a couple of food tins, with a metal clasp and a cracked, brittle neck strap.

'What's this?' I say, feeling the weight of it, sensing immediately that it's something precious.

'It's for you. For your job up in the treehouse.'

I click open the rust-speckled clasp and pull out a pair of heavy black and silver binoculars.

'They were my dad's,' she says, watching me lift them to my eyes and showing me how to adjust the focusing dial. 'For his birdwatching. They've been sitting in a drawer for years, but I want you to have them.'

At first I see only a blur, then a shelf of books at the far end of the room crystallises out of the murk. The titles become crisp and clear; even the creases on the spines are visible.

'They're amazing,' I say.

After I've experimented a little longer, Mum asks for a

go. As she raises the binoculars to her eyes, her face relaxes into a dreamy faraway expression.

'I remember the feel of them,' she says. 'Reminds me of being your age. He always took them with him on walks. If he saw anything interesting, he'd put the strap over my neck and try to show me. I hardly ever saw what he saw, but … wow, just holding them … I haven't touched them since Dad … it's like he's … I can almost feel his hand on my shoulder …'

She lowers the binoculars and she's smiling, but her eyes are glistening with a filmy sheen of tears.

'Sorry,' she says, handing back the binoculars and standing. 'Sorry. I wish you'd met him. He was a good man. He was kind. You would have liked each other.'

She swipes at her eyes quickly with the side of her thumb, turns away and walks out.

# The sweet spot

It's hard to say exactly what we do up there, but whole days drift easily by with the two of us right in the sweet spot between something and nothing to do, contentedly idle without being bored. Just watching the world go by, invisibly and from a secret height, is strangely and endlessly mesmerising.

Then, only minutes after getting home from her Wednesday half-day in the office, I see Mum march out of our front door with a determined, angry look on her face and cross the road directly towards us. My first thought is that we must have done something wrong, but she strides straight past the tree without even glancing upwards and heads into the commune.

I hurry down the rope ladder to see what's going on. As soon as I'm in the house, I can hear Mum's voice reverberating out of Dad's attic room.

I follow the sound up the stairs, and it's obvious (to me and probably everyone else in the house, if not the street) that they are arguing. Mum has evidently just listened to a voicemail on the landline at home from the 'HR department' (whatever that is) at Dad's work, saying that if he doesn't respond within twenty-four hours to the emails and phone messages regarding his unexplained absence, his employment will be immediately terminated.

In other words, Dad has been bunking off and they are about to fire him. It's not clear what Mum thought he was doing, or what she thought he had arranged with his work to allow him to muck around in the commune all day, but it's pretty clear she wasn't expecting this.

It doesn't feel right to go into his room in the middle of their argument, but I can't walk away either, so I hover on the landing outside, listening.

'Why didn't you tell me?' Mum's yelling.

'Don't worry. I'll sort it out.'

'Sounds a bit late for that. They're about to fire you.'

'They won't fire me.'

'The message says you've got twenty-four hours.'

'They're bluffing.'

'How can you be so calm! If you lose your job …'

'I'm not going to lose my job.'

'It looks to me like you are doing literally everything a person could possibly do to try and lose their job.'

'You have to do something really bad to get fired these days.'

'How is this not bad? They're not going to pay you to do nothing all day!'

'I'll tell them I'm having a nervous breakdown. I've seen it loads of times before. It always works.'

'Are you?'

'Am I what?'

'Having a nervous breakdown.'

'I don't think so.'

'Because it really looks like you are.'

'Then maybe you shouldn't be so angry with me.'

'Unbelievable! You're asking me not to be *angry*! While you sit around all day playing the banjo and making soup.'

'It's not a banjo, it's a guitar.'

'We need both salaries to pay the mortgage!'

'I know.'

'So what are we going to do when you get fired?'

'I won't get fired.'

This is when I realise that Rose is standing next to me on the landing. 'What's going on?' she whispers. 'Why are they talking about Dad being fired?'

'He hasn't been going to work, and Mum says they're going to sack him,' I say.

Mum now appears in the doorway.

'What are you two doing here? Are you eavesdropping?' she says.

'Has Dad been fired?' says Rose.

'Ask him yourself. If he's not too busy tuning his banjo.'

Dad shuffles out on to the landing, next to Mum. 'I don't know why you're all in such a panic. I'll call into work tomorrow and sort everything out.'

'He's going to tell them he's gone mad,' says Mum.

'Sounds plausible,' says Rose.

'See?' says Dad.

Mum's jaw drops open. 'What are you talking about?'

'Are you having a nervous breakdown or not?' I ask.

'If a nervous breakdown is doing things you actually enjoy, and being happy for the first time in years, and not living every minute of your day as a slave to other people's demands, then yes – absolutely – this is a nervous breakdown and it's bloody marvellous.'

'Was that a yes or a no?' I say, to Mum and Rose. They both shrug.

'How long are you planning to stay here?' says Mum.

'I just need to see this protest through. It's important.'

'Important on some kind of principle? Or just important that you're having a nice time?' asks Mum.

'When did you get so cynical?' says Dad.

'When did you get so totally insane?' replies Mum.

'Why did you even come here?' asks Rose.

'Well, I …' Dad tails away with a vague wave of an arm.

'Tell her,' insists Mum. 'Give her a proper answer.'

'OK. At first it was just to flush you out. Then I realised I like it here,' says Dad.

'Flush me out!? Like a turd?'

'Don't be ridiculous! This has nothing to do with turds.'

'You're the one that talked about flushing!'

'*Out*. Not *away*. You don't flush out a turd. You flush *away* a turd. It's a completely different meaning.'

'Well, I'm really flattered by the comparison.'

'That's not what I meant, and you know it.'

'I hate to interrupt this fascinating conversation, but I think we might be getting off the point,' says Mum. 'Shall we get back to your explanation of why you came here?'

Dad looks from Rose to Mum, then back again, thinks for a few seconds, then says, 'I thought me being in the commune might make the place seem less appealing, and you'd get fed up quicker and go back home.'

'So if I went home now, would you go too? Mission accomplished and all that?' says Rose.

Dad looks at her, chewing his lip, deep in thought.

'That's a tricky one,' he says.

'A TRICKY ONE!' yells Mum. 'YOU TOLD ME THAT WAS WHY YOU CAME! NOW SHE'S OFFERING TO GO HOME AND YOU'RE HESITATING.'

'I didn't say that,' Dad and Rose reply simultaneously.

'Didn't say what?' asks Mum.

'That I was offering,' says Rose. 'It was a theoretical question.'

'Someone else is living in your bedroom now, anyway,' I say.

'What? You gave away my bedroom?'

'I haven't given it away,' says Mum.

'TO WHO?' says Rose.

'Sky sleeps there sometimes, but I haven't *given* her the bedroom.'

'Sometimes as in every night,' I say.

'You can have it back any time,' says Mum.

'NO! I DON'T WANT IT! IF YOU'RE IN SUCH A RUSH TO SWAP ME FOR ANOTHER DAUGHTER, YOU CAN KEEP IT!' says, Rose, spinning on her heel and marching away.

'Why did you say that?' Mum says to me angrily.

'Just being honest,' I reply.

'Well, there won't be a bedroom for either of them if he doesn't keep up his half of the mortgage payments,' snaps Mum.

'Why is everyone being so emotional?' says Dad.

'Aaaaaarrrrrrggghhhhhhh!' growls Mum, throwing her arms in the air and eyeballing Dad as if she might throttle him.

Dad tries to hold her gaze, but fails.

'OK,' she says. 'We're going on holiday in a few days anyway. Why don't you just stay here till then and sort things out with work, then treat the time away as a chance to think about what you're doing, and how to resolve whatever weird thing it is you're going through? And after Spain we can all make a fresh start. Try to get back to normal. Does that sound like a plan?'

'Er … I suppose. Maybe that's the best way forward.'

'That's the most enthusiastic response you can come up with, is it?'

'No, I … er … great! Yeah! That's a good idea.'

Shaking her head, Mum turns and walks away down the staircase.

When she's gone, Dad shrugs at me and tries to pull his lips into a smile, but it ends up looking more as if he's about to vomit.

I look back at him, not smiling. I like Dad being a bit crazy, but getting fired from his job and living as a dropout is taking things too far.

'It'll all be OK,' he says, patting me on the shoulder.

'Not if we get thrown out of our house,' I say.

'That won't happen. And even if we did have to move somewhere a bit smaller, that wouldn't be the end of the world. You can't spend your whole life never doing anything you actually want. Well, you *can* – maybe most people do, but I'm not going to be one of those people. I can't do it any more.'

'Does that mean you're not going back to work?'

'It means I'm figuring out how to stand up for myself for once.'

With those ominous words he steps away and goes back into his tiny room, so I head downstairs and climb back to the treehouse, which is the only place I want to be. A few days ago it terrified me to be up here, now it feels like the safest place I know.

I can tell by the way Sky looks at me that she heard all the shouting. After giving me a while to sit and think, she says, 'What was that all about?'

'It's my dad – they're threatening to sack him, and Mum's not pleased. He's gone kind of nuts.'

'He seems fine to me,' says Sky. 'I like him.'

'He *seems* fine,' I say, 'if you've never met him before. But this isn't what he's supposed to be like.'

'What's he supposed to be like?'

'Like other dads. You know – boring.'

'Boring is better, is it?'

'Definitely. Well … I don't know … I think this version is kind of OK, but it drives Mum crazy, and the family's falling apart, and he might lose his job, so that can't be good, can it?'

'I suppose. I wouldn't really know. I've never had a dad.'

'Oh,' I say, trying to slam the brakes on my self-pity. 'I'm sorry.'

'I mean, he must exist somewhere,' says Sky, 'but I don't know anything about him.'

'Nothing?'

'All Mum will say is that he's an arsehole.'

'That's all you know? He's an arsehole?'

'Yup. That's it. Probably not enough information to track him down, is it?'

'I suppose you think I'm making a fuss about nothing, then?' I say, after an awkward silence.

'No. If I had what you had, then it started falling apart, I'd be heartbroken. I think you're being brave.'

For someone who knows nothing about anything, Sky has an uncanny ability to see into the heart of things.

'I suppose I should be grateful to have a dad at all, even if he is losing his marbles,' I say.

Sky shrugs, picks up the binoculars and stares out at the encampment of bulldozers and demolition machinery that has recently begun filling up one end of the street.

'Maybe it's just what dads do. They go off. Do their own thing,' she says.

'He's only crossed the street,' I say. 'He'll come back.'

'I hope so,' says Sky, lowering the binoculars and looking at me with a piercing gaze, as if she knows something I don't.

I sense that she's trying to reassure me, but her attempt is having the opposite effect. I always thought of my family as a single entity, like a machine with four moving parts, but now we seem more like four separate parts from four different machines, with nothing connecting us. Even if we were to end up back in the same house, I don't think the cogs would ever fit together like they did before – we'd be like a dismantled Mercedes reassembled into a pointless junkyard totem pole.

'Shall we go and take a look?' says Sky.

'At what?'

'The building site. See what's happening.'

'OK.'

I follow her down the rope ladder, and within a few minutes we're peering through the clamped-together sections of wire fencing that surround the two demolished houses at the end of the street.

Three small bulldozers are parked at the edge of a flattened patch of rubble-strewn land. A bigger one is closer to us, noisily clawing at a heap of bricks and twisted metal, which it dumps bite by bite into a waiting lorry.

A huddle of temporary buildings, long caravan-like boxes, have been piled at the edge of the site, and a man in yellow hi-vis gear is hovering by the doorway of one of them, having a conversation on a mobile phone.

Just in front of us on the other side of the fence, two

men are seated beside a heap of sand, silently sucking at cigarettes and gazing in opposite directions.

'All right?' says one of them, greeting us with a small upward jerk of the chin.

I nod, but Sky just stares at them with her huge other-worldly eyes.

'You from up the street?' says the builder.

'Yeah,' I say.

'Watch out for yourselves, OK?' he says. 'Things are going to get a bit tasty.'

'When?' I say.

'Soon,' he says.

'WHY DON'T YOU JUST GO BACK HOME AND LEAVE US ALONE!' shouts Sky suddenly, and the two builders stare at her for a second or so, then burst out laughing.

'You're a feisty one,' says the builder who hasn't spoken yet.

'WHY CAN'T YOU JUST BE NICE?' yells Sky, her voice cracking with emotion.

The builders burst into laughter again, and Sky marches away, her shoes kicking up a puff of dust as she spins on her heels. As an afterthought, she picks up a stone and throws it towards the builders, but it clatters weakly against the fence and falls near my feet. How to throw appears to be another thing she's never been taught.

201

'Why can't you just be nice?' repeats one of the builders, still laughing. 'That's priceless.'

I follow Sky away from the building site and back to our treehouse, thinking about the builder's warning, wondering what 'soon' really means.

I find Sky curled up in a ball, lying on her side in the middle of the platform.

'Are you OK?' I ask.

'We have to win,' she says, not moving or looking at me.

'Let's hope,' I reply.

'We *have to*,' she repeats, with a steeliness to her voice that I've never heard before. 'The bulldozers mustn't get through.'

She sits up, takes the binoculars and stares out at the building site again.

'Why do you care so much?' I ask. 'It's not like it's your street. When this is all over, you'll just go somewhere else, won't you?'

'Exactly.'

'So why is it such a big deal?'

Sky lowers the binoculars and finally turns to face me.

'Because if we lose and the demolition happens, Mum will drag me to the next protest, and it'll be the same thing all over again, but … not like this. Not like here.'

'You don't want to leave?'

'No. This is the first place I've been for years that feels like home.'

'So what is it you want? To win, or to keep the protest going?'

'I don't know. Both. The struggle is much more important than me. What I want doesn't matter, I suppose, but ...'

'Of course it matters,' I say. 'It matters a lot.'

'Not really. But ... thanks, anyway. You and your mum are ... what you've done for me ... it's changed my life.'

'It's nothing. Don't worry about it.'

'It's not nothing,' she says. 'It isn't.'

# Should I be worried about you?

Two days later, just as we're finishing dinner and getting ready to fetch down our suitcases from the loft, Dad bursts in with a big smile on his face. He's wearing accountant-on-holiday shorts and a vest-type-thing in the style of Clyde, except on Dad it looks less like a fashion choice and more like a forgetful middle-aged man has accidentally left the house in his underwear.

'Good news!' he says. 'Everything's sorted.'

It's fair to assume he's not talking about his outfit.

Mum looks at him sceptically, and says, 'What does that even mean?'

'With my work. The threatening phone messages. It's all dealt with. You don't need to worry about it any more.'

'They're not firing you?'

'I'm on sick leave.'

'Sick leave? But you're not sick.'

'Says who?'

'What are you ill with?' asks Mum.

'Depression!' replies Dad cheerfully.

'You don't seem depressed,' says Mum.

'Well, maybe not exactly depression, but I went to the doctor and told him about what's been going on, and how I've moved over the road into a kind of commune/slum-type place and how I can't bring myself to go to work any more, and how all the things I've spent my whole life caring about now seem completely hollow and meaning-less, and he said it sounded like a nervous breakdown, probably stress-induced, and I should give myself a period of complete rest, and consider medication if the symptoms don't improve. He wrote his diagnosis down, and I took the letter in to work, and *voila*. Sick leave.'

'So you're officially crazy?' says Mum.

'Yes!' says Dad. 'Except you're not supposed to use that word any more.'

'What is the word for it, then?'

'They didn't tell me.'

'Is this real, or not?' says Mum.

'Yes! Absolutely!'

'But you seem really happy.'

'I know! Crazy, isn't it?'

'I thought you weren't supposed to use that word.'

'You're not.'

'Are you faking this?' says Mum.

'No! If anything, the reality is that I've been lying my whole life, but now I've finally started to tell the truth. And what's the upshot? Society decides I've gone mad.'

'Have you?'

'I don't know. It depends whose definitions you accept.'

'You do seem kind of mad,' she says.

'Exactly!' says Dad proudly, turning towards me, but whatever expression I have on my face, it isn't what he's looking for, because his eyes flick away almost immediately and settle on the serving bowl of pasta in the middle of the table.

After a few seconds of awkward silence, he says, 'That looks nice.'

Mum stares at him evenly, but doesn't speak or move.

'Can I have some?' he asks.

She leaves him hanging for a few seconds, then shrugs, staring at him through narrowed eyes as if he's an image she can't get into focus. He fetches a plate, serves himself a large helping and sits down.

For a while we watch Dad eat. He seems oblivious to all the attention.

'People are saying it's getting close,' he says, through a mouthful of pasta.

'What is?' asks Sky.

'The eviction. We need to be ready. Vigilant at all times.

206

These two are doing a great job,' he adds, smiling at Mum and waving his fork in the direction of Sky and me.

'Pleased to hear that,' says Mum warily.

'Eagle eyes,' he adds. 'Mind if I have seconds?'

'Not getting enough food in the commune, then?'

'Eating like a king,' he replies, scooping out a generous portion.

'Are you sure you're OK?' asks Mum.

'Yeah, I'm fine. Never been better. I need to feed myself up because I might be chained to a tree for a while. Clyde says it's a good idea to carbo-load beforehand.'

'Should I be worried about you?' says Mum.

'That depends.'

'On what?'

'On whether you think life is a hole that you should sit in the bottom of, or a high wire you should walk along.'

Mum stares at him for a while, contemplating this idea, then says, 'Maybe I think life is neither of those things.'

'Is there any pudding?' asks Dad.

'Aren't you at all concerned about the example you're setting for Luke?' says Mum.

Dad turns to me, scrutinises my face for a few seconds, then says, 'Am I setting you a bad example?'

'I don't know,' I say.

'Do you want to spend the rest of your life just trying to conform and be the same as everyone else, or do you want to pursue something you actually believe in?' he asks.

'Do you want to have a job and work for your living,' says Mum, 'or sponge off other people by taking dodgy sick leave so you can sit around indulging yourself while you neglect all your responsibilities as an adult?'

I open my mouth to answer, but all that comes out is a sigh.

'What I want,' I say, after a tense silence, 'is for you two to stop arguing.'

Mum and Dad both go pale and still. For what feels like ages, all I can hear is the buzz of the fridge.

'Sorry,' says Mum eventually. 'This must be horrible for you. We'll sort everything out soon, I promise. Won't we?'

She turns to Dad, cueing him in, but he seems moment-arily lost for words.

'Yeah! It's all going to be fine,' he says after a while, nodding furiously.

'We're all human,' Mum continues. 'Your father's having a wobble at the moment, but the doctor says he just needs to rest and he'll be better soon. Isn't that right?'

'Kind of,' says Dad.

'And this time tomorrow we're all going to be sitting on the beach, in the sun, and everything will look different, won't it? The three of us will all be together, and we'll have fun, and swim lots, and do healthy things, and eat ice cream every day, and everything will begin to get back to normal.'

'Tomorrow?' says Dad.

Mum's face seems to freeze. 'Yes, tomorrow. We talked about this the other day. Please don't tell me you forgot.'

'No. Of course not,' he says. 'I just … didn't exactly remember. Days are going by so fast at the moment.'

Mum takes a deep breath and lets the air out slowly. I can see on her face that not saying the things she wants to say is, at this moment, about as easy for her as Olympic weightlifting.

'Well,' she says, standing up from the table, arranging her features into a rictus grin and taking a couple of steps towards the door, 'I think the best thing now is if we just stop talking and start packing.'

I follow her as she heads out of the room, but Dad doesn't move.

She stops in the doorway. Stares at him. Waits for him to speak.

'I can't,' he says eventually, head bowed, talking more to his hands than to us.

'Can't what?'

'Everything's coming to a head. I've committed to do certain things, so … I have to stay.'

'You've committed to do certain things?' she repeats acidly, shaking her head with what looks like disbelief.

209

'Sorry.'

Mum walks back to the table, sits opposite Dad, leans forward until he raises his head, then stares intently into his eyes like someone scouring the horizon for a lost ship.

Her voice is so quiet she's almost whispering when she says, 'Are you serious? You don't want to come?'

'I want to. But I can't. What Rose says is right. You can't live in an anti-airport climate change protest camp and hop on a plane to Spain for a week's holiday. It's not possible.'

'Did you say "live"?'

'Live ... stay ... visit ... same thing. I just meant you can't be a hypocrite.'

'So this is you living by higher ideals, is it?'

'I'm trying my best.'

'Are you?'

Dad drops his gaze to the floor and doesn't answer. Mum eyeballs him for a while, then turns to me.

'Looks like it's just me and you, then,' she says. 'We'd better start packing. Unless you'd also rather spend the week messing around in the commune, in which case I'll just go on my own.'

I think she means this as a joke, or, rather, a sarcastic barb towards Dad, but the fact is, now the demolition feels imminent, with me and Sky installed in our pivotal role as lookouts, I think maybe I would rather stay at home.

But I couldn't do that to Mum. It wouldn't be right. Someone has to stand by her, and the only person left who can do that is me.

'Of course I'm coming,' I say, adding, 'Wouldn't miss it for anything,' with as much enthusiasm as I can manage.

Nobody really knows when the demolition team is going to make their move, so I'll just have to pray they hold off another week. I'd hate to miss the big showdown.

'Great!' says Mum, and for a split second her eyes seem to fill with tears, then she claps her hands together forcefully and says to Sky, in a voice that's slightly too loud for the small space, 'Maybe I can get one of the names changed on the booking so you could join us.'

'That would be brilliant!' she replies, wide-eyed with delight.

'Do you think your mum would let you go?'

'Maybe. I've never been abroad. And someone else could take over as lookout, couldn't they?'

'Do you have a passport?'

'Er ... no.'

Mum's brittle smile falters. 'You'd need a passport. Sorry.'

'Oh. OK. Maybe ... one day ...' says Sky, her body seeming to shrink slightly inside her clothes.

Mum looks at her, takes a deep breath, then says, 'How about ... if you still want to sleep here ... we lend you a key. You could be our house-sitter.'

Sky thinks for a few seconds, biting her bottom lip. 'That's very kind,' she says, after a while, 'but I should probably be with Mum. She keeps saying she's missing me. It might be good if I spend a few nights there. And I'd be too worried about breaking something.'

'You don't need to worry about that,' insists Mum.

'It's fine. I'll go back over the road for a bit. I'll probably be in the treehouse most of the time, anyway. Got a job to do up there.'

'Sorry,' says Mum, again. 'I'll get hold of passport forms when I'm back, and we can fill them in together. So if you get another chance …'

'Thanks.'

Mum stands again, picks up the now empty pasta bowl, and says, 'OK, we should probably clear away the meal before we start packing. There's so much to do.'

Dad lifts his plate and walks towards the dishwasher. 'Not you,' she says, taking the plate out of his hands. 'You're a guest.'

He sits again, watches the three of us clear the table with an embarrassed look on his face, then says, 'Maybe I should go.'

'Maybe you should,' replies Mum, without even looking at him.

He slips away, wishing us a good holiday, but I'm the only one who responds.

# Sometimes you have to do these things

The first few days in Spain are strange. Mum tries her best to seem cheerful, but she's not a very good actor, and half the time talking to her feels like being at a bad panto. The resort is designed to have a constant supply of activities to keep kids and teens occupied, which, I assume, is why my parents want to come here every year, so other than during mealtimes and at night, I'm out on the water, mainly paddleboarding, sea kayaking and failing to windsurf. Every morning, as I set off for the beach, I notice that the instant I walk away, Mum's face falls and her body slumps, as if the cheerful act is costing her so much effort that she can't keep it going one second longer than is strictly necessary.

Whenever I return, she's on a sun lounger, asleep, with a book splayed across her stomach. Asleep is an understatement, to be honest. She's comatose. When I rouse her, it takes her several minutes to adjust to the waking world. For a spring-out-of-bed-and-get-on-with-things person like my mum, this is very out of character.

I text home every few hours to see if the demolition team has made their move, praying every time that the answer will be 'not yet'. And as the week creeps on, my luck holds. I don't say anything to Mum about the messages, because I don't want to hurt her feelings and make her think I'm not happy to be in Spain, though, in truth, the person who's giving little sign of enjoying the holiday is actually Mum.

Despite her efforts to be upbeat and chatty during meals, she seems like someone who is underwater, drowning in private thoughts she can't or won't share with me, exhausted by the struggle to fight her way back to the surface.

Then, with a couple of days of holiday left, she flips into someone else, suddenly transforming into the old Mum, only more so. Instead of picking at a couple of pieces of toast and a boiled egg at breakfast, she joins me at the buffet, loading up on potato waffles, sausages and baked beans, and even tries a pancake with me when I head back for seconds. As we eat, she apologises for being boring, and suggests that we head out on the water together, asking what I'd most like to do.

We spend the morning in a double kayak, come back for lunch, then head out straight away on paddleboards, which Mum is hopeless at, but she laughs every time she falls in (well, the first fifty times, anyway). When she finally gets the hang of it, we invent a game called 'paddleboard jousting', which gets increasingly violent and leaves us both bobbing in the water, helpless with laughter.

Mum ditches her panto-cheerfulness that evening, and we have a huge meal, talking over some of the more spectacular accidents and falls of the day, then turn in early.

We spend the whole of the next day out on the water again, taking a 'sea kayak safari' around the coast to visit some caves. As we're returning to our room, she suggests that we do something we've never done in all the years we've been coming here: go to the last night disco.

At first I think she's joking, but she isn't. I tell her there's no way I'm going, but she continues to persuade, cajole and beg as she changes into a slinky summer dress and starts to apply lipstick and eyeliner.

She then pulls out a short-sleeved shirt from my suitcase, still unworn, which I think she must have put in there, and lays it out on her bed.

'Pleeeeease,' she says, stroking the shirt.

With a sigh, I pull off my top and reach for the shirt. 'Ten minutes,' I say. 'Max.'

Mum grabs me and kisses me on the cheek, then returns

with a tissue to wipe off the lipstick mark she's left on my face.

We head down to the hotel bar, where she orders a glass of wine for her and a fruit cocktail for me. It arrives with a frosting of sugar around the rim and a paper umbrella on top, and is simultaneously delicious and disgusting.

We sit at a table next to the empty dance floor for a while, sipping our drinks, listening to the dreadful '80s music, which is impossible to talk over.

Every time a new song starts, Mum shouts, 'I REMEMBER THIS ONE!' at me, and I nod and smile, trying not to look as if I pity her for growing up in an era of such unbelievable cheese.

When there are a few other people for cover, with my ten-minute deadline long passed, Mum drags me out to the middle of the floor and tries to make me dance with her. I stand there, not moving, frozen with embarrassment, but it's such a relief to see her spring and zest back again, I don't want to break the spell by walking away.

So I stay put, making sure I don't catch anyone's eye, and shuffle from foot to foot in time to the music as a token gesture in the direction of dancing. Mum shimmies round me, sometimes inviting me to twirl and spin her, and for a moment our dance reminds me of being small, when Rose was at school, and Mum and I spent whole days just pottering around the house doing whatever came into our heads.

If anyone I knew was watching there's no way I'd let this happen, but here, away from everything, encouraged by Mum's totally unembarrassed over-the-top moves, I feel my self-consciousness ebb away, and I slowly begin to move my limbs a little more, letting her take my hand when she reaches for it.

Later, sweaty and content, we return to our seats. A slow song starts, filling the room with the high wail of a saxophone, and the dance floor transforms from a mass of flailing limbs to clumps of lumbering, swaying couples.

We watch the slow dancers, and I notice that Mum's face looks rigid, her smile frozen and stiff. I tell her I'm turning in, and she immediately says she'll come too.

In the lift up to the room, she thanks me and says she loves me, so I give her a swift hug, which I don't enjoy at all, but sometimes you have to do these things.

'I kept this for Rose,' I say, pulling the paper umbrella out of my shirt pocket. 'To show her what she missed.'

'She's going to be blown away,' says Mum.

When she's in the bathroom, I send one last text home, and an answer from Dad pings back straight away. The demolition is looking imminent, but it hasn't happened yet. Our flight is early tomorrow morning, so thankfully my holiday gamble has paid off. I haven't missed the big day.

\* \* \*

As soon as we get home, I head straight up to the tree-house. Sky, of course, is there, lying on her stomach with one arm curled around her sketchbook, drawing. She asks me all about the holiday, but I feel bad talking about it when she hasn't been able to go anywhere, so I quickly change the subject to the protest and what has been happening while I was away.

She tells me I haven't missed much, but that a couple of police visits to the building site have been taken as a sign that the eviction attempt is probably imminent. Word has been put out, and all week more protesters have been arriving on the street.

'Was it OK up here on your own?' I ask her.

'It was quiet,' she says. 'I'm pleased you're back.'

'Me too,' I reply, but this feels like an awkward conversation, so I change the subject again by asking to see her picture.

She hands over the sketchbook, which is open on a minutely detailed pencil drawing of the view from the treehouse, spread across two pages, complete with dangling branches in the foreground, a bird's-eye view of my home and garden, the commune with its wigwam and totem pole and the street stretching away into the distance.

'This is amazing,' I say. 'How long did it take?'

She shrugs and looks away. I leaf back though the sketchbook, paging through sketch after sketch: one of a hand; one of a squirrel so lifelike that I can imagine it leaping off the page; then a whole series of tiny images of the tree we're sitting in – leaves, twigs, bark, branches, light spearing through the canopy above – all of it so crisp on the page that the images look almost more real than the things themselves. Poring over Sky's drawings, the miraculous three-dimensionality of them, I realise that her skill isn't just the ability to do this with her hands, it's that she notices details which to me are just a blur, and it's these details that make a leaf a leaf, a branch a branch, a tree a tree. Those piercing eyes of hers really do see more than mine.

'I wish I could do this,' I say.

'I'm sure you could. If you had enough time on your hands.'

'I really couldn't. Not if I had a hundred years and a million pencils.'

Sky takes back her sketchbook, opens it to the page containing our view from the treehouse and continues to draw.

'I should probably go and see my dad,' I say.

'OK,' she replies, not looking up.

I head down the rope ladder, and inside the commune immediately feel that the atmosphere has changed. There are more people around, and a buzz of urgency seems to have filled the house. I sense the same tension you get just before a storm, a feeling of heavier-than-normal air, of slightly oppressive calm before an explosion of noise and energy. ✳

After a failed search of the house, I find Dad in the garden with Martha and a few others, making placards. He's sawing and nailing, Martha is painting. A heap of finished signs is stacked by the fence, each with a different slogan, ranging from specific calls to save this street and cancel the airport expansion to more general ones saying things like 'CLIMATE CHANGE ISN'T COOL', 'PLANE MADNESS', 'THINK GLOBAL, ACT LOCAL', 'LEARN OR BURN', 'THERE'S NO PLANET B' and 'THIS IS A MELTDOWN'.

'Hey! Luke!' says Dad, dropping his tools and rushing towards me with hug-intent in his eyes, but I do a sidestep and put my hands in my pockets.

'How was the holiday?' he asks.

'Good.'

'That's all you've got? One word?'

'It was fun. You should have come.'

'Well, I …'

He tails off, lets out a nervous chuckle, and his eyes flick towards Martha, who abruptly turns away and pretends she isn't listening.

I didn't plan this, but I now realise I have no desire to make this conversation easy or unembarrassing for him.

'So … you had a good time?' he says.

'Yeah. Bit weird with just the two of us, but it was nice.'

'And … how's Mum?'

'Fine. You can ask her yourself.'

'I will. Soon. And it's been all go here. Things are hotting up.'

'Yeah. Sky told me.'

'Er … do you want to help make some placards?'

'OK.'

Dad fetches a saw and hammer, directs me to a pile of wood and shows me what to do. I pitch in for a while, then drift away to look for Rose so I can give her my gift. She's in a meeting, of course, and just before I hand over the paper umbrella I suddenly lose confidence in the joke, finding myself unable to remember what was supposed to be funny about it, but I go ahead anyway. To my surprise, her response is, 'Thanks! I love it!' with a big smile, then she plants it in her hair.

After telling her that Mum has a Toblerone the size of an arm to give her, I head back up to the treehouse, where Sky fills me in on the newly finalised plans for eviction day. She shows me an orange whistle hanging on a nail in the trunk of the tree, and says that if we see signs of demolition machinery moving in, or any kind of police manoeuvres towards the commune, we should give a minute of long blasts, and this will alert all the protesters on the street to immediately proceed to battle stations.

221

A few other key people also have whistles, and if we're not in the treehouse when we hear the signal, at any time of day or night, we should climb up to our lookout post as fast as possible and immediately raise the ladder.

I lift the whistle off the nail and put it to my lips. 'I really want to do it,' I say.

'Not yet,' says Sky. 'Not yet.'

# The ranting middle-aged man chained to a tree

In the end it isn't Sky and me who sound the alarm. We're at home, asleep, when the whistle blows, and the first I know of demolition day arriving is when Sky runs into my room and shakes me awake.

'Get up!' she says. 'It's happening.'

My groggy morning brain takes a while to understand what she's talking about, but soon the sound of the whistle percolates through and wakes me up. I launch myself out of bed, into my clothes, and without pausing for food or even a glass of water we run out of the front door.

I get an immediate sense of crowds rushing around in a purposeful, excited way, but don't pause to look at who is going where until I'm safely up in the treehouse with Sky. Following our instructions, we pull the rope ladder after us and hook it over a high branch. Anyone who wants to force us down will have to be very good at climbing trees, or will need a crane.

I grab Mum's binoculars and scope the construction site to see what's in store. The gates have been opened wide and a row of vans is pulling up, snaking beyond the end of the street and on round the corner, out of sight, so it's impossible to see how many there are. As each one comes to a halt, the side door slides open and a team of ten or so men comes out, all wearing yellow jackets and hard hats. They're not police, but they don't seem like builders, either. All of them look young, and physically large. This must be the 'private security' we've heard people talking about, often with an edge of fear.

There's already a team of police surrounding the perimeter of the building site, arranged in a way that looks like they are there to protect the menacing security guards from us, the protesters, rather than the other way round.

I hand the binoculars to Sky and call Clyde to tell him what I can see. He takes in all the information rapidly, thanks me and tells me to call again if I have any more news.

Directly below us, the street is filling up with people. Even though it's not long after dawn, everyone from the commune has already come outside, and most of them are engaged in shunting the homemade barricade from the front garden into the road. I don't know where they found all the twisted metal and planks of wood it's built from, but by the time the roadblock is in place, stretching across the tarmac from pavement to pavement, it looks pretty solid. A few final adjustments are made by Clyde himself, using his welding torch.

Behind him the crowd begins to swell, mostly made up of people who have arrived in the last few days and filled up the remaining empty houses on the condemned side of the street. The most recent arrivals have ended up camping in front and back gardens, which has transformed the atmosphere of the whole street from suburban backwater to something that feels more like a festival.

A topless, heavily tattooed guy with a big African drum strapped over his shoulders begins playing, pounding out a rhythm which drifts upwards to our treetop perch, his beats mixing with snatches of singing and chanting that emerge from different pockets of protesters. Soon after he starts, Space appears out of the house carrying his own slightly smaller drum, and joins in. It is more or less impossible to play any drum anywhere near the commune without Space appearing and joining in. Just a couple of taps on a tambourine and he'd be there.

Then I notice Dad, directly underneath me, pressing his body against the tree trunk. Next to him is Martha, carrying a coil of chain. When Dad is satisfied with his position, Martha hands him one end, which he holds by his side, and she begins to walk round and round the tree, wrapping the chain around the trunk and my father, over his waist, legs, calves, then up around his stomach and chest. When the coil is finished, she picks up a padlock from the ground and fastens him into place. Martha holds out the key and they talk for a while, as if they can't decide what to do with it, then she puts it in her back pocket.

She checks the chains, pulling at them to make sure they're secure and not too tight, and while she's doing this, he says something that makes her laugh.

'YO, DAD!' I shout. 'YOU OK!?'

'AOK, BUDDY,' he replies. 'WHAT ABOUT YOU?'

'COOL!' I say, with a big wave and a matching grin.

'I'D WAVE BACK IF I COULD,' he says.

'HE'S BEEN A VERY NAUGHTY BOY,' says Martha.

'SO I KEEP HEARING,' I reply, which is a joke, and also not.

'ANY MOVEMENT FROM THE PIGS?' yells Dad.

'NOT YET! THERE'S LOADS OF THEM THOUGH. AND SECURITY PEOPLE. IT'S ALL GOING TO KICK OFF!'

'WE'RE READY!' says Dad. 'YOU'RE DOING A GREAT JOB!'

'Look,' says Sky, pointing across the street. 'It's that man! Your neighbour.'

Sure enough, Callum's dad, Laurence, looking like he's

dressed for a round of golf, is marching out of his house carrying not a set of golf clubs, but something that appears to be a large pot of glue.

He's greeted with cheers by a group of people outside the commune (which he seems to rather enjoy) and even a few hugs (which he's not so sure about). A conversation ensues between him, Clyde and Sky's mum, with the three of them pacing around the area of tarmac immediately behind the barricade.

After a bit of slightly uncertain joking around, the lid is prised off the tin of glue and it's poured out on to the ground in a stick man shape.

Just as he's about to lie down, Helena appears at a run from her house. I've never seen her run before, and she runs about as well as a seal walks.

I can't hear what's being said, but she clearly isn't encouraging him to carry on.

With barely a word of response to his irate wife, Laurence lies down flat on his back in the puddle of glue.

A huge cheer rises up, which Sky and I join in with.

Helena remonstrates a little longer with her husband and with the people who are cheering him on, but this only seems to make people laugh at her, and she soon retreats angrily back home.

'If you're not happy, write to your MP,' Sky's mum shouts after her.

As she goes into the house, I spot Callum peering at the street through the hall window, either forbidden from coming outside to see what's happening or too afraid. I wish he could see me up here, right at the heart of things, while he cowers at home with his mummy. Part of me wants to text him, asking who's the tough guy now, but I decide that would be petty.

The sound of a large engine roaring to life, followed by the scrape and clank of caterpillar tracks against tarmac suddenly diverts everyone's attention away from Helena's tantrum. Flanked by police, a bulldozer begins to inch out of the building site, heading directly towards the crowd.

The drumming and chanting rise in volume, and a stream of protesters surges in the direction of the barricade, swarming all over it like insects, making a human shield that spreads from one side of the road to the other.

The bulldozer keeps approaching, getting closer and closer, louder and louder, not even slowing down, as if the driver hasn't seen the mound of human flesh that lies in its path, or, more likely, as if he's trying to intimidate the protesters into backing down.

Nobody retreats. Most of them respond by beginning to dance and sing on the barricade. If they're frightened, which they ought to be, it doesn't show.

Time seems to slow down as the distance between the bulldozer and the dancing protesters closes, but at the last second before metal grinds into flesh, the machine comes to a stop and lets out a noisy sigh as the engine sputters out.

A raucous cheer rises up. A girl wearing rainbow shorts and a white vest top descends from the barricade and places a single flower inside the coffin-sized scoop of the bulldozer.

As she tries to climb back on to the barricade, a pair of security men dive forward and grab her by the ankles. A couple of her friends take her arms from above and a human tug of war begins, which keeps going as a piercing scream rips through the air. Two policemen waving truncheons come forward and mount the barricade. Their slashing swipes cause a quick retreat as a pocket of protesters step back to escape broken arms or cracked skulls, and within seconds the rainbow shorts girl is lifted up and carried away.

A wave of fear at this sudden flurry of violence seems to spread across the front rank of the protesters. Then they remember their strategy, and everyone who is still on the barricade lies down. The police now move forward and form a line in front of the bulldozer. For a while there's a tense stalemate, then the police clamber on to the barricade and start the cumbersome process of lifting the limp protesters down and carrying them to the waiting vans. Nobody fights back or resists arrest, but I can see how within the parameters of non-violence they are making it as hard as possible for the police. With at least four policemen needed for every arrest, clearing the barricade is a slow process, which, because of the continued singing and the celebratory atmosphere, certainly doesn't look like a defeat or even an annoyance for the people who are being arrested. It doesn't even look like a punishment. If anyone is having an unhappy time, it looks like it's the police.

It certainly seems that being arrested is a lot more fun than making arrests.

The police form a second line so a fresh wave of protesters can't come forward and take up positions on the barricade, but they've cleared away barely half of the people who are obstructing the bulldozer's progress when a TV news crew appears.

The police don't seem to like being filmed, but it looks like there's nothing they can do to keep the cameras away. The protesters, on the other hand, love it. Judging by their reactions, getting arrested on camera is the protester equivalent of scoring a premier league goal. Every one of them yells a different slogan as they are dragged away, mostly about climate change or the evils of aviation, but amid all the excitement, one of them seems to forget his lines and opts for 'HELLO, MUM!'

It takes hours to clear the barricade, and when it's finally done a team of security men clamber over and join the police on the other side, immediately in front of the remainder of the protest, which is now louder than ever.

The bulldozer fires its engine and begins to scoop up and drag away the barricade. After this is accomplished, the police retreat for a while, with the security guys still holding their line in front of the scratched stripe of just cleared tarmac.

For a while, nothing seems to be happening (apart from the hundreds of yelling, singing and dancing protesters), and Clyde calls us to ask if we can see what the retreating police are up to.

'I'm looking now,' I say, training my binoculars on the building site. 'Er ... it looks like they might be having a lunch break.'

'Ha!' replies Clyde. 'Brilliant!'

Not long after this, a couple of policemen who, judging by their age and uniforms, look like they might be senior officers, appear and examine the scene, staring out forlornly at the sea of bodies between them and the building that is the target of the demolition.

After several long conversations on mobile phones, the whole police and security enforcement team withdraws, and the bulldozer retreats into the building site. A huge cheer, followed by renewed surges of singing and dancing, accompanies their departure.

Through the celebrating crowd, I can just make out Laurence, still glued to the tarmac, being interviewed by a TV news reporter. He looks like he's having the time of his life.

The conflict seems to be over for the day, and Sky and I both feel like we're missing a party, so we decide to abandon our post and climb down. I get to the foot of the tree just as the news crew approaches my dad, who is still chained to the trunk.

They ask him why he's taking part in the protest, and he immediately comes out with a flurry of words so fluent and impassioned that, even though he's my own father, I almost don't recognise the man who is talking.

'You're asking me why I'm here?' he says, almost yelling the words. 'Well, my question to you, and to anyone sitting at home watching this, is – why aren't *you* here? Why would anyone stand by and let this happen? Because this isn't just about one runway and one airport! This is about all of us and the future of the planet. This is about whether we want to sleepwalk into a global catastrophe. This is about whether we, as a nation … as a species, want to be so blind and lazy and stupid that we are willing to sacrifice the lives of our children and grandchildren – throw away their chance of having a habitable planet to live on – simply because we're too addicted to satisfying our immediate shallow desires to care about the effect our selfishness is

232

having on the planet. The time has come that we *all* have to care about this. And not just care by sitting at home wringing our hands and doing nothing, but care by actually changing the way we live, and care by standing against the forces that are pushing us to accelerate faster and faster towards climate breakdown. That's why I'm here, and why I'm not leaving this spot until they drag me away by force.'

I look back at the interviewer to see what the next question is going to be, and she has the look on her face of someone who has just found a fifty-pound note on the pavement. I can see her struggling not to smile.

She thanks my dad and goes off to talk to other protesters, but however many interviews she gets, I'm pretty sure it's my dad – the ranting middle-aged man chained to a tree – who is going to make the cut. I don't know much about news, but even I can see that's great TV.

# A good day out

The party goes on all afternoon, with no further approaches from the police and security teams, so after a while the glued and chained people release themselves, ready to go back into position as soon as the next assault begins. Laurence somehow wriggles out of the clothes he's glued to the tarmac, to reveal an under-outfit of tennis shorts and a string vest. It's not an obviously fashionable look, but this doesn't stop him being high-fived and hugged by protesters young enough to be his kids. Bizarrely his glued-down golfing outfit remains in place, stuck to the road.

As the sky begins to darken, a meeting is called in the commune to plan for the next day. Everyone who has taken part in this kind of demonstration before seems pretty sure the police will return with reinforcements and a more aggressive strategy.

I don't normally go to commune meetings, but since Sky and I might be assigned a new task, we feel we have to attend, and, for once, we both actually want to. It's pretty clear storage jars won't be on the agenda.

The discussion soon moves to the problem of how to bring in increased protester numbers for what is sure to be an escalated confrontation the next day. It emerges that all the big social media platforms are alight with videos, photos, comments and likes on the topic of the day's protest. Huge numbers of people are saying they want to take part, but both ends of the street are now blocked by police, with access only being given to people with proof of residence.

Rose, who has been running the Instagram feed for the protest, says she's in touch with hundreds of people who have come to the area but can't get in.

For a long time the conversation goes round and round this topic without any useful suggestions, even though the solution is obvious. Eventually I put my hand up, but nobody notices until Clyde quietens the room with nothing more than a short cough and asks if I have a contribution.

'There's a secret way out,' I say. 'You can climb a tree at the bottom of my garden, which gets you on to some garages at the back of the new housing estate over that way. Then you can go along the garages and jump down into an alley that wiggles through the estate and comes out on the main road. I could meet people there and bring them in that way, so they wouldn't hit any roadblocks.'

A puzzled silence fills the room, as if nobody can quite believe what they just heard: an actual solution to the problem.

Clyde claps his hands together and rubs his palms in the manner of someone who has just been served his favourite meal. 'Great!' he says. 'Fantastic! Is everyone happy with that?'

'People will need a little time to get to the rendezvous point,' says Rose.

'Later is probably better, anyway, in terms of not being spotted,' replies Clyde. 'Shall we say ten p.m.?'

'That's pretty late for Luke. We should probably check with Mum,' says Rose.

'I'm your dad, and I give you permission,' says Dad.

'For Luke to set out at ten p.m., dodge police road-blocks and then bring maybe hundreds of complete strangers into our garden and through the house? You don't think Mum might want to know that's happening?' says Rose.

'OK. That might be a good idea,' Dad replies. 'But even if she says no, the answer's yes. I'll try to keep her onside though.'

'I'll go with Luke,' says Rose. 'We need someone there

who can check the people are who they say they are.'

'And don't put it out on social media,' says Clyde. 'The police will be all over our feeds. Just private messages on an encrypted platform to people you know. And tell them to spread the word the same way. Some of us are probably hacked anyway, but we have to do what we can to keep this under the wire. It's a quick turnaround, so we might get away with it.'

'I'll come too,' says Dad. 'Make sure you're both safe.'

'You don't have to,' says Rose. 'We'll be fine.'

'I want to,' he says.

'That's really not necessary,' says Rose.

'It might be helpful.'

'Unlikely.'

'You never know.'

Rose shrugs unenthusiastically.

'I'm not sure you'll be able to make it up the tree, Dad,' I say.

'Don't be ridiculous. I'm not *that* old,' he replies, with a slightly nervous laugh.

'I'll go and talk to Mum,' says Rose. 'Get her with the programme. Might be best if you stay here for that bit, Dad.'

'OK. Fair point,' he says.

Then Martha suddenly yells, 'WE'RE ON! WE'RE ON NOW!'

Everyone turns at the same time, and we see that she's staring at her mobile phone, on to which she's streaming the BBC news.

It's a while before I get to see it, because only so many people can look at one small screen at the same time, but her phone is passed around the room, with the same segment rewound and repeated, and when my turn comes I can barely believe my eyes. Everything I saw this morning from my perch in the treehouse is now in front of me again, but as part of a TV programme, as national news: the girl putting a flower into the bulldozer scoop and getting arrested; the police swarming over the barricade and struggling to drag away the protesters; the drumming and singing; then, most amazing of all, the interview with my dad. It's all there! Everything that happened in my little back-of-beyond suburban street! On TV!

When I lift my eyes from the screen, Dad is at the centre of a huddle of excited people, and I hear him say, 'Oh, it's only TV,' but his face is flushed and I can see that he's buzzing.

The strange thing is, TV is obviously less real than reality, but when you've seen something actually happen, then you get to see it in a news broadcast, it feels almost as if some higher authority has come along and stamped the events that took place in front of your eyes with a certi-fication that makes them more real than they were before.

The verdict on the news item from the commune members, who all try to play it cool but can't stop themselves squealing if they see anyone they know on-screen, is that the protest comes out well. It's the police, not the demonstrators, who look violent, and it's clear from the reporter's slant on events that the day represented a defeat for the demolition team and a victory for the climate rebels.

This publicity will add hugely to support for the cause. What nobody says (but maybe everyone is thinking) is that the whole thing looks like fun, which surely guarantees not just donations and kind words, but a bigger turnout for tomorrow's protest. After all, whatever you think about climate change, you can't beat a good day out.

# I want to be part of it

Just as the news broadcast celebrations are dying down, Rose appears and tells me that Mum has given the go-ahead for our clandestine excursion over the back fence of the garden.

'How the hell did you manage that?' I ask.

Rose gives a knowing smirk and raises one eyebrow. 'I charmed her,' she says proudly.

'How?'

'Just by ... I don't know ... being nice to her.'

'Is that all?'

'Pretty much. I haven't done it for months. She was so surprised I probably could have got her to say yes to anything. Totally blindsided her.'

'Wow. Would that work for me?'

'No. You have to put in weeks of groundwork, then it's pretty much a one-off. I think you should probably avoid her between now and when we set off. If she realises what she's agreed to, she might change her mind.'

'OK. I'll text her and say I'm having dinner in the commune.'

'She's here now,' says Rose.

'Is she? Where?'

'In the kitchen. She brought over a vat of soup for everyone.'

'Here? *Why?*'

'She was at the protest, and I suppose she noticed that nobody would have had time to make any food, and I think … maybe … she's beginning to see the point of the whole thing.'

'So now we're all here and the house is empty?'

Rose turns and looks out of the window. A flickering blueish light is glowing through our sitting-room window.

'Looks like Sky's there,' says Rose.

I hadn't noticed her leaving the meeting, but I suppose she must have drifted away at some point, unable to resist the gravitational pull of TV.

'I don't think Mum's staying the night here, if that's what you're wondering. It hasn't come to that,' she says.

'Yet. Feels like you're winning.'

'That's not going to happen. Trust me,' says Rose.

'I know. But I would have said that about Dad once.'

'Strange times.'

After dinner I decide to head home for a while to relax before our night mission, but as I cross the street I see a flash of movement at Callum's bedroom window, then, just before I've let myself into the house, he appears at a sprint and shouts my name from the pavement.

'What is it?' I say, turning reluctantly to face him.

'All right?' he says.

'Yeah.'

He stares at me for a while, shifting his weight from foot to foot, then says, 'Crazy day, eh?'

'Yeah, full on. OK, see you around.'

'Wait! I … er … can I … ?'

'What?'

'Ask you something.'

I'm pretty sure he's building up to some kind of trick or piss-take.

'What?' I say sceptically.

'Tomorrow, can I go up with you? To the treehouse?'

'You?'

'I want to do something for the protest. If your dad is and mine is, and they're getting on the news, I can't just sit at home and miss the whole thing, can I? I want to be part of it.'

'Are you serious?'

'Yes.'

'This isn't about getting on the news. It's about stopping the runway being built.'

'I know. And I want to help. Please.'

I've known Callum all my life, and I have a feeling this is the first time I've heard him use that word.

There's no way I want someone with his restlessness and constant one-upmanship in that small, precarious space alongside me and Sky, but the question of how to stop him is a tricky one. The ladder is right there, and nothing can prevent him climbing up. If he wanted to, he could even go ahead of us in the morning and raise the ladder, trapping us on the ground, so I need to keep him sweet.

'Er … I'd better ask Sky,' I say, thinking that if I play for time, I might be able to come up with a plausible reason to keep him out. Something other than, 'I don't like you and I don't trust you.'

'OK. Thanks. I'll wait here,' he says.

I go in, explain to Sky about Callum's request, and she responds with an immediate, 'No way.'

When I point out that he could get the jump on us in the morning and keep us out, she falls quiet and her face goes into chess strategy mode.

We rack our brains, searching for an excuse to keep him out, but neither of us can find one, so after a few minutes I head back outside. Callum is still in exactly the same spot, hovering nervously in a way that reminds me of how Sky used to wait for me outside the commune.

'Well?' he says, as soon as I emerge from the house.

With a heavy heart, I hear myself say, 'Er … OK.'

It seems crazy to let Callum come up to our private, sacrosanct lookout perch, but I console myself by trying to remember that it would be wrong to refuse him. The whole point of the commune, with its uncloseable front door, is that it welcomes everyone. Saying no to Callum would be against all the principles of the protest and, perhaps more importantly, it would be futile. When Callum wants to do something, that's what happens. Every time I've tried to stand up to him, not once has he given way without a fight. If he's determined to go up to the treehouse, that's where I'll find him tomorrow, whether I invite him there or not.

'Yes!' he says, punching the air (and reinforcing my doubts). 'I'll bring food. For all of us. Nice things. Is there anything else?'

'No. Just … be careful up there. It's high. We need to look out for each other.'

'I know.'

'Great. OK, see you tomorrow.'

'Sure will.'

With a grin spread across his face, he turns and heads home, pausing to give a quick wave just before he disappears inside.

Whether he means what he says, or is playing some cryptic power game, I have no idea.

# Rebel outlaw

Around the time I'm usually being told to go to bed, I set off out the back door, along with my father and sister, on our police-dodging night mission to bring in extra protesters. Rose has sent out word of a rendezvous point at a bus stop on the main road, and is expecting a good crowd, but we won't know how many people until we get there.

Before we leave, Rose checks with Dad at least three times that he really wants to go, and unfortunately he's adamant.

'It's almost as if you don't want me to come,' he says, the final time she asks him.

'Not almost. I don't want you to come,' she replies.

'OK – well, thanks for being clear.'

'Why *are* you coming?'

'To keep you safe.'

'We're perfectly safe without you.'

'I just want to be sure.'

'You don't want to be left out,' says Rose.

'That's ridiculous,' says Dad, without much conviction.

It's dark when the three of us head down the garden together, and despite Dad's unwelcome parental presence, an atmosphere of adventure is hanging in the air. I lead them to the apple tree in the bottom corner of the garden, then scamper up, crawl out along a branch and swing down on to the garage roof.

'OK!' I call down. 'I'm there.'

I find a spot at the edge of the roof where I can watch Rose's progress up the tree, and despite Dad's 'help', it takes her a while. Whenever she pauses, Dad chips in with advice Rose clearly doesn't want, and she seems to spend more time arguing than climbing.

'Up a bit with your left foot.'

'I *know*.'

'That's your right foot.'

'Stop talking! You're distracting me!'

'Bit higher.'

'I *know*!'

'Why are you snapping at me?'

'Why are you still talking?'

'Nearly there. Don't be scared.'

'I'm not scared.'

'You sound it.'

'This is the sound of annoyed. Scared is something else.'

'Just relax and it'll be a lot easier.'

'I'll relax if you stop talking to me!'

'OK. Fine … That's it. You're doing really well.'

'Stop!'

Eventually, Rose joins me on the garage roof, looking flustered, and Dad begins his climb.

A few seconds later, there's a loud snapping noise as one of the low branches gives way.

'Ow! Shit!' says Dad.

'Just relax and it'll be a lot easier,' says Rose.

'The bloody branch snapped.'

'Don't be scared. You're doing really well.'

'That's not funny, Rose.'

'It is though,' she replies, laughing.

Dad continues his climb, with lots of grunting and swearing, like a man struggling to lift something that's too heavy for him, which is exactly what's happening, the thing in question being his own body.

'When I said you were doing really well,' says Rose, 'you do realise I was lying, don't you?'

'Maybe I was too,' snaps Dad.

'Ooooh! Touchy!'

'I helped you! And all you're doing is laughing at me!' says Dad.

'Yup,' replies Rose. 'Listen, we don't want to be late. Why don't you catch us up?'

'Wait, I'm nearly there!'

'No offence, Dad, but I think you're too heavy for those branches.'

'They're very thin.'

'Just like you. OK – we're going to head off now.'

'Wait for me!'

'No time. Bye, Dad.'

'This is really mean!'

'Unlucky! We won't let on to your new friends,' says Rose. 'We'll tell them you were the big hero – hauling us up with your huge muscles. Or maybe not.'

'I'll stand guard here, then,' says Dad.

'Thanks. That'll be a massive help,' says Rose, with a cackle, as we turn away and head across the garage roofs.

'Do you think you were a bit hard on him?' I say, once we're out of earshot.

'He deserves it.' Then she suddenly stops dead and adds, 'Are you sure these roofs are strong enough to hold our weight? They're bending.'

'I guess we'll find out, won't we?'

'Probably best Dad isn't here, after all.'

We walk slower and a little more tentatively than at first, but it isn't long before we reach the last garage, from where I jump to the top of a brick wall, then slide down a lamp post to the ground. Rose follows, landing awkwardly as she hits the tarmac, but when she straightens up, she has a wide smile on her face.

'It's cool you thought of this,' she says, looking me right in the eye.

I feel my cheeks reddening as I smile back at her, and I can't think of an answer.

We head along the path to the main road, snaking through a chain of small car parks, but just as we're reaching the exit from the housing estate, a police car comes into view, driving slowly towards us.

'Should we hide?' I mutter.

'No. Keep walking. We live here, and we're just heading out to the shops.'

'Bit late for that, isn't it?'

'Just look relaxed. Brother and sister out for an evening stroll.'

The police car approaches, an officer in the passenger seat staring at us as they pass by, but they don't slow down or stop.

'Oink, oink,' whispers Rose.

We carry on towards the main road, but when we see the bus stop, Rose's face falls. Instead of the crowd we're expecting, there are only a couple of people.

Rose looks at them, and they look at Rose, but nobody speaks. They're ordinary-seeming, late-teens or early-twenties, in jeans and T-shirts, and look like they could easily be climate protesters, or just as easily not care in the slightest about the entire issue.

We approach warily and, after an awkward moment, the girl says, 'Are you Rose?'

Rose nods. 'You're here to get into the protest site?'

'Yes.'

'There's just two of you? I thought there'd be more.'

'There are,' the girl says, nodding to a brick wall that encircles the front perimeter of the housing estate. 'There's a patrol car sniffing around, so we thought it best to keep everyone out of sight.'

'Oh. We saw it just now. They're in the estate,' says Rose, letting out a sigh of relief.

'Let's just sit it out here, then,' says the girl. 'Like we're waiting for a bus. When they move on, we can go for it.'

'OK. This is my brother, Luke, by the way.'

'Hi, Luke,' says the girl. 'I'm Amy. This is Rob.'

We all shake hands, then sit on the bus-shelter bench. Rose chats to them about the protest – where they heard about it, how long they're planning to stay, what they're expecting for tomorrow – while I eye the street where the police car is likely to emerge.

A few minutes later, it comes out, pauses at the junction, and drives away.

When it's out of sight, Rob lets out a wolf whistle. A

swarm of bodies clambers over the low wall – a dozen, then another, then another, until there's a crowd of more than fifty of us huddled around the bus shelter.

'Is that everyone?' says Amy.

There's a general murmur of assent.

'OK. Follow us,' says Rose, and we head off at a fast walk, back through the housing estate, then along the path to the lamp post.

'We'll need a bunk-up here,' says Rose. 'Who's strong?'

Rob steps forward and forms his hands into a cup for the first climber.

'OK,' says Rose. 'Luke will go first, I'll bring up the rear. We're going over these roofs, then down a tree into a garden, where we'll all reassemble, before heading on through our house. We don't think these roofs are strong, so keep apart – one person at a time on each garage. OK?'

Everyone nods. I put my foot into Rob's hand-stirrup and launch myself up. As I head across the top of the garages, I turn and see a spaced-out snake of people following me. Just before pulling myself up into the apple tree, I get out my phone and take a quick photo of all the protesters crossing the roofs in my wake. It's too dark for much to be visible, but I want to remember this moment – capture the thrill of feeling like a leader, like some kind of rebel outlaw, fighting for justice, battling against the destruction and wickedness of the planet-destroying Establishment. No new high score or getting-to-the-next-level on any game has ever come close to matching the buzz of this.

I show the person immediately behind me where we're heading and swing up into the tree, then across and down. It occurs to me, as I'm landing, that this might be the most fun I've ever had.

By the look of things, Dad has got bored of 'standing guard' and gone into the house. Amy from the bus shelter is the first person to jump down after me.

'Nice garden,' she says.

'Thanks,' I reply, thinking that if it wasn't dark, and she could see the overgrown mess surrounding us, she'd have to think of something different to say.

Another person then drops out of the tree and introduces herself as Crystal. She has spiky blonde hair and a beautiful smile.

'This is cool,' she says, just as another person crashes down to join us, introducing himself as Anthony. He sounds extremely posh, even though his trousers are held up with string, and stains from several different-coloured meals are splattered across the front of his T-shirt. He gives Crystal a lingering, flirty greeting, to which she responds with not one nanosecond's interest.

'Have you come far?' says Anthony to Crystal.

'Not really,' says Crystal to the garden fence.

'Things are going to kick off tomorrow, big time,' he says,

but she gives no indication of having heard him, even though he's right in front of her. I'm no expert on romance, but even I can spot the body language for *Don't even think about it.*

With a rustle of foliage, another person tumbles from the tree, lands with a thump and falls backwards into a bed of weeds-that-used-to-be-herbs.

This is the strangest social gathering I've ever been part of, but nobody has given me any instructions as to what to do now, so the only thing I can think of is to stand there until Rose appears.

By the time she does, the whole of our parched and unmown lawn is covered with people. The atmosphere feels halfway between a party and a dentist's waiting room.

'OK, everyone,' says Rose, to the assembled crowd. 'Thanks so much for coming along to join the struggle. We really appreciate it. I'm going to lead you through the house now and take you to the demo site. If you need help finding a spot to bed down, I'll be around to give you a hand.'

Rose leads the way into our house through the back door, and this time I bring up the rear. There's no sign of Mum when we file through the kitchen, but just as I'm following everyone out through the front door, she appears in the hallway.

'Luke!' she says, too loudly for me to pretend I haven't heard her. 'Bed!'

I turn round and smile innocently. 'Bed? Now?'

'It's almost eleven.'

'Is it? I'm a bit busy though.'

'Busy?'

'Yeah. The whole route for getting these people in was my idea, so I just have to finish ...'

'You don't have to finish anything. They're here. You did a great job, but now it's done.'

'I'm not tired.'

'That's what you always say.'

'And it's always true.'

'There's going to be an early start tomorrow. Let's go upstairs and you can tell me about your trip over the garages. How many people did you bring in?'

'Lots.'

'Did everything go to plan?' she says, edging towards the stairs.

I can't be sure if her sudden interest in my rooftop adventure is genuine or just a lure to get me to bed, but I decide to go along with the ruse and follow her upstairs.

By the time I've cleaned my teeth I realise that I'm shattered. Too tired, in fact, to get undressed, and I flop down on top of my duvet fully clothed. Mum hauls me up, ignoring my protests that she should leave me alone, hands me my pyjamas, and seconds later I'm fast asleep.

# You've had your last warning

It feels as if no time at all has elapsed until the next thing I'm aware of, which is Sky bursting into my bedroom and yanking open the curtains. Before I even open my eyes, I hear a series of long, high whistle blasts coming from over the street, and I'm somehow up, dressed and out of the front door before having any real idea of where I am or what I'm doing.

It's barely light, but as soon as I step outside into the eerie, blueish early morning haze, I see that the street is filled with people, all of whom seem to be running around in states of confusion and excitement. There's lots of shouting, but not like the celebratory rumpus of the day before. Straight away, I can sense panic in the air.

Clumps of security men in bright yellow jackets have already got much closer to the commune than they achieved in the whole of yesterday. They're moving in packs, scouring the street and dragging away anyone who crosses their path, pulling them roughly across the ground, frogmarching them with arms bent behind arched backs, or prodding them forward held in chokeholds. Screams of pain and outrage are coming from all directions, and there's a bloodthirsty tang in the air – a feeling that yesterday was a game the protesters won, but this is a fist fight they seem set to lose.

'What are we going to do?' I say.

'Run,' replies Sky, setting off into the street battle without waiting for my answer. Her age and size seem to act almost as an invisibility cloak, and she cuts through the swirl of scrabbling bodies untouched. Hoping the same magic will work for me, I set off behind her at a sprint.

As I pick my way through the mayhem, darting left and right to avoid being caught or hit, I catch a glimpse of something unexpected on the faces of the lunging security men: enjoyment. They're having fun, like long-restrained dogs finally let off the leash.

By the time I get to the tree, Sky is already halfway up to our lookout platform, and without waiting for the ladder to be free, I climb up after her, ignoring my panic and breathlessness, pushing myself up from rung to rung as fast as my aching muscles will allow.

Sky reaches down and hauls me, panting, on to the platform. From here, I can see protesters streaming towards the centre of the conflict, surging in from down the street, and within minutes the balance of numbers (if not of aggression) seems to have shifted against the invading security team.

I lean over the edge to haul up the ladder, but just as I'm about to pull, someone appears around the trunk and grabs hold of the bottom rung. My first instinct is to try and yank it away, then I recognise the person and remember: it's Callum. He's wearing a pristine red tracksuit and carrying a matching backpack.

'Quick!' I yell. 'We need to get the ladder up!'

'OK! Coming!' he shouts.

But he doesn't come. He gets a short distance into the air, then stops.

'Hurry!' I shout.

He takes a few more slow steps upwards, then, two or three metres off the ground, he freezes.

'What are you doing?' I call.

'There's something wrong with the ladder!' he says. 'It's swaying too much.'

'That's just what it does. You have to keep going!'

'I can't! My legs are swooping in!'

'Keep going!'

'I think I'm too heavy for it!'

'You're not.'

'I am.'

'Either come up or go down.'

'I can't.'

'Up or down! You can't just stand there!'

'The backpack's putting me off balance.'

'So leave it behind.'

'I can't. I'm stuck.'

'Go down or come up! I need to pull in the ladder.'

For ages, with the noise of the arrests and the protesters' fightback getting louder and louder, Callum doesn't move. Then, very slowly, with shaking limbs, rung by rung, he goes back down to the ground. Without saying anything or even looking up, he walks away, head bowed. As I pull up the ladder, I watch him circle the crowd of bodies that has filled the street near the foot of the tree, walk back home, go inside and close the door.

'Probably for the best,' says Sky.

'Definitely.'

The volume of drumming and chanting continues to build, and today it sounds angry, maybe even desperate, without the playfulness of the day before. A battle line forms between the tree and the position of the now obliterated barricade, with protesters pushing against a phalanx of police who stand shoulder to shoulder behind their riot shields, which they are steadily hitting with truncheons – the regular pound of the police beat competing with the syncopated rhythms of the protest drums. It feels simultaneously thrilling and frightening, this raw, brutal sound of two warring factions trying to intimidate each other with the power of noise.

More people continue to emerge on to the street, forming a dense mass of bodies that stops the police making any forward progress. Just behind them, I see my dad hastily chaining himself to the tree with Martha's help. Laurence has already glued himself to the ground again, assisted by Rose. Whether this means Rose is back on good terms with Callum's family, or the opposite, I'm not quite sure.

Sky, who has the binoculars, suddenly grips me by the elbow and points.

'Horses!' she says.

I follow the line of her finger, and can just make out a team of mounted police approaching through the building site.

'But ... they'll flatten people,' I say.

'We have to warn them,' says Sky. 'Give me the phone!'

She brings up Clyde's number with shaking hands and places the phone to her ear.

Her eyes fix on a point in mid-air, as she says, 'Clyde! Call us back. There's horses! Police on horseback! They're coming any second! Answer your phone!'

She hangs up, looks at me with an expression of dread on her face, and dials again.

'He probably can't hear it,' I say, looking down at the mayhem unfolding beneath us. Police and protesters are engaged in what looks like a crude shoving contest, with truncheons slashing down above and between the riot shields. For the people now trapped against the police line, pushed forward by the mass of protesters behind them, there's no escape from a beating. Even from up here, over the noise of drumming and chanting, I can hear their shouts of anger and cries of pain.

My front garden looks like it has become an improvised first-aid station. A young guy with long hair in a pony tail is sitting on the small patch of grass, looking dazed, with blood streaming down his forehead and face.

Mum comes out of the house with a bowl of water, some cloths and bandages, and begins to clean his wound. A girl who doesn't look much older than Rose is flat on her back. I can't see any blood, but she doesn't seem to be moving. A boy is kneeling beside her, holding her hand and yelling frantically into a mobile phone. A few others, with blood-stained clothes, are sitting or lying on the paved driveway.

'PICK UP!' Sky yells pointlessly into Clyde's voicemail.

'It's too late,' I say.

Sky leans over the side of the treehouse and screams, cupping her hands around her mouth, 'WATCH OUT!

HORSES! HORSES ARE COMING!' The veins in her neck and temple stand out through her pale skin as she yells, but nobody seems to hear and, seconds later, the wall of shield-carrying police parts in the middle to let through a charge of horses, which causes instant panic from the protesters. The drumming and chanting stop. Screams fill the air. Several people are knocked off their feet in the chaotic scramble to escape. Some of them curl up in a ball to avoid being trampled, others try to scurry away on hands and knees. Everyone who remains upright runs. A guy in a green T-shirt who stands his ground, maybe as an act of crazy bravery, or perhaps because he doesn't realise fast enough what is happening, is whacked across the shoulders by a mounted policeman's truncheon and crumples to his knees.

Within a couple of minutes, the body of the demonstration has been forced back down the street, and a wave of police pushes through behind the horses to arrest anyone left behind. They start with the green T-shirt man, making no allowances for the fact that he is still on his knees and looks like he might be on the brink of passing out. Two officers grab him by the upper arms and drag him away to a police van, his feet trailing limply behind.

Another group of police swarms around Laurence. They cut him free from the ground using what looks like a large pair of garden shears and pull him up. He's now wearing a pair of boxer shorts and a white vest, and, probably in deference to his age, they spare him the dragging-away business, instead handcuffing his wrists behind his back and marching him swiftly towards the building site.

He must have known his protest was likely to end in arrest, but he still has a stunned and outraged look on his face, as if he can't quite believe what is happening. A news crew circles around him, filming the arrest, but it looks like the police shove away the journalist before she can get close enough to ask any questions.

The shriek of metal against metal now rises up from below us. I have to lean right out to see what is happening, gripping on to the guard rail to make sure I don't fall. A spurt of orange sparks flashes across my vision, and for a moment I can't figure out what this might be, until I make out a man with a circular saw cutting through Dad's chains.

The TV crew rushes to the foot of the tree, filming the whole thing, as the chains fall layer by layer to the ground. Dad is grabbed roughly by two policemen, handcuffed and yanked from his spot beneath us to the row of police vans, which are rapidly filling with arrested protesters. He yells something to the journalist as he's pulled away, but I can't make out the words.

Yesterday felt like a victory; today is already a crushing defeat.

From our vantage point in the tree, we have a

depressingly clear view of the next stage. With a wall of police in full riot gear holding the line against the pushed-back crowd, a wave of men in hi-vis jackets comes out of the building site and swarms purposefully into the commune. Stuff soon begins falling out of every window: furniture, books, mattresses, clothes, paintings, cooking pots and everything else that belongs to the people who have been living there over the last months.

A truckload of bricks and a cement mixer are then brought into the front garden, and one by one, faster than you would have thought possible, the windows are bricked up. At the same time, a team of men climbs up on to the roof and sets about tossing down all the roof tiles.

In front of my eyes, the building that was the beating heart of the protest is transformed from a home – a vibrant hub of life and laughter and music and resistance – into an uninhabitable shell.

Due to the noise of the crashing roof tiles and the louder-than-ever yells of the protesters, it takes me a while to pick out the significance of a new noise – a high-pitched buzzing. Then Sky tugs at my arm and points downwards. A man wearing a helmet and visor is revving a chainsaw at the foot of our tree.

We both scream down at him to stop, but he doesn't hear.

Mum sprints out of our front garden, but a policeman

blocks her path, and when she tries to push past him, he grabs her and holds her back. It looks like she's about to get arrested too, but I can see her yelling and yelling, red in the face, pointing up towards Sky and me in the treehouse.

The policeman, suddenly understanding her panic, lets go of her and runs to the tree. He grabs the workman by the shoulder, they have a brief conversation and the chainsaw is switched off.

The two men step back and stare up at our treehouse. Mum is next to them, looking like she's halfway through a heart attack.

'ARE YOU OK!?' calls Mum, though she barely has enough breath to get the words out.

'WE'RE COOL!' replies Sky, giving a thumbs up over the side of the treehouse.

'Are *you* OK?' I say, because it really looks like she isn't.

'NO! They were about to cut down the tree!'

'We saw!' I say proudly. For some reason, the mortal danger of our situation seems to have hit my mother, but not Sky or me.

'You're going to have to come down!' says the policeman.

'Bite me!' replies Sky.

'What did you say?'

'It means no,' I explain.

'It wasn't a question, it was an order. As an officer of the law, I'm ordering you both to come down.'

'And as a child who doesn't want to see the planet destroyed, I'm saying no,' says Sky.

'You don't have a choice in this,' says the policeman.

'Yes we do!' I say. 'And our choice is to stay here.'

'How long do you think you're going to last up there?'

'How long do you think the human race is going to last if we don't change our priorities?' says Sky.

'Er … that's not what we're discussing here.'

'It's not what *you're* discussing, but the failure to have this discussion is the exact reason why we're here.'

'The point is, you have to come down.'

'The point is, we won't,' I say.

Only now do I notice that a TV crew is right there, recording this whole conversation, watching the policeman go redder and redder in the face.

'This is your last warning!' he says. 'If you don't come down willingly, we'll have to resort to other methods.'

'You've made your point,' Mum shouts up. 'I think it's time to come down now.'

Sky looks at me. 'You want to go down?' she says.

'No way,' I say. 'You?'

She smiles at me and shakes her head. I look back down over the side and call out, 'We've made a decision!'

'You're coming down?' says the policeman.

'Guess again.'

'You're making a very big mistake,' he says. 'Wasting police time is a criminal offence.'

'And what kind of an offence is it to destroy a planet?' says Sky. 'I'd say that was a pretty big mistake too.'

'Right! You've had your last warning!' says the policeman, before marching away to confer with a group of colleagues.

'And you've had yours!' I call after him. He doesn't hear, but it feels satisfying to have the last word.

# No defeat! No surrender!

Around the middle of the afternoon, a mobile crane trundles into view and inches towards our tree. As it positions itself below the treehouse, a chorus of boos and jeers rises up from the crowd of protesters, which still seems as noisy and large as ever, despite being squashed into the bottom end of the street.

After a dip in energy at the sight of the commune being ripped apart and bricked up, the protesters have now found their voice again, and all of them seem to be looking up towards us, as if we are the last stand of the commune, which I suppose we are. It's hard to make out the words, but some of the chants that rise from a crowd around the topless drummer seem to be about the treehouse and saving the tree.

After a brief debate at the foot of the trunk, the policeman who has already tried and failed to persuade

Sky and me to come down gets on to the crane's platform, which is like a small open-air lift surrounded by a waist-high metal rail. He's accompanied by a guy who appears to be the crane operator, and they slowly make their way up towards us.

A chant of 'NO DEFEAT! NO SURRENDER!' begins to boom out. It's clear we're no longer peripheral observers, but have somehow become the very heart of the demonstration. Hundreds of people are looking up at us, waiting to see what we'll do, shouting and singing their support.

I keep thinking there must be someone else up here who's the focus of all this attention – an adult … someone who has a plan – but there isn't. It's just me and Sky.

'What are we going to do?' I say to Sky, as the crane begins to force its way into the crown of the tree, crunching through a layer of branches that splinter and crash downwards.

'Stay put,' she says.

'What if they just grab us?'

'We fight back.'

'But … if we fall …'

'We can't let them win. We can't!' says Sky, without a glimmer of doubt in her voice.

After much buzzing, clicking and readjusting, the crane lift finally comes to a standstill, positioned one step of empty air away from the treehouse. Sky and I retreat to the opposite side of our platform. She gives the policeman her narrow-eyed death stare.

'NO DEFEAT! NO SURRENDER! SAVE THE TREE!' chant the protesters.

'OK, fun's over,' says the policeman. 'You're coming down with me.'

'No, we're not,' snaps Sky. 'And this isn't about fun. It's not a game.'

'You don't have a choice. If you don't come in the next ten seconds, I'm going to arrest you.'

'I don't need ten seconds. You can arrest me now.'

'OK. I will.'

'Good. Go on then.'

'Give me your hand.'

'No.'

'Don't make me come and get you.'

'You can't come and get me. This platform isn't strong enough for a grown-up. And if I fell, you'd be a murderer.'

'That's why you need to step this way,' says the policeman.

'And that's why I won't,' says Sky.

She's good at this. If it wasn't for her, I don't think I'd have the guts to resist. The policeman's face is now clenched into a dark scowl, and I may be imagining it, but there appears to be a hint of a smirk hovering around the mouth of the crane operator.

'Do you have any idea how much trouble you're in?' says the policeman.

'I do. It's a dire emergency. The planet's dying.'

The crane operator lets out a splutter of laughter, which the policeman cuts off with an angry glare.

'I'm not talking about the planet. I'm talking about you.'

'Well, maybe you need to open your mind and think about what's really happening to the world, and do something about it, instead of wasting your time trying to arrest children who haven't even done anything wrong.'

'I'll be the judge of that.'

'*I'll be the judge of that,*' says Sky, mocking his voice. I can't help but burst out laughing, and so does the crane operator.

'Resisting arrest is a serious crime,' says the policeman.

'You'd better arrest me for it, then,' replies Sky.

The policeman removes his hat and scratches roughly at his receding hair. This obviously isn't how he'd been expecting his crane mission to go. He walks to the edge of the lift platform, which wobbles as he moves, and looks down through the gap between where he's standing and the treehouse. He only has to take one small step, but it's a long drop and he has no idea how strong the treehouse is, and the prospect of getting into a wrestle with two children at this height is clearly not a tempting one.

He steps back from the edge and grips his safety rail.

'How long are you planning to stay up here?' he says.

'I guess that's what we're about to find out,' says Sky.

'You're a cocky little so-and-so, aren't you?' says the policeman.

'*You're a cocky little so-and-so, aren't you?*' she replies.

'What about you?' he says, looking at me. 'Are you coming down, or are you as much of an idiot as she is?'

'If I'm an idiot, you're twice as much of an idiot, with bells on,' says Sky.

'You! Come down!' says the policeman, jabbing a finger at me.

'Can't,' I say.

'Why not?'

'Because we're a team.'

'You're making serious problems for yourself, young man, unless you come down with me right now.'

'No, thanks,' I say. 'I'm here on important business.'

'Yup!' says Sky. 'Important business. Couldn't put it better myself.'

With a shake of the head, the policeman orders the crane operator to take them back down.

As soon as they emerge from the high branches, having visibly failed in their attempt to get us to come down, the crowd of protesters lets out a huge cheer. The crane operator glances up and throws us a sneaky wink.

I look at Sky, and she looks at me, and we smile at one

another for a while, listening to the sound of the demonstration.

'I think they're cheering for us,' I say.

'Weird, isn't it?' she says.

'Our mums will be down there somewhere.'

'Mine probably got arrested,' says Sky. 'She likes getting arrested. It's kind of a hobby.'

'She'll be proud of you,' I say.

'Hm,' says Sky, looking as if she's trying to shrug off the idea.

After a moment's silence, she adds quietly, 'I suppose that would make a nice change. She thinks I've gone over to the dark side.'

'What's the dark side? Me and my family?'

'Yeah. Jobs, cars, possessions, school, plastic bags … all that stuff.'

'Have you? Crossed over?'

'Don't know. But I needed to at least see it. Just once. To find out what it is.'

'So what do you think? Are you going to go straight and become an accountant?'

'Nah, that's not me. And I'm useless at maths.'

'What, then?'

'No idea. Looks like I'm stuck living in a tree for now.'

I look down at the ground far below, and at our rope ladder looped over a branch, hanging in mid-air, and I realise that she's right. We're stuck here. We can't leave.

'What are we going to do?' I say.

'Just wait, I suppose,' she replies.

'For what?'

'I don't know.'

'Are you hungry?'

'I don't know.'

'You're always hungry.'

'I suppose I must be, then.'

I look in our snacks box, and it's pretty depleted. Underneath a layer of empty chocolate and biscuit wrappers, all I can find is two packets of crisps, then a layer of the healthy stuff my mum gave us, which has been ignored until now – apples, raisins, oat cakes and nuts.

'How much food have we got? How long do you think we can stay before we get too hungry?' she asks.

'Do you think they'll try to starve us out?'

'Don't know. If they do, I reckon I can miss one meal, tops.'

'Me too. Just talking about it is making me hungry,' I say.

We take an apple and a bag of crisps each, then sit at the edge of the treehouse with our legs dangling down, watching the dismantling of the house and the raging of the protesters.

The crane creeps noisily back to the building site, and

the policeman who tried to negotiate with us disappears from view.

Hours trickle by in what feels like a mixture of both mayhem and tranquillity, with a strange feeling hanging over us that we are at the centre of a battle, and also somehow far away from it, floating on another plane, untouched by the shouting, the violence and the destruction. This huge old oak, which has been here far longer than any of the houses on the street, longer than the street has even existed, feels like a sanctuary – a place apart from the angry human drama playing out below.

By the end of the day, the commune building has been rendered uninhabitable. Windows and doors have been bricked over, roof tiles ripped off, floorboards torn up and thrown outside. When this job is complete, the human wall of police officers that was holding back the protesters retreats into the fenced-off building site, leaving behind just a small team guarding the tree. Though I suppose it's not really the tree they're guarding – it's me and Sky.

It could be that they want to stop other people coming up to join us, or perhaps they want to arrest us if we come down, or maybe they just want to prevent anyone sending up the food and water we need to continue our protest. Whatever the reason, it feels like something of an honour to have your own police guard.

As the light begins to fade, Mum appears from our house carrying a couple of Tupperware boxes, which even from this distance I can tell is a meal for Sky and me. The police stop her before she can get near our basket-drop position and, even though she remonstrates with them vociferously, she fails to persuade the officer in charge to let her through.

When she eventually gives up on the argument, she tilts her face upwards and yells, 'I'VE GOT FOOD FOR YOU, BUT THIS MAN WON'T LET ME SEND IT UP! EVEN THOUGH YOU'RE CHILDREN.'

'WE'RE OK,' I reply. 'Lots of snacks.'

'THIS MAN HERE,' she repeats, turning towards the street, which is still filled with milling protesters even though the shouting and drum-banging has long since stopped, 'IS HAPPY TO DENY TWO HUNGRY CHILDREN THEIR FOOD, JUST TO PROTECT HIS JOB.'

A wave of boos spreads outwards from the tree.

'TWO CHILDREN! HUNGRY CHILDREN!' adds Mum, eliciting more boos.

The policeman appears unmoved by this, though he must surely be shrivelling up with embarrassment inside, and my mum walks away. I know her too well to think for even a second this might be her giving up.

My guess is that she's simply moving on to her plan B and, sure enough, a few minutes later my phone rings.

'Hi, it's me,' says Mum. 'Are you OK?'

'Great,' I say.

'When are you coming down?'

'Don't know.'

'You can't spend the night up there.'

'Why not?'

'It isn't safe.'

'Says who?'

'What if you fall out?'

'We won't.'

'You might.'

'We won't.'

'I never would have let you go up there if I'd had any idea you were going to do this!'

'I'd better stay here, then.'

'Please come down. I won't be cross, I promise.'

'You're already cross.'

'Only because you won't come down. It'll be dark soon.'

'There are street lights.'

'It's not safe.'

'We're staying put.'

I turn to Sky and she gives me a firm nod.

Mum spends another few minutes trying to persuade me to come down, but I hold firm and change the subject to Dad being arrested (which is surely worse than me being in a treehouse). When I ask if there's any news from him, she just tells me I mustn't worry, and that he'll be out soon. Eventually we get on to the important topic of food, and how to get it up to the treehouse.

'We've made a plan,' she says. 'I'm going to stay out of sight, because they already know who I am. A team of Rose's friends are going to create a diversion. We don't think the police know you have a basket, so get it as low as you can now without it being visible, and when you see that the distraction has worked, drop it down fast. Someone will be at the spot ready to put the food in, you pull it up and … bingo! What do you think?'

'OK – we'll get ready.'

Sky stealthily lowers the basket two-thirds of the way down the trunk, and a crowd of people (including Rose and some of the group we brought in over the garages) soon appears next to the policeman who seems to be in charge of guarding the tree. They begin singing stupid songs, then Rose takes the policeman's hat and puts it on, dancing in front of him, just out of reach.

He tries to take this with good humour, and Rose keeps up her playful demeanour but refuses to give the hat back, continuing to dance just out of reach as he steps forward to try and retrieve his hat.

Soon the other police around the tree are sucked into the argument, arrest is threatened, and at that moment a crouching figure darts out of a bush and positions himself directly below us. It's Callum, carrying a well-stuffed back-pack. Sky lets the basket plummet to ground level. Callum chucks in the backpack and we immediately pull, as hard as we can, both of us straining to get the heavy load up and out of sight.

Nobody seems to notice what Callum has done. He turns and slips away, giving a furtive thumbs up to Rose, who immediately returns the police helmet to its owner and melts back into the crowd.

Seconds later, the basket is in our hands, and we spread out our feast on the treehouse platform: two huge Tupperware tubs of creamy chicken pasta, a big thermos of soup, a cling-film-covered slab of sandwiches, a family pack of KitKats and several bars of chocolate, two big cartons of juice and assorted bags of crisps, sweets and popcorn. There's even a power-bank charger for my phone.

We both pile into our pasta and I text Mum as I eat: 'Thnx. Best meal ever! xxxxx'

'Enjoy!' she replies. 'Stay safe! I love you! xxx'

Sky asks me what the reply says, but I leave out the last bit.

After a while, Mum sends another text, saying, 'You have been very brave and you've made your point. I really think you should come down now.'

I text back: 'Got sleeping bag, blankets and cushions. We'll be fine. Thanks again for dinner.'

'This is a really bad idea,' she texts back, and I don't reply.

A few minutes later, a text comes through from Rose, saying, 'Mum says I have to text you to tell you to come down, but DON'T. Stay there! You're doing a great job. I'm proud of you. Everyone says they're proud of Sky too. There have been many tears today, but you two are our brave shining lights. We all send big hugs to both of you.'

When I read this out to Sky, a shiver of contentment seems to pass through her whole body.

# Move with the tree

After eating our pasta, washed down with an epic quantity of chocolate, Sky and I make a nest of cushions and blankets and bed down for the night. It's the first time I've used my sleeping bag since I lent it to Rose at the start of the summer holiday, which now feels like a lifetime ago. It smells smoky, with faint wafts of spicy food, incense and unwashed human body, but I don't really mind. It occurs to me that this is the smell of the commune, which, as of today, no longer exists. The scent of my sleeping bag is a last remnant of something unique and beautiful that has just been smashed.

I breathe it in, and imagine myself walking through the now stripped and destroyed rooms, reconstructing them in my head.

The sounds of singing and guitar-strumming float upwards as the night darkens. Sky's mum calls on my mobile, asks me to hand over the phone, and the two of them have a muttered chat which I try to avoid eavesdropping on, though it's impossible to miss Sky promising over and over again to be careful, or not to notice that she signs off with, 'I love you too.'

Apparently, despite her best efforts, though she did get shut in a van for a while, Sky's mum wasn't arrested after all. Every hobby has its challenges, I suppose.

Some of the protesters drift away for the night, others bed down in tents. From our vantage point high up in the tree, Sky and I watch the now homeless commune members pick through the remains of their possessions, which are strewn across the ground outside their destroyed home. There's lots of hugging and a considerable amount of weeping. Almost everyone I know from the street – including Helena – comes out to help them, providing cups of tea, food, comfort and even suitcases for their belongings. Mrs Gupta keeps emerging from her house with tray after tray of brownies.

I watch my mum have a long conversation with Clyde, jotting things down on a piece of paper, then she goes up and down the street, ringing on doorbells. One by one, everybody from the commune leaves the mournful gathering under the tree and goes into one of the homes on the street, lugging with them the salvaged remains of their belongings.

Last to find a bed for the night are Clyde and Sky's mother, who are led into my house by Mum. I imagine Rose must be sleeping in her own bedroom for the first night in weeks, so presumably one of our guests will be in my bed and the other on the sofa in the living room.

All change again, I think to myself, as I begin to doze off. Commune people sleeping in my house with Mum and Rose, the commune empty, me and Sky up a tree and Dad in a police cell. I didn't see that arrangement coming. When my parents set out to bring Rose home, I'm pretty sure this isn't what they imagined, either.

Sleep won't come though. Lying still in the dark, it begins to feel as if the platform is moving. Even though it's a relatively windless night, up here the whole tree seems to creak and sway. Whenever my body begins to drift into unconsciousness, a panic reflex telling me I'm going to roll off and fall to the ground kicks in and jolts me awake.

With the street silent at last, quiet enough for me to hear the leaves above my head jostling against one another, I turn towards the moonlit silhouette of Sky's motionless body and whisper, 'Are you asleep?'

'Sort of,' she says. 'You?'

'Can't sleep. I feel like we're moving.'

'We are.'

'It's weird.'

'It's natural,' she says. 'Why do you think people rock babies to soothe them?'

'I don't know.'

'Because we're monkeys. Fancy monkeys who think we're cleverer than all the other monkeys, but this is where we belong. In trees.'

'Speak for yourself.'

'It's true.'

'According to who?'

There's a long silence. For a while I think Sky has fallen asleep, then she says, 'You know I said this is the first place I've been for years that feels like home? It happened once before. There was a man, when I was small. We lived with him in a tent. It was a protest camp in a forest down south. About a road, or something. A bypass. He was called Aidan. Me, Mum and him in one big tent, which he called a yurt. It had a wood stove in the middle and a hole in the roof for the smoke. He's not my dad, but he felt like it for a while. It was him that taught me how to play chess, with pieces he carved himself. We went out into the forest every day. Searching for firewood and food, or just walking. Looking at things. He taught me which mushrooms you can and can't eat, and where to find them. Same thing for berries. Also all sorts of stuff about birds and how to spot the tracks of deer and foxes. If he saw a spiderweb he liked the look of, we'd all stop, examine the shape of it, talk about how it was made.'

Sky pauses for a moment, lost in a distant memory, then carries on in such a quiet voice it's almost as if she's talking to herself. 'Everything he saw, he had a story about it, or sometimes just questions. And he always listened to my answers, which usually led to some other story, probably about plants or insects or wild animals ... but most of all he loved trees. He taught me how to identify them from their leaves or bark or even just buds. He had a hammock, and sometimes the three of us would climb really high, and he'd tie us on and we'd all lie there. Listening. Just being there. It was amazing. I was never bored. Not for one minute in that forest was I ever bored.'

'How long were you there?'

'I don't know. Probably less than a year, because I remember it getting too cold. I think that's why we left.'

'What happened to the man?'

'Aidan? I don't know. He stayed, we left. That was that. Mum was different then. More fun. I don't often think of him now, but ... he was nice. I know people think I'm stupid. They think I don't know anything about anything, but that's not true. I just know different things.'

'I don't think you're stupid.'

'You did at first. I saw it in your eyes.'

There's no answer to that, and I'm glad it's too dark for her to see my face, because I know she'd see that she's right.

After another long, sleepy silence, Sky says, 'Did you know that trees talk to each other?'

'You really believe that?'

'Not in words but in scent. There's a tree in Africa that sometimes gets eaten by giraffes. The giraffes only nibble for a short while though, then they walk away, not just from that tree, but from all the others close by. When scientists studied it, they learned that after the tree starts to get eaten, it sends out a bad-tasting toxin to the leaves which puts the giraffe off. But not only that – it also gives off a scent warning to other trees nearby, and those trees pump their leaves with the same toxin before the giraffes even bite into them. The trees help each other.'

'Is that really true?'

'A hundred per cent. Aidan told me, and he never lied. He loved stories like that. Did you know that in a forest, underground, all the roots of all the different trees intertwine and connect? An ill tree will be sent nutrition by its neighbours to help it recover. Aidan always said a forest, however big, was actually like one organism endlessly rebuilding itself over time frames that humans can't even imagine. He said that if you walk in a forest and all you see are individual trees, then you don't know what a forest is. That's how trees are supposed to be, and that's how the whole world looked until humans came along and started cutting everything down. This oak we're in now, it's an orphan. They don't like being on their own.'

'Well, it isn't now,' I say. 'We're here.'

'I'm tired,' she says.

'Me too.'

'If you try to stay still while the tree moves, you'll never sleep. You have to accept where you are. Move with the tree. Be part of the tree. If you do that you'll have the best sleep of your life.'

'I'll try.'

'Night night.'

Silence descends, until I whisper one last question.

'Are you frightened?' I ask.

'No,' she says. 'No.'

# How long do you think we have left?

I don't even notice myself falling asleep, and the next thing I'm aware of is a sound that I at first think is an alarm clock, until my eyes open to a bright shock of sunlight and I realise my phone is ringing.

'It's me,' says Mum. 'Look down.'

I peer over the edge of the treehouse, and there's my mother, in the middle of the street, holding a basket of food. She gives me a big wave.

'Are you OK?' she asks. 'Did you sleep?'

'Yeah. I'm fine.'

'I know this is going to sound weird, but there's someone here who wants to talk to you.'

'Who?'

'It's some TV news people.'

I peer over the edge again and notice that Mum is

standing directly in front of a camera crew as she's talking to me.

'What do they want?'

'Well, I've been trying to get some breakfast up to you, but the police here won't let me, and these news people think this is a good story, so they want to ask you how you feel about being starved out of your protest.'

'Starved?'

'Well, you can say whatever you want. Shall I hand you over now?'

'OK.'

There's a rustling sound, and a younger female voice comes on the line. 'Hello, is that Luke?' she says.

'Yup.'

'I'd like to ask you a few questions about your protest, if that's OK.'

'Sure,' I say, still not entirely believing what's happening to me. Even on a normal day I find the world confusing at this time in the morning, and though I've only been awake for less than a minute, it's already clear this is very much not a normal day.

'How was your night in the tree?' she asks.

'Fine,' I reply. I know I ought to think of something more interesting to say, but I haven't yet found the on switch for the part of my brain where words are kept.

'Your mother's been trying to send food and water up to

you, but she's being prevented by a police cordon. How do you feel about that?'

'Er … angry,' I say. 'It's … really bad. I'm starved. And I'm only thirteen. That's not right, is it?'

'Absolutely not. Do you have a message you'd like to give to the authorities who are trying to starve you out?'

'Yeah … er … just … don't be stupid. Don't be mean. But this isn't about me, anyway. It's about the planet. It's the most important thing there is, and everyone my age feels the same way about it. We need a future. Can we … talk about this later? I've just woken up.'

'OK. We can try. Thank you, Luke.'

Then the line goes dead.

'Who was that?' says Sky, rubbing her eyes and yawning.

'Them,' I say, pointing down at the TV crew. 'News people.'

'Wow,' she says. 'You're famous.'

'Hardly. They said they might call back. Maybe you should do the talking next time.'

'I won't be any good,' she says.

'You'll be better than me.'

'You were great!'

'Apart from the fact that I couldn't remember any words. As soon as she said who she was, I basically forgot how to speak.'

'No, you didn't. I heard the whole thing.'

289

'Well, that's what it felt like. Anyway, apparently Mum's trying to send up breakfast but they're not letting her.'

'It's OK. We've got loads left from last night.'

This is certainly true. We unpack the food we've hidden away from marauding squirrels and begin to pick at what turns out to be a rather lavish and prolonged breakfast. We're certainly far from hungry when a text message pings through from Mum, saying that the police have caved in to the 'PR calamity' (whatever that means) of blocking her attempts to send up food, and that brunch (whatever that is) will be on the way soon.

Before I even have time to reply, a second message arrives saying that I should open the parcel carefully, because there will be a fragile surprise in there.

By this time a demolition team has arrived to continue their work of dismantling the commune. An enormous digger with a brick-chewing pincer on the end of a hydraulic arm shoves and bites at the structure of the building all morning, first pulling out the roof beams, then setting about the work of crunching down the walls. There's something mesmerising about the slow, inexorable destruction this machine can wreak, pulling apart an entire house in front of my eyes.

The protesters have been pushed back away from the demolition site, but they're still present in large numbers, and as the morning progresses they seem to find their voice. We can't quite make out the words of their songs, but there are moments when both of us think they're singing about a treehouse, and we may be imagining things, but from time to time we even think we hear our names.

When Mum reappears from the house, she's carrying two bulging carrier bags of food, and she walks confidently towards the tree. The police cordon parts to let her through, and I watch her thank the policeman in charge with what I can tell, even from a distance, is extravagant sarcasm.

Sky drops our basket down, and together we haul up three loads of supplies. The last one contains a padded envelope with our address scribbled out on the front, and above that the words 'OPEN CAREFULLY', in Mum's handwriting.

Inside is an iPhone and a letter saying that the phone will ring at midday with a video call from a news anchor, which will be recorded and put out on the national lunch-time bulletin.

'You're going to be interviewed on TV!' says Sky.

'We are,' I say. 'Both of us.'

'I won't have anything to say.'

'Yes, you will. And even if you don't, people should see you.'

'I don't know if I want them to.'

'I'm not pretending I'm up here alone. That would be a lie.'

'OK. I suppose.'

'How do we look?' I ask.

She shrugs. 'We look how we look.'

'You're right,' I say. 'We are who we are and we look how we look.'

A slow smile creeps across Sky's face. 'I can't believe this is happening.'

'Me neither.'

'We'd better think of something good to say. All my life I've been around people who are protesting about one thing or another, and nobody ever listens to them,' says Sky. 'I've seen hundreds of demonstrators spend whole days on marches where they shout their heads off to absolutely nobody. Now we're going to be interviewed on TV. We have to *say* something.'

'You're right.'

'There's never going to be another chance.'

'I know. And they're probably going to talk down to us because we're kids.'

'You can still give smart answers to stupid questions,' she says. 'It doesn't matter what they ask us. This is our moment, and we just have to say what needs to be said.'

'You're going to be brilliant. I know you are. I'm going to forget how to talk.'

'Between us, we can do it,' she says. 'We just have to plan out what to say.'

'OK.'

There's a long silence.

'Maybe we should eat first,' I say.

The iPhone sits on the platform between us as we chew, both of us glancing at it warily, as if it might explode at any moment.

A couple of times we try to discuss what we should say in the interview, but the conversation goes nowhere, even though there clearly isn't anything else to talk about. Eventually, having decided we'll just have to wing it, we sit there in ruminative silence, working our way through the giant picnic sent up by my mother.

The morning creeps on painfully slowly. From one dragging minute to the next, I veer between willing midday to arrive and dreading it.

Eventually the phone rings, and from the small screen in my hand I'm greeted by a news presenter whose voice is so familiar it feels almost as if he's a member of my family. Sky positions herself next to me, and I hold the screen at arm's length so we're both in shot.

'Hi!' I say, scarcely believing this familiar TV face is someone I can actually converse with. 'Can you hear me?'

'Loud and clear. You're Luke, are you?'

'That's me,' I say. 'And this is Sky. It's a joint protest.'

'So I heard.'

'Have we started yet?' I ask. 'Is this the interview?'

'Well, we're recording,' he says. 'We're ready to begin as soon as you two say you're ready. The sound isn't great, so remember to use big voices. OK?'

'OK.'

'Ready?'

'I guess.'

He goes still for a second, waits for some kind of signal off-camera, then turns away from us, gives an introduction about the protest and explains who we are. I try to listen to what he's saying but my mind goes blank, blurring into a fizz of panic, which only partially clears when I see him turn back to stare at us directly through the phone screen and ask a question which passes straight through my brain without me registering any sense of what he's asked.

Luckily Sky must have been managing to focus better than me, because she replies, in her usually chirpy voice, 'Fine! We're absolutely fine! What's being built here is an atrocity and it shouldn't be allowed, and we're both very pleased to be taking a stand against it. My mum brought me up to believe that I shouldn't let people push me around, so that's what we're doing.'

'So do you really think that two kids up a tree can stop a multi-million-pound airport expansion going ahead?'

'I don't see what our age has to do with it. And no, we probably can't stop it, but we're already delaying it, and also making people aware of what's going on. Not just us, but everyone who has come here to protest. This is a subject everyone should be thinking about and talking about – and here we are, talking to you, which is proof that what's happening here is already some kind of success.'

'Are you aware of how much protests like this cost the taxpayer? Don't you think that now you've made your point you should come down?'

I feel I might be looking like an idiot, sitting here saying nothing, so I jump in with a quick answer. 'No! For years people having been asking politely for politicians to do something about climate change, and nothing ever happens. Until you get in the way of somebody making money, nobody even notices you're there.'

'For older people this whole thing is just an idea – a news story – but for us it's our lives,' says Sky, in a voice that reminds me of an engine shifting up a gear. 'Unless something drastic changes very soon, by the time we're your age, in maybe 2050 or 2070, the world as we know it will have been totally destroyed by people of your generation who didn't feel like giving up fast cars and weekends in Paris and plastic-wrapped fruit flown in from New Zealand. We're going to have to live with this. You can't understand how we feel.'

'I think we can,' the presenter says.

'You can't and you don't, and every young person in the world knows this, and we aren't going away. It's our world, and we're not going to just sit there politely and shut our mouths while people like you destroy it.'

Sky's voice is wavering with emotion now, and I can see by the look on the interviewer's face that he's torn between being offended by her combativeness and delighted by the drama.

'And when you ask about the cost to the taxpayer, that shows how much you don't get it,' I say. 'Because the cost of doing nothing is so huge you can't even measure it.'

'I can see you both feel very passionately about this,' says the interviewer, glancing down at his list of questions and hesitating for a moment, apparently finding that none of them fits the way the interview has panned out.

'It's not just us. It's everyone here, and everyone of our generation, and everyone who hasn't got their head up their bum,' says Sky. 'There's no Planet B, and there's no more time to waste. Something has to change. *Everything* has to change.'

'Well, thank you for sharing your opinions and your enthusiasm—'

'*Opinions and enthusiasm?*' interrupts Sky. 'These aren't opinions! They're facts. Science.'

'There are two sides to every story.'

'Not this one. How long do you think we have left?'

'Er …'

'If nothing changes, how long will the world as we

know it last? Twenty years? Fifty? Seventy? If we do nothing, in my lifetime how many people will lose their homes or die? How many millions? One? Ten? A hundred million?'

The presenter takes this as his cue to end the interview, and without any kind of goodbye, the line is cut and the screen goes blank.

Then there we are again, up in our treehouse, alone together, shortly to be broadcast all over the country.

We look at each other in stunned silence for a few seconds, then suddenly, I don't know why, we're both overtaken by hysterical laughter.

'How do you think that went?' says Sky, when we finally recover.

'You were fantastic,' I say.

'I shouldn't have said bum. People don't say bum on the news, do they?'

'Not usually. But apart from that it was great.'

'You think? I have no idea what I said.'

'I can't remember, either. The whole thing's a blur. I feel like it lasted about five seconds, or maybe like it didn't really happen at all.'

'It definitely happened,' says Sky. 'Whatever it was, it happened.'

There doesn't seem to be anything else to do now except carry on eating, so we reopen the food box and begin to snack, jumping from sweets to crisps to sand-wiches to sausage rolls and back again.

When I can't eat any more, I flop on to my back and gaze up at the shimmer of blue that dances through the shuffling layer of leaves, luxuriating in the way that up here it seems as if time slows to a crawl. Nothing-to-do hours in the treehouse feel almost like lolling in a warm swimming pool. I breathe deeply, pulling into me the clean, woody scent of this tree, which I don't ever want to forget.

Will this be our last day up here? I feel as if we don't have much longer. Someone will force us out. They must know that if they start cutting, we'll have to climb down.

How much longer will this tree be alive? It seems like an immense responsibility that Sky and I are the only things holding back the murder of this beautiful giant, and feels unspeakably sad that soon we will be beaten and the axe will fall.

Picturing the trunk of this tree cracking open as it crashes to the ground makes my eyes prickle with sorrow and fury. One human with a small, buzzing tool bringing to an end hundreds of years of life in a matter of minutes: how can that be possible? How could a person do that?

Without shifting position I reach out, pluck a leaf and rub it between finger and thumb, feeling its two textures: rough on the dark green surface and smooth but ridged on the pale green underside. With a fingertip I trace the perfect taper of the silky-smooth central stem as it shrinks to a hair's breadth at the leaf's tip.

Holding it up to the light, my eyes follow the veins that branch off this tiny spine, and the veins that branch off them, and the minuscule filaments that split off yet again, barely visible. As I examine this pattern of perfect ever-shrinking smallness, my mind suddenly spins out to picture this vast tree cradling me high in the air, and the thousands upon thousands of leaves it has grown over century after century, every single year, creating and dropping these same leaves on this same spot when I was a baby, and when my parents and grandparents were babies, and their grand-parents, on and on. Until now. And I have a sudden sense that this tree, which has become my temporary home during what will be the last few days of its unimaginably long life, is speaking to me about the interconnectedness of everything – telling me that big is small and small is big, and the whole planet, from the tiniest bug to the largest mountain, is one thing. I can't quite fully capture or under-stand this thought, but I feel it, in my fingertips and blood and heart.

This daydream is interrupted by the ping of my mobile phone receiving a message, then, almost immediately, another and another. There's one from Mum, another from Sky's mum, rapidly followed by a torrent more from Rose,

Clyde and seemingly every other person who has my mobile number, all of them compliments on what we said, or variations on 'You were amazing!'

None of these messages quite sink in. My eyes slip over this seemingly endless stream of words as if they have little to do with me, as if it's someone else who is being congratulated, then one flashes up from Grandma. My dead Grandma. For a second I think I must have gone mad, then I remember that she shared her mobile phone with Grandpa, even though he never seemed to use it. I haven't been texted from this number since she died, and I had no idea he still owned the phone. The message says, 'You showed them, big guy! Proud of you! Grandpa x'.

I'm not sure why, but the sight of these words hits me in the guts, and I feel my eyes welling up. I turn my head so Sky can't see, pondering how to reply, but I can't think what to say, so after a minute or two I just send back a smiley emoji and a thumbs up.

Not long after that, Dad calls to say that he's been released without charge, and that I don't need to worry about him (which, as soon as he says it, is something I realise I had completely forgotten to do). He then says he's heard I've become a celebrity.

I don't really have an answer to that, but he tells me he's on his way home and he's impressed by my courage and he can't wait to see me. As I'm hanging up, it occurs to me that I can't remember him ever saying this to me before.

That night, again, I can't sleep. It's for a different reason though. The gentle swaying of the treehouse no longer bothers me, and even the intermittent creaking of the platform's wooden joists has come to feel soothing rather than worrying. The new problem is that I feel as if my whole body is fizzing with a crackling energy that won't let my mind shut down. Everything that has happened over the last weeks has been spiralling me towards this supercharged instant in time, and now the spiral has found its centre.

I've never felt like a nobody, because the idea didn't mean anything to me. It never crossed my mind that I could be a somebody. But now I'm at the heart of something big, and it feels like an electrical pulse has buzzed into my veins. I am the focal point of attention for people I don't even know, and I realise this is just a fleeting, freak occurrence which will pass, and will never happen to me again, but it's happening now. Right now. It's as if I'm a firework filling the sky with a brief flash of beautiful colour, and if I close my eyes for a second I'll miss it.

In the dead of night, the clatter of a bin lid pierces the silence, and I look down over the edge of the platform. A sleek, silent fox wanders insouciantly across the road, followed by two skittish cubs.

Sky sits up next to me, also wide awake, and we watch the three animals until they slip out of sight under a hedge.

'Still awake, then?' I say.

She nods, rolls on to her side, and says, 'How much longer do you think we can last up here?'

'Not much, probably. We can't leave though, can we? As soon as we do, the whole protest is finished, and the tree will be cut down.'

'I know.'

'We can't do that.'

'I know.'

After a long silence, I say, 'When this is all over, where will you go?'

She turns on to her back and thinks for a while, looking up at the flicker of leaf shadows against the slate-grey sky, then says, 'Just move on, I suppose. There's always a next place.'

It's a long time, and Sky's breath has gone slow and deep, before I say, 'I'll miss you.' There's no reply, so I have no idea if she hears me.

# Say what needs to be said

It's the pitch of the sound that wakes me up. Voices, lots of them, not shouting or singing, just talking, but at high frequency.

I look over the edge of the platform, and at first I can't quite understand what I'm seeing. The whole street is filled with a crush of bodies. Hundreds and hundreds of people. I can barely see a single patch of tarmac. Only heads.

I switch on my phone and call Mum.

'You're awake!' she says.

'What's going on?'

'Have you seen?'

'Who are they?'

'Just people. Mostly teenagers. I'll hand you over to Rose. She'll tell you.'

There's a clatter as the phone is passed over.

'Luke?' says Rose.

'What's happening?'

'After the news thing yesterday, you and Sky exploded online. The Instagram feed for the protest went crazy. People all over the world love what you're doing and what you said. Lots of them were saying they wanted to come and be part of it, so in the end I put something up about how to get here via the garages, and apparently there's so many people turning up the police haven't been able to stop it. From the crack of dawn this morning, they've been flooding in over all the back fences. Everyone on the street has opened their garden doors and let them through. The whole thing's insane. And it's not the usual protester types, either. They're mostly young, but it's just normal people. It feels like the whole world has turned up.'

'Wow.'

'You're famous.'

'But I haven't done anything.'

'You have. You and Sky said what every environment-alist has been saying for years, but something happened, and this time people listened. It got heard.'

'Why?'

'No idea.'

I wake Sky and show her the crammed street below us. With every minute, the crowd gets thicker, and spreads further down the street in both directions. A forest of flags and placards waves above the heads of the demonstrators, displaying calls to action, howls of anger, messages of hope, jokes, slogans and demands. Pockets of singing and chanting rise up and fall away. The four policemen around the tree, now pressed in close to the trunk, look uneasy about being this heavily outnumbered.

There's no way the demolition work can continue today. An impenetrable blockade of bodies is filling every inch of ground between the bricked-up remnants of the half-destroyed commune and the fenced perimeter of the building site, where the first few workmen are now beginning to appear. You couldn't possibly drive any kind of bulldozer down the street now, or bring back the police to arrest this number of people. I can't see how you could even clear the area, because there isn't any space for the protesters to retreat to. Sending in horses again would be lethal.

All it takes is for me or Sky to give a wave over the edge of the platform and a huge cheer passes through the crowd.

My phone keeps ringing and buzzing with calls, messages of support and updates on what's happening below. Everything we hear is essentially an excited repeat of 'MORE PEOPLE!' until around the middle of the day, when Clyde calls and tells me to put the phone on speaker so he can talk to both of us. He then says that a government minister is planning to come to the site. Apparently if we agree to come down when he visits, the minister will grant immunity from arrest and will promise to save the tree. He won't cancel the airport expansion, obviously, but plans can be adjusted, and the tree will be saved.

'What do you think?' says Clyde.

'I don't know. What do *you* think?' I reply. 'I mean, we have to come down at some point. Probably quite soon.'

'Yeah – I think this is your moment. This story's never going to get more exposure than today, and the best we can hope for from this is to spread the word. The whole struggle is about awareness and communication as much as it's about anything else. So I guess what we have to do is accept the minister's plan, but make sure it plays as a victory, not a defeat.'

'How do we do that?' says Sky.

'You have to do to him what you did to the news guy. He thinks he's just going to shake hands with a couple of kids and be the hero of the hour for resolving a stand-off. You have to change the conversation. Say what needs to be said in front of the cameras. And this time it's not just the UK. People around the world are following this. You can do that, can't you?'

'We can try,' says Sky.

'What should we say?' I ask.

'You don't need me to tell you. I couldn't have done

better than you two did on the news yesterday. Just do that again.'

I look at Sky. She nods.

'OK,' we both say.

'So shall I set it up?'

'Yeah.'

'Great. And remember – think about what you're going to say, and say it. Don't let the guy shut you up or change the subject or make it sound like he's got the better of you. Don't be patient and don't waste time trying to be polite, because he's coming here to try and play you. You have to get in first and beat him at his own game. You might have less than a minute. Say your piece straight away and speak from the heart.'

We spend the afternoon sketching out our attempt at a speech, pulling in everything we know, putting it down on paper, then trying to refine it and distil it to a few short points. The only disagreement is over who is going to speak. I think it should be Sky because she did so well last time, Sky says it should be me because she isn't confident with public speaking and thinks she'll mess it up. We end up agreeing to divide it in two and to memorise our own sections. Getting the precise words is less important, we decide, than following Clyde's advice to speak from the heart.

* * *

Towards the end of the day, a bustle of activity at the foot of the tree lets us know that something is up. An area is cleared in the press of bodies, and a gaggle of photographers and cameramen appears at one edge of the empty space, which now has a branching cluster of microphones in the middle of it.

I text Clyde to ask what's going on. He calls back to check that we're ready, and tells us that the minister is about to arrive. 'Don't move till I say though,' he says. 'I'll text you when it's time. Make him wait. It's for you to make an entrance.'

After a while, a large black car surrounded by police on motorbikes becomes visible, inching through the dense crowd, which reluctantly parts to let it through.

'Ready?' I say to Sky.

'No,' she says. 'You?'

'Not really.'

'I can't believe I've spent my whole life surrounded by protesters, living with people who have dedicated their lives to shouting from the sidelines, now finally the cameras and microphones are pointing in our direction, and people out there finally want to know what we think, and it's up to me to speak up. Why me?'

'You're better qualified than me. Why should it be me?'

'We mustn't let them down.'

'Who?'

'My mum. Clyde. Aidan. Everyone.'

I look into Sky's eyes and see something I've never seen there before: fear.

'You won't let anyone down,' I say. 'You're good at this. And maybe it's not a coincidence that it's you and me people are listening to, because this is our lives. It's not just theory for us – we're going to have to live with this. Look at all the people down there. They're young.'

The ping of an incoming text message rises from my phone. It's Clyde, telling us it's time to come down.

'You want to go first?' I say.

She looks at me, and now something different is in her eyes – a steely glint of total concentration and focus.

'OK,' says Sky, then she slides herself off the edge of the platform and begins to descend the rope ladder. With every step she takes, the cheers from the crowd get louder and louder.

I reach the ground seconds behind Sky, and the minister is right there in his immaculate suit, waiting for us with a smug grin on his rosy, well-fed face. The only crack in his facade of smarm is a slight twitch of the nostrils as we approach. It's been a while since we washed.

The crowd around us hushes, and I can sense them craning in to listen.

The minister extends an arm to us, offering a handshake, and I'm about to give him my hand when Sky steps ahead

309

of me and says, 'We don't want to shake your hand, because shaking hands with someone is a sign of mutual respect, and we feel that you're only pretending to respect us, and we find that insulting. In fact, we think you're only pretending to respect our whole generation. We want a future. We want the opportunities that you have had, and if the planet heats up by two degrees, that isn't going to happen. Every scientist who isn't a puppet working for oil companies agrees on this, and the only way to achieve this is to stop burning fossil fuels right now. To change everything NOW.'

No niceties, then. Sky's clearly not in the mood for chit-chat and has immediately come out with the first chunk of our prepared speech, plus a little no-handshake improvisation.

The minister is no longer smiling, and he's momentarily lost for words. Flashbulbs are popping around us, and I feel as if I can hear a shocked but thrilled silence pulsating out of the listening journalists. It's up to me to say the next bit, and Sky jabs an elbow into me, nudging me into action.

My tongue feels dry, as if glued to the roof of my mouth, and for a moment I'm worried that I won't be able to get any words out. My heart is racing as if I'm in the middle of a sprint, but my breath feels strangely slow – out of sync with my galloping pulse. I cough, rub my face to try and force some normal sensation back into it, and push out the first few words. 'There's a tipping point coming in ten years,' I say, weirdly loud, but now I've started, I immediately feel a sense of purpose and control descending, a total determination – powered by the horror of the facts Sky has taught me – not to mess up this fleeting, unrepeatable opportunity. 'When we reach our early twenties, melting permafrost will start to release so much methane that global warming will be irreversible. After that, nothing can be done. Nothing. The reason why there are so many people here today – young people – is because we need changes to be made *immediately*, but we have no power. You have power. You are in charge. So do something. Don't just stand here shaking hands with two children and making empty promises. Do something. Use your power to force big business to change its priorities in a way that makes ordinary people change how they live.'

That's the end of our speech. We stare at the minster, giving him the evils, and he looks back at us, bewildered, like an actor who's walked on stage and found himself in the wrong play. This is clearly not how he expected our conversation to go.

'Well … those are very interesting points, and … you make them very powerfully. This is an important debate,' he says.

'It's not a debate. That's the whole point,' says Sky. 'There's nothing more to discuss. Something has to be *done*.'

311

'Yes. Quite. We are working as hard as we can towards our commitments …'

'It's not enough. How long do you think we've got?'

'To do what?'

'The human race – if we carry on doing nothing to save ourselves. Fifty years? Eighty?'

'I don't think we can put a number on it.'

'I think you should. And I think you should ask yourself if you're happy with that number. And with what happens when that year arrives. Which it will.'

Sensing that the minister is on the brink of making a run for it, I decide that I should speak up and make a final point. 'Only one generation has the chance to stop this catastrophe, and it's not ours. It's yours. If you do nothing, for us it will be too late.'

'Well, er … thank you for your time,' he says, 'and … it's wonderful to have you back on terra firma, so to speak, and, good luck with … er … thank you.'

Within seconds, he's surrounded by his team of suit-wearing handlers and is swiftly ushered to the waiting car.

He and his team drive away, and the next thing I know, the street has erupted in cheers, and I'm being hugged by Mum and Dad and Rose, and after that by a stream of people I've never even met.

After my tranquil, quiet days up in the treehouse, this heady whirl of raucous congratulation soon feels like too much. Nobody seems to notice when I slip away, head home and run myself a deep hot bath.

For a moment I wonder if this makes me a hypocrite, using all this hot water straight after making that speech, but … well, you have to wash. And I really do need a bath.

I climb in, and through the half-open window I hear the now familiar sound of a crowd walking the line between anger and celebration.

Even with my head underwater, I can still hear it.

# Two Years Later

# The call

If you are asking people to change everything, maybe you are asking too much. Maybe that's an impossible request, even when it's our only hope. We got people's attention for a short while – which is as long a time anyone's attention seems to settle on anything, however important – then things carried on as before. Or seemed to, for a few months.

But then, the following year, everything did change, though not in a way anyone wanted or expected. Of course, you all know that story – the virus, the lockdowns, the strange aftermath.

Building work stopped on the airport expansion when everything else stopped, but when the world began to go back to normal, construction didn't restart. Months crept by, and the bulldozers at the site stood there, unused, then were eventually taken away. Nobody seemed to know what was happening.

Then, a year and a half after the protest ended, it was quietly announced that in the light of changed economic circumstances and shrinkage of the aviation industry, the project had been cancelled.

This didn't exactly feel like a victory, but we had won. The first objective of the protest was to stop construction of a runway, and even though the commune had been smashed, its goal was now achieved.

The other objective – making more people think and care about climate breakdown – had its moment and was pretty successful in its way, but the world moves on, and I had to move on too.

After our confrontation with the government minister at the foot of our tree, which was watched hundreds of thousands of times all over the world, Rose handed over the treehouse protest Instagram account to me and Sky. We had a huge number of followers, but Sky wasn't interested in that side of things. I kept it going for a while, but participating in that whole world made me feel like a fake, as if I was claiming to be some kind of hero, which I know I'm not, so even though I continued to look at it, I stopped posting.

People from the commune were now scattered all over, most of them still in protest camps, keeping up the fight. Clyde was living up a tree in Germany, in the path of a planned autobahn.

Sky had moved down to Devon with her mum, who after the end of the protest decided to settle in one place and train as a nurse. Sky began going to school, which she was initially ecstatic about, but school is still school, and by the sound of her messages the ecstasy did fade after a while.

We kept in touch by text, but over the months the gaps between messages got longer and longer. The last I heard from her was on my birthday. I don't know how she knew the date, but on the day itself a parcel arrived containing her drawing of the view from the treehouse, mounted and framed, with no message or card, just 'S *xxx*' written on the back.

It went straight up on my wall, positioned where I can see it when I'm lying in bed. And it's still there today.

Just when it's beginning to feel as if those crazy few weeks didn't really happen, one evening, as we're clearing away dinner, Mum's phone rings. It's Clyde. She puts him on speaker, and he congratulates us on the good news about the airport, then goes on to propose a street party to mark the success of the campaign, timed for the second anniversary of the day it all came to a head, inviting everyone who was involved. 'Even if we're still a long way from winning the war,' he says, 'it's important to remember that we have won a few battles. Sometimes you have to celebrate.'

'I'm in,' replies Mum immediately. 'A hundred per cent.'

'Me too,' adds Rose, who's home for the whole summer, working various jobs to try and keep her student loan down.

When Mum hangs up from Clyde, Rose whoops with delight and begins to rattle off the names of all the people she's most excited about seeing again. She doesn't mention Space.

So I do.

'Ughh! Don't remind me. What was I thinking? Just the sound of his name makes me feel clammy.'

'Ah, first love!' says Mum.

'Not all it's cracked up to be,' replies Rose.

'Even with a maestro of the drums?' I say.

'Specially with a maestro of the drums,' she replies, tossing a soggy dishcloth at my face.

# The party

Mum leaves it to me to invite Dad, but instead of calling him I wait till it's one of my weekends at his flat. At first I didn't like going there. It felt strange – boxy and empty – with hardly any furniture and a slightly eerie atmosphere of false cheerfulness. Whenever I walked in, the place always smelt like it had just been sprayed with nostril-burning quantities of air freshener, and the chemical smell of fake lemons somehow reminded me of his mood: plastic happy masking something bad.

After the protest ended and he lost his job, he was edgy and off-kilter for quite a long time, constantly trying to prove to me that everything was now better than it used to be, even though it obviously wasn't. After a while he got a new job, bought some furniture for his flat and, more importantly, stopped pretending that everything was always great. He began to seem like a new person – a hybrid of the old downbeat him combined with a few elements of the crazy commune version. I can't say I exactly prefer this new Dad, but at least it feels real, and it's certainly better than the I'M-REALLY-HAPPY personality that took over when he first moved into his weird flat.

These days, my weekends with Dad aren't so bad. I wish he still lived with us, but you can't have everything, and if I'm ever feeling hard done by I remind myself of Sky never even meeting her father, and how things could be a whole lot tougher.

Dad and I still visit Grandpa together, which is always a reassuring reminder that even when life changes so fast that it feels impossible to keep up, some things never change at all. Grandpa and I have almost the same conversation every fortnight, and still play the same card games, and he and Dad go through their familiar repertoire of old arguments as if it's a playlist of favourite songs.

When I tell Dad about the party he's ridiculously pleased.

'So you'll come?' I say.

'Of course! Wouldn't miss it for the world. And … Mum's happy for me to be there?'

'She told me to invite you, so …'

'That's good. That's good.'

'And Rose will be there,' I add.

322

'So, all of us in one place, then,' he says wistfully.

'Plus fifty or so other people, yeah.'

On the day of the party, Rose sets up a sound system to blast out of her bedroom window on to the street, while Mum and I, along with Helena, Callum, Laurence, the Guptas and a couple of other families, set out a row of tables along the pavement and load them up with sandwiches, crisps, cakes, biscuits and drinks.

It feels odd that Callum joins in with the party preparations. He's never once mentioned to me his failed attempt to climb the rope ladder, or his role in the scheme to get food up to the treehouse. He pretends the whole thing never happened, but when we bump into each other on the street, he is a shade more polite than he used to be. You might almost say he talks to me as an equal.

It's one of those scorching summer days when you know there's no chance of even a single cloud, and everyone seems to be in a good mood. With nobody in particular hosting the party, and nothing resembling an actual invitation ever having been written, no one knows who will be coming, or when, or how long they'll stay, which Helena seems particularly irritated by, but she also manages to appear relatively cheerful at the same time, in her own tense way.

Mid-afternoon, the first guest arrives. It's Space. I look

around, but there's no sign of Rose. Whether or not she's seen him coming and has run away, I'm not sure.

He greets me with a 'Yo!' and a complicated handshake, which I get wrong.

'It's Mr Hero-of-the-Hour,' he says, maybe sarcastically, maybe not. Or perhaps he just can't remember my name.

'The drum master himself,' I reply, aiming to match his 50/50 sarcasm.

'Didn't bring it today, unfortunately,' he says.

'Unfortunately,' I reply, pushing up the sarcasm to around 80/20, but he doesn't appear to notice.

'Rose around?' he asks.

'Yeah, somewhere,' I say. 'Back in a minute, I expect.'

He drifts away to make an early start on the snacks, and I immediately text Rose a warning. She doesn't make an appearance for another half hour, by which time there are enough other arrivals for her to melt into the background.

Everyone greets me fondly, even people who I don't think I've ever seen before in my life, but the only one who sticks around to talk to me is Clyde. He's keen to know how I settled back into school after my moment of fame. I tell him it was exciting at first, then awkward for a while when some people turned against me, as if I needed cutting down to size for some reason, and eventually everything just went back to normal.

He tells me he's pleased to see me looking so well, then leans in, places a hand on my arm, gives me one of his intense stares, and says he's proud of what I did. Proud and impressed. 'You made a difference,' he says.

I know I ought to thank him, but I feel momentarily lost for words, so I just look at him, and he looks at me, and I realise I don't need to say it. My thanks, and my gratitude for the way he inspired and guided me, are right there in the air between us, and nothing needs to be said.

Over Clyde's shoulder I spot Dad approaching with a walk that's so bouncy and excited it's almost a skip. He greets me with one of his usual fleeting hugs, then he spots Clyde, and the two of them fall into each other's arms like long-lost brothers.

I slip away, leaving them to it, and pace the edge of the party, feeling uncomfortably as if I am both the centre of attention and a peripheral outsider.

After a while I spot a teenage girl, slightly taller than me, with short hair and piercing eyes, who I half recognise. She stares back at me, also briefly puzzled, and after this instant of confusion, I realise it's Sky, completely transformed since I last saw her.

The conventional-looking woman next to her, wearing jeans and a fleece, no longer sporting even a trace of a half-shaved head, must be her mother.

Sky and I step towards each other, and there's an

325

awkward moment when I'm not sure whether or not to hug her, but she solves the dilemma by reaching out and giving me a quick squeeze.

'You've grown about a foot. I almost didn't recognise you,' I say.

She shrugs and looks down, smiling.

'It's good to see you,' she says.

'You too. Still at school?'

'Of course.'

'Still loving every minute of it?'

'It's good. A lot of people think I'm weird, and feel like they have to keep telling me, but ... you learn to ignore the idiots, don't you?'

'First thing school teaches you.'

We stare at one another, appraising the physical transformations we've both been through in the last two years, but neither of us seems to know what to say, until I tell her that the treehouse is still in one piece.

'You ever go up there?' she asks.

'Never,' I say.

'Why not?'

'Don't know. You want to go now?'

She looks around uncertainly, taking in the crowd of people, all way older than us, intensely locked into their clusters of excited gossip and reminiscences, and says, 'OK. Why not?'

I lead her to a gap in the construction site fence that now runs along one side of the street, and we pick our way across the bare, levelled ground that used to be the front garden of the commune, towards the spot where we first met, which is identifiable only by the oak tree we briefly lived in. Where the house used to stand there's just soil now, dotted with stones, lumps of crushed concrete and a ragged sprouting of weeds.

Amazingly the rope ladder is still there, wrapped around a branch, slightly green with mildew, but otherwise exactly how we left it. I pull it down and step on to the lowest rung. It feels creaky and not entirely safe, particularly since I'm significantly heavier than the last time I climbed it.

I give a couple of small jumps to test the strength of the ropes, and it squeaks but holds firm.

'What do you think?' I say. 'Shall we risk it?'

'Up to you,' she says.

It doesn't feel entirely sensible to attempt the climb, but I also have a powerful feeling that we can't just walk away. We need to go up into our tree one last time, together. I have a sensation of something unfinished hovering around us, like an unsneezed sneeze.

Carefully placing hand over hand and foot over foot, I begin to ascend the rope ladder. It's slippery underfoot, and still sways alarmingly, but I grip hard, push on and eventually make it up to the platform. After testing the boards with a few shoves and thumps, I clamber on to its rough, rickety surface, and am instantly taken back to that moment of fear when I first climbed up here.

I lie on my stomach, look down at Sky and call, 'I'm on! It feels solid.'

After Sky has finished her slow, careful climb, we look around at the still familiar view, though of course half the street has now been demolished, but the branches around and above us are unchanged. The oak, of course, is magnificently oblivious of its last-minute stay of execution. It has no idea that we saved its life.

'So weird to be back here,' she says, after a long but not uncomfortable silence.

'Happy memories?'

'Absolutely. I've lived lots of places, but this one was special. Happiest I've ever been,' she says.

'Are you talking about the treehouse or the commune?'

'Both. And your home. Your family changed my life.'

'It goes the other way too. You helped hold us together when everything was coming unstuck.'

'And now? Is it fixed?'

'Not really. After the commune was demolished, Dad never moved back home.'

'Sorry to hear that. Is he still around?'

'Yeah, I stay with him every other weekend,' I say, before adding swiftly, 'So I'm lucky, really.'

'Must still be hard,' she says.

A cheer from below rises up through the leaves. We look down and see that everyone at the party has gathered around the front of my house, where Clyde is standing on a coffee table, holding a small microphone which seems to have been rigged up to Rose's speakers. It looks like he's beginning to make a speech. We can't hear what he's saying, but every other sentence elicits ripples of laughter and occasional rounds of applause. We watch, both of us sitting with our legs dangling over the side, until the rhythm of his speech changes and the crowd starts turning their heads, looking up and down the street. That's when we realise that Clyde is saying, 'Where are they? Sky? Luke?'

More people start to call our names, and for a short while we just watch, then Sky lifts the unused orange whistle from the nail where it is still hanging and gives a single sharp blast.

All the heads down below turn in our direction, but at first nobody sees us.

'We're up here!' I yell, with a wave.

There's a ripple of laughter and the whole crowd waves back, then calls us to come down.

'We need to celebrate you!' Clyde shouts into the mic. 'Come and join us!'

'Better go back to the party, then,' I say.

Sky looks at me, takes a deep breath, gives a tiny little quarter-smile, then shrugs and says, 'OK.'

Clyde's speech continues as we climb down, with more bursts of laughter, and as we approach, he says, 'Come up here, you two! Join me!'

The crowd parts, and as we walk towards Clyde everyone begins to applaud and cheer. Sky's cheeks redden, and I can feel mine doing the same. As we pass through, people keep reaching out to shake our hands or pat us on the back.

When we get to Clyde, he says, 'Our two brilliant spokespeople!'

A noisy round of applause bursts out, complete with whoops and wolf whistles, as Clyde pulls us up on to the table and draws us into a three-person hug.

As the noise subsides, he says, 'Sometimes, doing what we do, caring about what we care about, which often feels like a lost cause, it can be hard to stay hopeful for the future. But with young people like these two poised to take the reins of power from the fools and monsters we currently have in charge ... honestly, how can you not feel hope? This is the generation that is going to change everything. I just pray that it isn't too late, and that my lot haven't destroyed everything by the time you take over. Because I believe in you, I really do.'

There's another cheer, and Clyde pulls us close to him,

330

asking if we have anything we want to say. Sky shakes her head, but I say yes and he hands over the microphone.

Suddenly there's silence and everyone is staring at me, waiting for me to speak.

I cough, momentarily regretting my decision, then say, 'I've been thinking about this party over the last few days, and about seeing all of you again – people from all over the country who heard what was happening on our little street and decided to come and help – and about how you didn't just talk about doing it, you actually came. Every one of you changed what happened here. And I know you've all moved on now, but … I took a look the other day and the Instagram feed for our protest is still there, and it still has lots of followers, and I know most of you have other feeds in other places … so now that the airport project is dead, I thought maybe we should see if it's possible to raise some money to try and get back the land where the commune was, and to grow something there. A community garden or something. Not some pretty little park for picnics, but a nature reserve. Somewhere we could grow trees to be a family for the one that gave Sky and me a home for those few days. A tiny forest. A garden of hope. Maybe we could make another totem pole to go in the middle. Will any of you help me do that?'

A wave of noise sweeps over me, clearly a resounding yes.

'Thank you,' I say. 'Thank you. I know it's a small thing, insignificant and maybe almost pointless, but it's not nothing. And maybe, together, we can make it happen. So thank you.'

I switch off the microphone, and as we jump down from the table, music begins to pump out of the speakers. Sky's mum appears in front of us, tells me I'm a good kid, and pulls me and Sky into an embrace.

I feel the threat of more hugs looming from all quarters, so I ask Sky if she's hungry, and the pair of us slip away in search of food.

By the time we've eaten a couple of platefuls of sandwiches, cakes and crisps, everyone else at the party seems to be dancing, which isn't something I feel comfortable doing with Sky, so I ask if she wants to watch TV and she swiftly agrees.

We head inside, and that's where we spend the rest of the evening, sitting on the sofa, watching old episodes of *Friends* and half listening to the increasingly loud sounds of the party outside. It feels good to be with her again, together but not having to talk. We only knew each other for a very short time, but somehow she's part of who I am, and I have a feeling she always will be.

I thought we'd drifted apart, but sitting next to her on the sofa, feeling her physically transformed yet utterly unchanged presence alongside me, I realise that even if months or years pass without any messages or phone calls, there's a connection between us that will never break.

When people ask me what happened that summer, how I ended up on TV screens all over the world, I can't explain it. I can go through the events that took place, but I can't get across how it changed me and made the whole world around me slide into focus in a new way. I think the only person who will ever really understand is the one who was up there in the treehouse with me.

After a couple of hours, we go back outside to see what's happening. The food and drink tables are now more or less bare. Most people are flopped on the rugs and blankets that have been laid down in front gardens, lolling around chatting. Only a hard core is left flailing their bodies around the patch of space below Rose's speakers, and right in the middle, lit by a street lamp, is a middle-aged couple dancing cheek to cheek, in time with some slow inaudible rhythm of their own which bears no relation to the thumping dance music filling the air. I stare at these two people, my mother and father, holding one another for the first time in years, and wonder silently to myself what will happen next.

Sky reaches out a hand and holds it in the air in front of me, palm upwards. 'Want to dance?' she says.

# Acknowledgements

Thank you, Hannah Sandford, Felicity Rubinstein, Beatrice Cross, Anna Swan, Nick de Somogyi and Fliss Stevens.

Thanks also to Peter Wohlleben for his fascinating and informative book *The Hidden Life of Trees*.

Thank you, Saul, Iris and Juno.

Above all, thank you, Maggie O'Farrell.

# Have you read

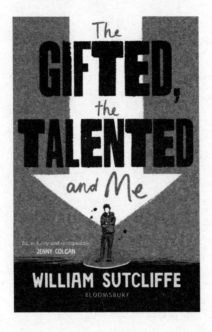

# Because we can

'COME DOWNSTAIRS, EVERYONE! FAMILY MEETING!'

Even though I was mildly curious about why Dad was back from work so early, and what a 'family meeting' might involve, I stayed put in my room.

'PIZZA!' he added. 'Last one down gets the Hawaiian!'

Doors slammed, footsteps thundered down the staircase and I leaped up. After a brief tussle with Ethan in the kitchen doorway, during which Freya somehow managed to crawl between our legs and get the first slice, we all assembled around the table, eating straight from takeaway boxes spread over a layer of drawings, uncompleted homework, unopened letters and unread magazines.

Ethan, who was seventeen and hadn't worn any colour except black for the last three years, announced through a mouthful of pizza, 'I don't mind who gets custody, but I'm not moving out of my bedroom.'

'Custody?' said Mum.

'Yeah. I'm not leaving, and I'm not going anywhere at the weekends.'

'You've got the wrong end of the stick, love,' said Mum. 'We're not getting divorced.'

'Oh,' said Ethan. 'So what's all this about a family meeting?'

Freya, who lived in a seven-year-old's fantasy universe populated exclusively by fairies, unicorns and cats, temporarily tuned in to reality and began to cry. 'You're getting divorced?'

Mum jumped out of her chair, dashed around the table and lifted Freya into her arms. 'We're not getting divorced. You mustn't worry.'

'But Ethan said you are!'

'Ethan's wrong.'

'How do I know you're telling the truth?' said Freya. 'How do I know you're not just saying that to protect me?'

'Ethan!' snapped Mum. 'Look what you've done. Tell Freya you made it up.'

'I didn't make it up.'

'You did! Nobody said anything about divorce until you piped up.'

2

'I worked it out for myself.'

'INCORRECTLY! WE'RE NOT GETTING A DIVORCE!'

'Why not?' said Ethan.

'What?' replied Mum. 'You're asking me why we're *not* getting a divorce?'

'If you can't even think of an answer, maybe we should be worried,' said Ethan.

'STOP!' said Dad. 'Rewind. Stay calm. There's no divorce. I called this meeting because we have something to tell you.'

'Trial separation?' said Ethan.

'No. It's good news.'

This shut everyone up. The idea of good news hadn't occurred to us.

'I sold my company,' said Dad, leaning back in his chair, with a grin spreading across his face.

Ethan, Freya and I stared at him blankly.

'You have a company?' I said.

'Yes! Of course I do! What do you think I've been doing every day for the last six years?'

I shrugged.

'Well, until last week I had a company. But now I've sold it!'

He beamed at us, waiting for a response. None of us had any idea what he was talking about, or why he was making such a performance of this fantastically dull information. Freya, losing interest in the entire conversation, pulled a notebook from her pocket and began to draw.

'For a lot of money,' he added.

Ethan's eyes rose from his pizza.

'When you say a lot … are you saying … ?'

'We're rich!' said Mum, leaping up with Freya still in her arms and beginning to dance around the kitchen. 'We're rich! We're rich! Goodbye, Stevenage! Goodbye, cramped, boxy little house! It's going to be a whole new life! Nobody believed he could do it, but he did! He made it! We're rich!'

'How rich?' said Ethan.

'Comfortable,' said Dad.

'Stinking,' said Mum.

'Not stinking,' said Dad. 'Mildly smelly.'

'Can I have a new phone?' said Ethan.

The only clue this might have been about to happen was Dad's job. Or lack of one. When Freya was still a baby, he walked out on whatever it was he was doing back then – something that involved wearing a tie and getting home after I was in bed – and installed himself in the shed at the bottom of our garden. He spent months on end squirrelling around down there, dressed like he'd just crawled out of a skip (which, in fact, he often had), and from this point on, when people asked him what he did for a living, he said he was an 'entrepreneur'. If he was trying to sound interesting, he sometimes said 'inventor'.

He was always coming and going with random bits of machinery, then occasionally he'd turn up in the kitchen wearing a suit, and we'd all be kind of, 'Whoa! Who are you? How did *you* get into the house?' But after making fun of him for looking like an employable adult, none of us ever remembered to ask him where he was going.

One of those meetings must have generated a source of serious money, because at some point he stopped tinkering in the shed, upgraded his wardrobe from skip-diver to blind-man-stumbling-out-of-a-jumble-sale and went off to work in a warehouse somewhere. Or maybe it was an office. I never thought of asking him. He was just my dad, going out to work like everyone else's dad. What this actually involved didn't seem important. As long as he showed up at breakfast and weekends, and drove me where I needed to go, it didn't occur to me to wonder what he did all day.

Then there was a week when he flew off to America, carrying brand-new luggage and a floppy suit bag I'd never seen before. This time I remembered to ask what he was up to, but he just said 'meetings'. There was something in the way Mum wished him luck as he set off that did seem

5

odd – the way she said it, like she genuinely meant it –
but a couple of minutes later I forgot all about the whole
thing.

It was just after he got home from America that our
first-ever family meeting was called.

'Hang on,' I said, interrupting Mum's celebration dance.
'What do you mean goodbye, Stevenage?'

'You don't think we're going to stay here, do you?' said
Mum. 'Rich people don't live in Stevenage. They live in
London! Dad's sold his company, I've handed in my notice
at work, and we can finally get out of this dump and move
to London!'

'But I like Stevenage,' I said.

'The only people who like Stevenage are people who've
never been anywhere else,' said Ethan.

'I've been to the same places as you.'

'No, you haven't. And you've barely read a book in your
life. Your idea of culture is ten-pin bowling.'

'What's that got to do with liking Stevenage?'

'See? Ignorant.'

I looked across at Mum for support, hoping she'd take
my side, but it looked like she hadn't even heard. Her
expression reminded me of the thing you see in cartoons
when people's eyeballs turn into dollar signs.

'So we're moving?' I asked.

'Yes!' said Mum. 'As soon as we can! To a place I've been dreaming of all my life. There are beautiful Victorian houses, and it's in London but it's near an enormous park, and even though it's expensive, it's filled with artists and musicians and publishers and creative people. It's called ...' her voice dipped to a reverential whisper '... Hampstead.'

# About the Author

William Sutcliffe is the author of thirteen novels, including the international bestseller *Are You Experienced?* and *The Wall*, which was shortlisted for the CILIP Carnegie Medal. He has written for adults, young adults and children, and his work has been translated into twenty-eight languages. His 2008 novel *Whatever Makes You Happy* is now a Netflix Original film starring Patricia Arquette and Angela Bassett. It was released under the title *Otherhood*. His first funny novel for teenagers, *The Gifted, the Talented and Me*, was described by *The Times* as 'dangerously funny' and by the *Guardian* as 'refreshingly hilarious'. It was shortlisted for the YA Book Prize 2020 and was the *Sunday Times* Children's Book of the Year 2019. He lives in Edinburgh.

@Will_Sutcliffe8